HOMELAND

Also by Barbara Hambly

PATRIOT HEARTS
THE EMANCIPATOR'S WIFE
A FREE MAN OF COLOR
FEVER SEASON
GRAVEYARD DUST
SOLD DOWN THE RIVER
DIE UPON A KISS
WET GRAVE
DAYS OF THE DEAD
DEAD WATER

HOME LAND

A NOVEL

Barbara Hambly

BANTAM BOOKS

Ham

Published in the United States by Bantam Books, an imprint of The Random House Publishing Group, a division of Random House, Inc., New York.

Library of Congress Cataloging-in-Publication Data
Hambly, Barbara.
Homeland / Barbara Hambly.
ISBN 978-0-553-80552-9
eBook ISBN 978-0-553-90687-5
1. Female friendship—Fiction. 2. United States—History—Civil War, 1861–1865—Social aspects—Fiction. 3. United States—History—Civil War, 1861–1865—Psychological aspects—Fiction. 4. United States—History—Civil War, 1861–1865—Women—Fiction. I. Title.
PS3558.A4215 H66 2009
813/.54—dc22

Printed in the United States of America on acid-free paper

www.bantamdell.com

2 4 6 8 9 7 5 3 1

First Edition

Book design by Glen M. Edelstein

For Victoria

ACKNOWLEDGMENTS

Special thanks are owed to my dear friend and advisor on nineteenth-century housekeeping, Victoria Ridenour; to the staff and guides of the Travelers' Rest, Cragfont, and Wynnewood Plantations, for their friendly helpfulness; to guide Dick Toll at the Andrew Johnson Homestead and to Daniel Luther at the Dickson/Williams House, both in Greeneville, Tennessee; to Connie Wiberg of the Deer Isle–Stonington Historical Society; to Gene Larson; and especially to my editor, Kate Miciak, for her patience and vision in shaping this book to be what it is.

HOMELAND

1861

Susanna Ashford, Bayberry Run Plantation
Greene County, Tennessee
To
Mrs. Cora Poole, Blossom Street
Boston, Massachusetts

THURSDAY, APRIL 25, 1861

Dear Mrs. Poole,

Please, I beg you, tell *no one* what you saw.

You said it was nothing, and I pray that's the truth. I wish there had been time to speak to you before you got on the train. I will always be so grateful to you for helping me as you did, and did not dare imperil *your* situation by even a day's delay. But, you being Emory's bride, I know you've heard the stories.

[~~*I'm afraid*~~–crossed out.]

Please forget.

I enclose this in a package of the books Emory's father says he is sending you. I hope that it reaches you in safety and that you enjoy the books. I am *killed* with envy that you're getting his copy of *The Hunchback of Notre Dame*!

You are the only person here—the only person I've ever met, really—who has truly and disinterestedly acted as my friend. I don't want what happened to destroy that. Please tell me it's really all right.

Your friend,
Susanna Ashford

P.S. Enclosed is a sketch of us going to Nashville.

Mrs. Cora Poole, Blossom Street
Boston, Massachusetts
To
Miss Susanna Ashford, Bayberry Run
Plantation
Greene County, Tennessee

Monday, May 6, 1861

Dear Susanna,

Did we not agree, when I escorted you down to Nashville in March that we were to be Cora and Susanna? So far as I am concerned, that has not changed. Indeed, after eight whole weeks of matrimony I still find the thought of being Mrs. Anything unsettling. Our Lord said, "Let your Yea be Yea, and your Nay be Nay," and when I told you, "It's nothing," I meant it. I may be a "mealymouthed Abolitionist bluestocking," as your Aunt Sally so tactfully put it at that *frightful* tea-party, but having grown up in an atmosphere poisoned by gossip, I have no wish to either spread it, or credit it. Be reassured, I will keep the thing I saw to myself. Yet I cannot pretend that I am not profoundly disturbed by it, and more than a little concerned for your safety.

Your letter arrived Saturday. The books that accompanied it were consigned to the attic, for I do not read novels.

When I wrote my letters of thanks to my kind hostess for the tea-party, I felt I should write one to you, as well. Mrs. Johnson and your sister-in-law offered warm Southern hospitality, but in you I sensed actual friendship. Thank you for it, from the bottom of my heart. To excuse my delay in responding I plead the exigencies of setting up housekeeping for the first time: sewing curtains, learning which farmers in the market can be trusted not to water their milk, setting up account-books with grocer, butcher, and the man who delivers the coal, and finding a servant-girl who is honest. Back on Deer Isle, everyone knows the girls who "help" and can complain of them to their mothers if they misbehave. Here, most prospective "helpers" are immigrant Irish or German girls, and their mothers speak little or no English.

I trust our efforts in Nashville have borne fruit, and your admission to the Academy is secured? I know you were apprehensive. Yet I cannot see how your father would object to your hope of attending the Academy, much less of going on to advanced training in Art. Were you your father's *son,* rather than a daughter, there would be no question of keeping you from the technical training that shapes ability into excellence. One look at your sketchbook convinced me how extraordinary your talent is.

Forgive me if I write too warmly. My own father took great care, and suffered no small amount of criticism, that I should have an education equal to my brother's, and it is a matter very close to my heart. Please let me know, as soon as you hear.

And thank you, for your concern not to delay our departure. Happily, our train was not stopped by the militia bands one hears of. I trust that all remains quiet in your section?

Please extend my best wishes to Mrs. Johnson when next you see her, and thank her again for her hospitality.

Ever your friend,
Cora Poole

[N.B. April 12–14, 1861, Fort Sumter was shelled by Confederates and taken.]

Susanna Ashford, Bayberry Run Plantation
Greene County, Tennessee
To
Mrs. Cora Poole, Blossom Street
Boston, Massachussets

MONDAY, MAY 20, 1861

Dear Cora,

Thank you, thank you, thank you! I still don't know what to do—or even what to think—about what happened at the depot.

[~~*I can't let*~~—crossed out]

I bless you for your silence.

There have been *housekeeping exigencies* here, too, largely having to do with getting the tobacco seedlings transplanted. We have three hundred acres in tobacco, and about half again as much in corn, and my oldest brother, who oversees the day-to-day work of our plantation, leaves tomorrow to join the Army.

And thank you, more than I can say, for your words about going to the Academy. It's so true: were I a boy there would be no question whether I should go to the art academy in Philadelphia, even if it is in Enemy Territory now. There certainly wasn't any about my brother Payne going to the Virginia Military Academy.

I've kept house here since my Evil Stepmother died when I was nine—Pa likes the way I manage the servants, and do the accounts. When Julia was getting ready for her wedding, and didn't need me for a companion anymore, she was happy to tell Pa how nice it would be for me to go to the Academy. But now that Tom has gone into the Army, and Julia is home again, she doesn't want me to leave, either. When Pa shakes his head and sighs, "Now, Babygirl, there isn't a thing they teach at that Academy that you can't learn right here at home," I sneak up to my room and read and re-read your letter, to remind myself that he says so only because I'm a girl. That I have as much of a right to be an artist, as a boy would.

Friday, May 24

I can't imagine *not* reading novels. When I was little, I would tag after Payne when he'd go up to Crow Holler to go hunting with Emory, and I'd sit on the dog-trot and read Mr. Poole's books. Some of them I couldn't understand (a lot were in Latin and French and Greek), but sometimes Mr. Poole would come out of the woods and help me with them. Then at night I'd tell the stories back to Julia and Payne, or make up other stories about the characters. Even though I know you don't read them, I'm glad to know Mr. Poole's books are safe in your attic. The Secesh militia has been burning the houses of Unionists.

Didn't you even read *Uncle Tom's Cabin*?

Your friend,
Susanna

P.S. I enclose a sketch of your train being attacked by the Secesh militia. That's Julia down in the lower corner, fainting into President Lincoln's arms. (Does he still have a beard?)

Mrs. Cora Poole, Blossom Street
Boston, Massachusetts
To
Miss Susanna Ashford, Bayberry Run
Plantation
Greene County, Tennessee

Monday, June 3, 1861

Dear Susanna,

Had I known—as I now do, thanks to your sketch—that Confederate militia bands include elephant corps, chariots, and archers firing from balloons, I would certainly have been even more apprehensive than I was at the thought of them attacking our home-bound train. I will treasure your sketch, and take it to show the ladies of my Tuesday night Soldiers' Aid Society. What on earth is a "dog-trot"?

". . . there isn't a thing they teach at that Academy"—fiddlesticks! I heard that from every one of our neighbors when I was preparing to go to the Female Seminary on the mainland: "What's wrong with the schools right here on Deer Isle?" Your father doubtless thinks there are plenty of drawing-teachers in Greene County, as good as anything you'd find in Philadelphia, or Paris for that matter!

Of course I except *Uncle Tom's Cabin* from the general category of novels, written as it was with a higher purpose than mere frivolity. Even my father excepted it, once *I* had lent *my* copy to *him*. This was after my school-friend Elinor thrust it upon me and declared she would never speak to me again, until I read it. And please forgive me my assumption that you would follow your family's lead on the question of Secession—an assumption unworthy of Mrs. Wollstonecraft, and Lucretia Mott, and other champions of the right of women to think and speak after the promptings of their own hearts. Or do I mistake your words? I am extremely curious to know what you thought of the book? I wept and wept over it.

Tuesday, June 25

An interruption. Only days after the receipt of your letter, my mother wrote me from Deer Isle that my brother Oliver quite astonishingly announced his intention to wed, and Emory and I took the train back to Maine to attend the wedding. (Mother is fit to be tied.) It was good to see again the friends with whom I grew up, though my darling bossy Elinor could not attend, being great with her second child. Most of the men were out with the cod-fleet, and all my aunts and cousins and second-cousins deep engaged in the cultivation of their gardens.

The talk was of nothing but the War, and of the parade when the first of the Maine regiments marched south; of how we will "make the Southerners pay for their audacity." Flags float from every public edifice and most private ones as well. Despite the joy of having milk and butter from our own cows, and good country vegetables—despite the beauty of the wildflowers in our woods and the pleasure of working in Mother's garden again—I was conscious as never before of how primitive is the life on our island, and how narrow the focus of its dwellers, though they be people that I love. Nowhere did I hear even the suggestion that *all* Southerners might not be degenerate slave-holders.

I am profoundly glad to return to Boston. I sorely missed the variety of its newspapers, and the chance to read more than one view of a subject: here in Boston I read not only our own *Transcript* and *Harper's* but several New York papers as well. Sorely, too, I missed the opportunity to hear lectures other than the Sunday sermon at church, or music beyond the level of the choir singing a hymn. How far I have come from that world!

We travelled up with my older brother Brock, his wife, and their children. Army recruiters were active on the island; fifteen of our men have enlisted, including four of my cousins, our hired man, Elinor's husband Nathan, and my friend Deborah's fiancé Charles. Most of those who signed up for the three-month enlistment were married men, many with children.

I send this in care of Eliza Johnson, who writes me that though postal service between the States of the Confederacy, and those of the Union, is now severed, men cross over the mountains in secret. I understand her husband made good his escape—surely the Confederates would not actually have *hanged* him? I pray this reaches you.

Emory bids me send his love to your beautiful sister.

Affectionately,
Cora

1861

Susanna Ashford, Bayberry Run Plantation
Greene County, Tennessee
To
Mrs. Cora Poole, Blossom Street
Boston, Massachussets

MONDAY, AUGUST 5, 1861

Dear Cora,

Your letter at last! And, Saturday, the letter came that I am accepted at the Nashville Female Academy! Tho' I don't dare approach Pa on the subject until after the tobacco is harvested.

Men do indeed cross over the mountains all the time. Hundreds are fleeing to join the Union Army in Kentucky. Mr. Poole is widely rumored to be one of the "pilots" who guide them across, despite the guards the Confederate government has set on the border, to keep them in. I have instructed Mr. Poole to ask Pa for my hand a week before I show Pa the letter from the Academy: Pa would see me in Perdition, never mind a Female Academy "full of uppity Yankee women" (sorry), before he would risk an alliance with "that d–Lincolnite Poole." If all goes well, I will leave for Nashville at the end of this month.

Thank you, thank you for your good wishes and prayers!

I read *Uncle Tom's Cabin* because everyone was making such a fuss about it, but nobody I talked to had actually read it. I had to hide it behind the paneling in Payne's bedroom. Much in it is so dreadfully inaccurate! My family has owned slaves all my life; I grew up playing in the quarters, and no black person I've ever met, slave or free, is as blindly trusting as poor old Uncle Tom. I know he's supposed to be an honest Everyman, like Christian in *The Pilgrim's Progress,* but to me he just seems like a simple-minded child who should know better. And I wanted to drown Little Eva in the rain-barrel.

I don't think the book is really about black people at all. I think it's about the way white people *regard* black people: how whites talk and think about slavery.

I can't say I agree with the Abolitionists, because I honestly don't believe men and women who've been slaves all their lives would stand a chance of making a decent living if they were just all turned loose one day, without any schooling or anything. But I've met too many of Pa's friends who, if you let them put off emancipating their hands til they were "ready," would find some good reason, and then another, why they weren't "ready" until Kingdom Come. So I guess that's why it's so hard to come up with a good solution to the problem.

Whenever anybody talks about how reading novels is bad for girls, I think about *Uncle Tom's Cabin.* No sermon in the world could have done what that novel did, in opening people's eyes. (Pa takes that as proof that novel-reading *is* bad for girls.)

What do they say in Boston about the battle?* Pa and Regal talk as if the Federal Army was slaughtered to the last man at Manassas, except for the cowards who ran away.

Thursday, August 8

Henriette and Julia and I have been putting up blackberries—what a horror! Of course it's the hottest week of the year, and only Cook and Mammy Iris to help us. All the rest of the house servants are out in the fields. Six of the main gang are down sick, which always happens at harvest. I think there's got to be something in the tobacco sap that makes them sick, especially the children, but Pa says they're just lazy. I will be very glad to be gone to Nashville. Since Manassas, everybody's saying, "The War will be over by Christmas."

By next year, I should be able to apply to the Pennsylvania Academy of Fine Art in Philadelphia.

You forgot the other thing they always say to girls: "You'll forget all about that Art nonsense when you have your own darling little babies to raise." Except nobody has ever expected me to get married. Why would they, with a nose like mine? I was just supposed to stay home and be Julia's companion.

Enclosed is a sketch of Mr. Poole's house at Crow Holler. The south side of the cabin has been nailed up shut as long as I can remember. That's me when I was five years old, sitting reading on the dog-trot, which as you see is that breezeway between the two halves of a cabin.

Your friend,
Susanna

[N.B. The Battle of Bull Run/Manassas Junction was fought Sunday, July 21, 1861.]

Susanna Ashford, Nashville Female Academy
Nashville, Tennessee
To
Mrs. Cora Poole, Blossom Street
Boston, Massachussets

MONDAY, SEPTEMBER 9, 1861

Dearest Cora,

Though I have had no letter from you, I *must* write. Truly, no one else could understand how happy I am! Not even, strangely, the other girls here at the Academy; I think I'm the only one who actually *wants* to be here. You are the only other person I have met who has ever spoken of the pleasure of learning, not to have "accomplishments" or to "make Papa proud," but for "the life of the mind," as you call it, in itself. Mr. Cameron, who teaches drawing, is a marvel. He studied with Rembrant Peale, and knows everyone in Nashville who has paintings from Europe for me to study and copy. Nobody in America paints as they do in Italy and France! Except the people who *studied* in Italy and France. Mr. Cameron is only the third person I've ever met—after you and Mr. Poole—who doesn't think I'm crazy and unwomanly to want to paint pictures for my living. He knows a *very* wealthy lady here—a Mrs. Acklen—who has an entire art gallery! He has promised me to introduce us. I can hardly wait!

The Academy is a squat brick building with all manner of corridors and wings, and backs onto the Nashville and Chattanooga Railway tracks. From the windows we girls can see troops coming and going from the depot at all hours. The streets are full of soldiers and Army wagons, and everyone here, without exception, is a Secessionist: teachers, girls, Dr. and Mrs. Elliott—the kindest people imaginable—their daughters, most of the servants, and even Mr. Cameron. Sunday Mrs. E takes us for calls on all the "nice folks" in town, and the talk is of nothing but Yankee perfidy and the Justice of Our Cause. They say girls shouldn't talk about politics, but that actually means, "Girls can talk about politics all they choose so long as they favor the Rebellion." I smile, nod, and pretend I am a Spy in Enemy Territory. And think of you there in Boston, studiously reading your newspapers. They frown heavily on novel-reading here, too. Really, I've never understood what's wrong with it.

On Saturday evenings we write letters, and Mrs. Elliott reads them to make sure they're grammatical, and that that stuck-up Nora Vandyke isn't penning love-notes to her beaux. I'm writing this secretly in my room, after evening prayers—I bribed my room-mate not to tell. I write *her* letters to her Mama and sisters; I can copy anybody's handwriting in the school, practically.

Julia writes to me (it has never been scientifically proven that

Pa *can* write) saying how desperately she misses me and that the plantation is a shambles without me there. I re-read your letter, how if I was a man they wouldn't feel they had the right to demand I stay home, but I feel like a traitor. I suppose, legally, I *am* a traitor, but I don't notice the Confederacy making *women* take their Loyalty Oath.

Your own Spy,
Susie

THURSDAY, SEPTEMBER 19

Dearest Cora,

I have done a wicked and terrible thing, and there is no one but yourself I dare tell; yet I feel I *must* tell someone. Here it is: Instead of going to tea yesterday evening with Mrs. Acklen, I dressed myself as a boy, and convinced Mr. Cameron to take me "down the line," that is, down Spring Street to the landing, where all the soldiers' taverns are. I promise you, this was not for purposes of dissipation (if it had been the stink would have cured me *forever*!). If I am to be an artist, I need to see as much of the world as I possibly can—even the parts "nice girls" aren't supposed to know about.

We went early in the evening, and Mr. Cameron took very good care of his "nephew." He understands why I need to see these things. Please, please, tell me you understand also! The men weren't dashing or heroic, and the women weren't beautiful, and this morning I found a *louse* in my hair! I paid one of the maids to fine-comb my hair four times and an extra twenty-five cents not to breathe a word to *anyone*. Please don't think I'm bad.

Your penitent,
Susie

Mrs. Cora Poole, Blossom Street
Boston, Massachusetts
To
Miss Susanna Ashford, Nashville Female Academy
Nashville, Tennessee

MONDAY, SEPTEMBER 30, 1861

Dearest Susanna,

Your letter leaves me troubled, and of two minds—or three, or four—as to what I ought to reply.

First, my heartiest congratulations on your acceptance to the Nashville Academy! They are saying here, too, that the fighting should be over by Christmas. President Lincoln has called for one million new troops, so I cannot imagine how this will not prove so. Whether Philadelphia is then in your native homeland once again or in a foreign country, you must be able to go there to study your Art. Though nothing could make me regret being Emory's wife, there are times when I wish that I might also have been permitted by Fate to continue my own education. I do so *hunger* for new learning, and the life of the mind.

Second, thank you for your frank opinions on *Uncle Tom*. You are quite right, that it opens the eyes by winning the heart—unlike, I fear, the vast majority of novels. You are the sole person I have met who has both lived in the world Mrs. Stowe describes, and has read the book. Emory's experience of growing up in Greene County was enlightening, but, as you know, his father held no slaves. The men and women of color whom I met in Hartford while at the Seminary, and when I visit Papa at Yale, were freedmen of several generations, not Southern-born or bred. Deeply as I revere the book and all that it has brought about, I suppose I am now enough a lawyer's wife to ask, *Is this testimony correct?*

Please forgive me if I trespass on the bounds of friendship, when

I say that after seeing your sketch of the house where he was born, Emory told me things about his father that disturbed me very much. I had heard some of them in Greeneville, as I know you must have as well; stories of Justin Poole's madness, and wild rumors concerning the death of his wife. In the five years I have known Emory, he has spoken of his father exactly three times, and one of those was only to say, "Pa's a strange man." After his revelations, the estrangement between father and son no longer surprises me. And yet, you have known Justin Poole in the five years since Emory fled, and I know you to be a level-headed young woman.

Pontius Pilate asked, "What is truth?" and washed his hands. But I say only that what my husband told me of his father leaves me deeply concerned, that you have anything to do with this man.

There! Forgive me writing of this, and if you wish, tear this letter up and burn it. I swear I will not bring the matter up again.

Tuesday, October 1

Emory has just come home, with word that my brother Brock has quit the law firm, to join the Army.

Come what may, ever your friend,
Cora

Susanna Ashford, Nashville Female
Academy
Nashville, Tennessee
To
Mrs. Cora Poole, Blossom Street
Boston, Massachusetts

MONDAY, OCTOBER 14, 1861

Cora,

Awful news. Julia writes me that our brother Payne was wounded in a skirmish in Virginia, his right arm so badly broken by a minié ball as to have been amputated. It doesn't seem real. It's even more horrible because every person at the Academy feels they have to tell me about people they know who were wounded and had limbs cut off, and died of it. I just want to cover my ears and run away. Please don't tell me you'll pray for him, or how sorry you are, or about anybody else you know, or how lucky he is to be still alive, or it's a small price to pay for the honor of defending his homeland . . . Nothing. Please.

WEDNESDAY, OCTOBER 16

Another letter from Julia. *Still* no letter from you. Payne is to be furloughed home. I want to weep, thinking about Payne without his arm. I remember holding his hand, a thousand nights when we were little, when he'd come creeping into our bedroom to listen in the dark to my stories about the fairies in the woods and the barn. Now that hand doesn't exist anymore. I try to do my Latin verbs, or read my history books, and all I can hear is the soldiers marching to and from the depot.

Yesterday all I could do was sit in a corner of my room, reading *The Hunchback of Notre Dame* again. Being with those people, those old friends, Quasimodo and Gringoire and the Beggar King that I also used to tell Payne and Julia stories about. Being anyplace but here. I cried for Quasimodo's hopeless love, and Esmeralda's undeserved death, cried until I was almost sick. Then I slept, and when I woke up I felt better.

Tuesday, October 22

I think the Rebels must have seized and burned your letter. I pray, pray it isn't because you've changed your mind about what happened at the depot in April.

Shopped all over town for good linen, to make a shirt for dear Payne when he comes home. I *hate* sewing (buttonholes were invented by the Devil), but all the officers we see on our Sunday calls say that new, whole clothing is prized among the men. Mrs. Elliott went with me, and Mr. Cameron. Because of all the soldiers in town and the teamsters and sutlers and *females of a certain sort* who follow armies it isn't thought safe even for groups of women to be about on the streets without male protection. I couldn't find anything I could afford, on account of the blockade (I've been trading Nora Vandyke for drawing-paper for weeks), and finally settled for calico, at a price Julia used to make Pa pay for silk!

And of course, it's all the perfidious Yankees' fault.

Sunday, October 27

Julia writes that our Payne is coming home next week.

Yours,
Susie

Mrs. Cora Poole, Blossom Street
Boston, Massachusetts
To
Miss Susanna Ashford, Nashville Female Academy
Nashville, Tennessee

Saturday, October 26, 1861
Night

Dearest,

This is so hard to write. Emory promises he will see to it that this goes into hands that will carry it safe to you. My darling husband leaves tomorrow, to join the Army. By Thursday, I, too, will be gone.

I have seen this coming, from the moment we stepped off the train in Greeneville last March, and Emory re-encountered the friends of his boyhood: Tennessee men who were ready to fight to preserve the Union. This evening when Emory came home he said to me, "I cannot stand this another day. I must go, Cora."

Yesterday I would have put my hand on the Bible and said, "The Union must be preserved at *any* cost." I still believe this with the whole of my heart, Susanna, even if the price be my husband's life.

I cannot believe I just wrote those words. Please forgive me for them–you whose brothers fight for the Confederate cause. Please do not think me your enemy, because Emory has taken up arms. I write to you because you are from his world, and know better than anyone of my acquaintance what his choices are.

Tonight I try to imagine Emory and myself, white-haired and smiling, sitting together years and years from now at the dawn of another century, saying things like, "Remember how scared you were, you goose, when I went off to fight in the War?" But there's only darkness. I try to see God's hand guiding Emory to wherever he needs to go, guiding me . . . and there's only darkness. Emory sleeps now, his back to me. Tomorrow night the pillow will be empty, the sheets cold.

On Thursday I will return the key of my precious little home to its landlord, and take the train north to New Haven to meet my father. My Uncle Mordacai will meet us in Belfast, Maine, in his sloop the *Gull*, to carry us across to Deer Isle. I will stay with Mother, Ollie, and his bride Peggie until the fighting ends, or until Emory comes home. I have chosen not to tell him what I have only begun to suspect: that I might be with child. His mind is in torment enough. We have had one "false alarm" already, and I would not put him through the pain of decision a second time, for what might only be another. If there *is* a child, she will be here when my darling returns.

Please, my dear friend, write to me on Deer Isle, care of the Post Office in Southeast Harbor. Snow will be flying, by the time I arrive.

Yours,
Cora

Susanna Ashford, Nashville Female Academy
Nashville, Tennessee
To
Mrs. Cora Poole,
[~~*Blossom Street*~~
~~*Boston, Massachusetts*~~—address crossed out]
Southeast Harbor
Deer Isle, Maine

THURSDAY, NOVEMBER 7, 1861
NIGHT

Dear Cora,

This morning as we girls were coming out of prayers Mrs. Elliott touched my shoulder, said, "Would you come into my office for a moment, Susanna?" and I knew by her voice that Payne was dead.

He'd been home at Bayberry for three days. I was going to take the train Sunday to see him. He got there Monday; Julia wrote me that he seemed well, only quite weak. She said he was growing whiskers, and couldn't wait to start practicing shooting with his left hand.

I keep thinking he can't really be dead, because I didn't get to see him. This has to be a mistake.

The last time I saw him was Christmas, my first grown-up ball. Payne was in his VMA uniform and danced with me, the first time we'd danced together except in classes as children. He said, "Good Lord, Susie, you're getting all grown up." I wanted to say the same about him. When he left for the Academy he and I were the same height–I was fourteen, he sixteen. At Christmas he was taller than me.

Regal (my middle brother) met me at the depot this afternoon. He said Payne died oh so quickly. "Damn it, he was on the mend. God damn f–n' doctors." Regal always has to blame somebody for things that just happen. It's the closest I've ever seen, to seeing him cry.

The fences haven't been fixed at Bayberry, nor the woodpile re-stocked. There are hardly any cows or pigs left, and the hen-runs are mostly empty. Payne's coffin is in our parlor, the windows all curtained. Before I could step through the door from the hall Pa came out of his office, seized me in his arms: "This place is not the same, Babygirl, since you've been gone!" Henriette came running down the stairs saying how I must go up and take care of poor Julia, who had wept herself sick.

That's where I am now. I've been here all evening, altering mourning clothes for us both and trying to make sense of Henriette's bookkeeping. All Julia can say, over and over, is, "What will I do if Tom should be killed, too? How could God let this happen?" It was hard not to cry, being here in this room again, where Payne would lie at the foot of the bed listening to me tell stories.

FRIDAY, NOVEMBER 8
EVENING

Oh, Cora. I don't even know how to write this. I am so sorry.

When it came time to wash and dress and ride with Payne's casket into town, all Julia could do was cling to me and cry, "I can't, I can't! And I won't let you leave me." Henriette said, "She'll make herself ill, poor darling!" (Julia is expecting in the spring.) "Besides, someone must stay here to make sure the food is laid out ready for company afterwards." And Pa said, "That's my good girl! I knew we could depend on you, Susie!" It's what he always says.

So I stayed. I tell myself it doesn't really matter. Payne and I said our farewells last Christmas, when he got on the train to go back to Virginia. Anyway, that isn't really Payne in that coffin, any more than Payne was the arm they cut off. The least I can do for him is make sure everyone has a clean house to come to after his funeral.

I asked Colfax our butler and Mammy Iris, could I maybe ride into town and at least see the procession to the grave? But they said no, there's bush-whackers in the woods, even this close to town. Two of Regal's men—he's a captain in the Secesh militia—rode behind the buggy back from town yesterday. Then Mammy Iris said, "If it's Mr. Emory you're hopin' to see, Miss Susie, he'll be here after the funeral's done." And for just one second I felt so happy, that your Emory would bring me a letter from you. Then it came to me what it means that he's *here,* in Tennessee, instead of in Kentucky where all the Unionists are escaping to. I felt exactly like someone had slammed me up against the wall, and I guess I just stared at them both like an idiot.

Your husband's been staying in town with Mrs. Johnson. He stopped here Monday, to ask Julia if he could take any messages from her to Tom, whose regiment he'll be joining, and stayed in town because of our poor Payne. Emory was one of the first to arrive, riding Charley Johnson's horse. He wore one of Charley's coats, too, since he didn't bring a black one of his own. For a minute we just looked at each other on the front step. Then I said, "I can't say it's good to see you here—but it's good to see you." Emory put on a little grin and put up his hand, as if he would have pinched my cheek except he remembered now I'm sixteen and a young lady. "That's my Susie," he said. I had to go greet other guests then, though it was nearly an hour before Pa and Henriette returned and almost another hour after that, before Henriette came down from her room. Julia didn't come down at all. I found Emory out in Henriette's garden. It's bare and cold now, and all the leaves gone, so we were alone.

"It made my blood boil, to hear Yankee recruiters talk about 'killing Rebels' as if it was foxes and rats they spoke of, not men with wives and farms and homes," he told me. He looked like he hadn't slept in a week. "I believe in the Union, Susie. I truly believe, with all my heart, that it is the only way our country is to survive. Yet when it came down to it, it didn't make one bit of difference. I can't fight against my homeland. Can't step back and watch other men invade it. Not even if I know the cause is good."

It's only now, with fall of dark, and everyone leaving, that I've been able to read your letter he gave me.

Cora, what can I do? How can I make what's happened easier for you to bear?

You'll be on Deer Isle by now, with your family. Emory *has* to have told you that he didn't go down to the nearest Union camp and sign up. I *pray* this isn't the first news that you get about where he is! I pray so hard that your vision is true, about you and Emory with white hair, holding hands as the Twentieth Century dawns, surrounded by your grand-children, saying, "It was a horrible time but we got through it."

I pray for your little child, who'll be there when Emory returns. What are you going to name her? Or him, but it's really got to be a Her.

I'm glad you described your parents' house on Deer Isle for me—do they *really* pile pine-boughs all around the walls to trap the snow like you described, so the house will stay warmer? Enclosed is a sketch of you in your snug little bedroom behind the stairs, listening to your family's voices from the kitchen, like you said you did as a little girl.

I'm going to try to have our stableman escort me up to the Holler tomorrow, to see if I can find Justin Poole, to give him this letter. Please, please write of how you are. My oldest brother Gaius is coming home on furlough a few weeks before Christmas, and I'm afraid they're going to find some reason to keep me here until then. Then they'll find a reason to keep me until Christmas, and then . . .

I'll find a way. And wherever I am, I'll be with you in my heart.

Love,
Susanna

Emory Poole to Cora Poole, Boston

SUNDAY, OCTOBER 27, 1861

My most beloved—

Forgive me. That first, and above all else.

Parting I quoted that trite, true Lovelace chestnut that every man trots out for his beloved, when he deserts her to hazard his life for the life of his homeland: "I could not love thee, Dear, so much, loved I not Honor more." Its meaning is as true now as it was then: that the man you love is the whole man, good and bad together. That the man who loves you so desperately is also the man who with equal desperation loves the land of his birth. One man, not separable into husband and patriot.

That much I told you.

What I did not and could not tell you, my darling, was that it wasn't a Massachusetts regiment that I was going to join. That I wasn't going to be fighting shoulder to shoulder with your brother Brock. When I parted from you on the threshold of our home, it was not to walk to the recruiting office, but to the depot, to begin my journey back to Tennessee to join the Army of the Confederacy.

I believe in the Union of the States. I believe that our nation is unique and holy, molded by God's inspiring hand as no nation has been in the history of nations. Were any outside tyrant to assail it I would unhesitatingly pour out my blood in the Union's defense.

But it is not the Union which is being attacked. It is my home. And my home is Tennessee. I cannot stand by and let my home be invaded, not even by the government of the Union that I hold so dear.

My beloved, I wish I could have told you all this last night. But God forgive me, Cora, I could not. I so feared you might guess my intent. I wanted my last sight of you—if it is to be my last sight—to be of your smiling courage, not of pleas that would lacerate my heart without altering it.

I will write to you when I can, and I beg you to understand why I must do as I do. My only regret is the cowardice that shut my lips on this final lie; that, and the anguish I know you will feel.

I love you to the last drop of blood in my heart.

Forever,
Your Emory

Susanna Ashford, Nashville Female
Academy
Nashville, Tennessee
To
Cora Poole, Southeast Harbor
Deer Isle, Maine

Tuesday, November 12, 1861

Dear Cora,

Your letter of October first was waiting when I reached Nashville this evening, the one written before Emory's departure, warning me against Mr. Poole.

I wasn't even born when Patsy Poole went over that cliff. I've seen the cliff–it's called Spaniard's Leap and it's really quite high–and one of the first things Emory told me about his Pa, was, "He killed my Ma." When I first met Mr. Poole, I was five, Payne was seven, Emory twelve. Justin Poole was still living in the woods then and sleeping up in Skull Cave most nights, tho' he'd work the farm in the daytimes, with his hair all down his back and twigs in his beard. I think I was the only person he would talk to. After Emory went to Yale Mr. Poole did start coming into town sometimes, and dressing in regular clothes. Tho' he still sleeps on the ground with the dogs. The big one's Sulla and the ugly one's Argus. I knew he was crazy when first I met him, but I never was afraid of him, so please don't credit all the terrible stories they tell of him.

The night of Payne's funeral, the Lincolnites burned the bridges all along the railroad line. All the mountain counties rose instantly in revolt against the Secesh government in Nashville. There was supposed to be a Federal Army invading, too, only they never showed up. Pa not only sent me back to Nashville, but packed off Julia and Henriette and all the children here, too, to stay with Henriette's mother and sisters, whom Henriette *hates*. She keeps asking, Why can't Pa write to Aunt Sally in Vicksburg, and they go stay there? Because Aunt Sally has a big house and six plantations and a *lot* of money. I guess Pa doesn't feel up to telling Henriette that Aunt Sally *despises* children and won't have Leonella and Tristan in her house.

Would you have gone on with your education, Cora, if women were allowed to go to college? I know people say a woman isn't suited for any of the professions because she has to take care of her children, but what about all the women whose husbands [~~*leave them to go to war*~~–heavily crossed out] turn out to be drunkards or gamblers or wastrels? They *have* to take care of children *and* do something to earn money, don't they? And every slave woman works in the fields and takes care of her children, too. What's the difference between hoeing tobacco all day and seeing your children only at night, and teaching or mixing medicines all day and seeing your children only at night?

Monday, Nov. 18

Sunday dinner yesterday with the Russells, Henriette's family. I didn't really want to go. Since Payne's death I find myself getting angry very suddenly at little things that didn't used to bother me at all, like Julia's chattering, but Julia sent a note begging me to come, "so we can comfort each other." But talking about Payne *doesn't* comfort me, much less listening to what Julia would do if Tom were to be killed. (Die, too, she vows. She and Henriette spent a tedious hour planning their mutual tomb.) And all Henriette's mother and sisters could talk about was the blockade and how they can't get any coffee or sugar. I came back to the Academy feeling worse than if I'd spent Sunday here alone. Is there something wrong with me, for feeling like this?

Today Mrs. Elliott let me spend nearly the whole afternoon at Mrs. Acklen's, copying an Italian painting of St. Peter in Chains. Enclosed is my sketch—quite clumsy—and a study of Mrs. Acklen's dog sleeping.

I hope all is well with you on your Island tonight.

Your friend always,
Susanna

Cora Poole, Southeast Harbor
Deer Isle, Maine
To
Susanna Ashford, Nashville Female
Academy
Nashville, Tennessee

TUESDAY, NOVEMBER 12, 1861

Dearest Susanna,

As cold waters to a thirsty soul, so is good news from a far country. Your letter must have reached Boston only days after I left the city.

Needless to say, I fainted with horror at your shameless conduct in going "down the line." Nothing less will do for you, wicked girl, than to forever after wear a large red "C" sewn on your garments for, "Curiosity." Did you don a false mustache? How did you disguise your voice? It has always amazed me that the men in Shakespeare's plays never caught on to the fact that there was something a trifle dainty about "Cesario" and "Ganymede." Did you smoke a cigar? I search in vain for even one sketch.

It has been snowing heavily since yesterday noon. We feared Papa might be trapped here when the storm came on in earnest. Ollie has stretched ropes to the barn from the back door, so that Mother and I hold on to them when we venture out to feed the hens and milk the cows and goats, without fear of straying in blowing snow.

THURSDAY, NOVEMBER 14

Still snowing. With the house "banked" in spruce-boughs, the shutters stay closed from November to March, and the dim daylight can only be seen in the attic. As a child I thought nothing of this, but once I went to the Seminary on the mainland, I would look back on these dark winters, and wonder how I could have endured them.

In truth, I had good need for the cheer your letter brought me. Upon my return last week, Elinor and Deborah came to the farm to welcome me. The silence that fell on them when I said that my Emory had joined, not the Union Army, but the Confederate, went to my heart like a dagger-blow. They recovered quickly, and gave me loud and angry commiseration, assuring me I will still be welcome to the Ladies Reading Circle that we three founded when we were barely schoolgirls.

But as they were leaving, Elinor took me aside, and told me, quite seriously, that I had grounds to divorce Emory, for desertion.

Mother had put me to work at once, helping her finish her cheeses, and then make the soap. Between aching shoulders and washing the grease from my hair, I had little occasion to think. Yet now, snowbound, my thoughts return to their silence, and the look on Elinor's face. No one here speaks of Emory. Mother reads the Bible to Peggie and I offered to teach her writing and ciphering, but she manifests no interest in it, preferring to sew. With the house closed up, everything in it smells of smoke.

Saturday, November 16

Sunlight this morning like the trumpets of angels, but oh my, it is bitterly cold! Ollie and I donned snowshoes and dug out the path to the "house of office," filled with childish delight to be out-doors again and able to breathe fresh, sweet air. The summer kitchen is stacked with cut wood to its low ceiling, and more heaped around the barn. All afternoon Ollie and I have lugged in buckets of snow to melt for water, for baths tonight. This means the parlor will have a fire this evening, and there will be oceans of spilled soapy water to be mopped from the kitchen floor before we can go to bed! The weather looks to hold clear for church in Northwest Harbor tomorrow. Mother and I will bake, for coffee in the church hall between services, the scent of ginger and molasses almost better than the cakes themselves. I will drop this letter into the post-box at Lufkin's store, for Will Kydd to take across to Belfast on his mail-run Monday.

You may always say what is in your mind to me, Susanna—anything you wish. As I hope I may, to you, should I ever chance to do anything as outrageous as yourself.

Your friend always,
Cora

Cora Poole, Southeast Harbor
Deer Isle, Maine
To
Susanna Ashford, Nashville Female Academy
Nashville, Tennessee

WEDNESDAY, NOVEMBER 27, 1861
LATE NIGHT

Dearest Susanna,

The thought of you in Nashville—smiling and politely nodding while all around you rabid Secessionists shout their heads off—is the only thing that lets me breathe a little easily tonight. I trust that further meetings of the Southeast Harbor Ladies Reading Circle will go better!

TUESDAY, DECEMBER 10

Your letter came. Oh, my darling, I will take the liberty of disregarding your first request, and will pray for your brother Payne! For both of your brothers! And for yourself. I hope things go more easily for you now?

Another snowstorm last week. The house and barn are but dimpled mountains of snow. Even during daylight hours the house is dark, for the sun rises well past eight and is vanished by four. We keep the wood-box filled, prepare our simple meals and eat them, endeavor in vain to keep the house clean of soot. With the hired man gone, Oliver works very hard keeping the cows fed and the barn clean and fresh. The cows are nearly dry, so there is no butter to be made, only salted from the cellar, and last fall's eggs taste of brine. As the well is frozen hard, Ollie scoops up buckets of snow, to melt in the kitchen for our use and that of the animals. In the evenings we knit or sew, while Ollie sharpens tools and mends snowshoes and harness, and keeps the brass polished. He and Mother take turns reading to us from the Bible. I sometimes read the Portland newspaper, but much of what it contains is diatribes about Southern cowardice and degeneracy. Like you with *Uncle Tom's Cabin,* I *know* this is not accurate!

I took the precaution of purchasing material before I left Boston, for clothing for Little-Miss-Fidgets or Little-Master-Fidgets. Fabric is always dearly expensive on the island, the more so now that the Confederate sea-raiders are burning coastwise shipping. Peggie confided to Mother last night that she suspects she may be with child herself. Ollie walks around with a dazzled look on his face that is almost comical.

Mother reads, and we sew, and the banked spruce-boughs clogged with snow almost muffle the shrieking of the wind.

Friday, December 13

And now it is for me to confess shocking, shameful, and outrageous behavior.

A storm again, darkening even the windows of the attic where I sit in what used to be Peggie's tiny room. I have brought up a lamp with me, and this end of the attic, above the kitchen and close by its chimney, is comfortably warm. Yesterday Elinor visited, to ask me to speak at the Ladies Reading Group. "The women need to hear you," she told me. "You need not let shame keep you silent. For the good of the Union, Cora, you must speak out about how you truly feel towards this traitor who has tricked and deserted you. You must show the other women that you are one of *us*."

I replied, "I am not ashamed. Emory made his choice. That does not alter either my love for him, or my loyalty to the Union. Have you not always been first to champion a woman's right to hold views that differ from her husband's?" But Elinor was profoundly shocked at my disloyalty. In the end I gave a half-promise to speak, but her embrace upon departure left me feeling more alone than ever.

I do not wish to dwindle into one of those people who is forever complaining, "In the City we did so-and-so . . . Back home it is like this . . . " Yet when I woke last night to the muffled howl of the new storm outside, I felt such a longing for Boston, with its lectures, its newspapers, its concerts, and its crowds, that I nearly wept. Instead I lighted my candle, and re-read your letters: wanting only, as you said in your latest, to be anyplace but here. Yet reading last week's newspaper brought no distraction—accounts of skirmishes in South Carolina, of bloodshed and incompetence. At length I climbed to the attic, and opened Mr. Poole's trunk of books, and sought for one of those novels that gave you such comfort. Upon finding it, I thought that the title *The Hunchback of Notre Dame* sounded rather lurid, yet surely a title like *Pride and Prejudice* connoted grave respectability.

After two chapters I *had* to continue, and pursue the fate of the Bennet sisters and their ridiculous mother. There was hopeless love there, too, and I grieve for Elizabeth and her Mr. Darcy. As I read on, bundled up in my quilts, I did feel much better.

You were quite right, dearest Susie, about the power of novels to lighten a heart. I never knew!

Your enlightened friend,
Cora

Susanna Ashford, Bayberry Run Plantation
Greene County, Tennessee
To
Cora Poole, Southeast Harbor
Deer Isle, Maine

THURSDAY, DECEMBER 12, 1861

Dear Cora,

Tho' there has been no reply yet to any of my letters, I must seize this chance to write one more, while I can. Justin Poole will take this letter across to Kentucky, and this time he won't be back.

I'm at Bayberry again, tho' thankfully will not be staying. Even Pa agrees that it's too dangerous. We're having Christmas here early, because of Gaius's furlough. Then Henriette and Julia will go back to Nashville with me, and Pa will take the train in the other direction, to Richmond, to see if he can get a dispensation (or whatever it's called) to sell our tobacco.*

It apparently never occurred to Pa to write to any of us that Regal's militia company is now camped around our tobacco-barn. We may be safe from bush-whackers this way, as Pa boasts, but it makes my hair stand on end, to see the men harass the maids when they go down to the servants' out-house. Pa says, "It's just the boys having a little fun. They don't mean any harm by it." But I've told the women servants that it's all right for them to go down in pairs.

The men from the camp relieve themselves in the weeds along the snake-rail fence. That's in full sight of the window of my and Julia's bedroom–which it didn't used to be, but all the trees that surrounded the house have now been cut down for firewood.

I feel like I'm in a bad dream: one of those where you're with a total stranger, and everyone around you keeps saying, "No, no, that's your mother–" (or Julia or Payne or whoever) and you *know* they're lying.

From the window of what used to be Payne's room I sketch the men, eating or playing cards or cleaning their rifles. As you can see from these, I don't get any too near. They hold cockroach races on hot skillets. I bet they don't wash the skillets afterwards, either!

I'm making a drawing of Gaius, as a Christmas present for Henriette. My brother is much thinner than he was last April, and he moves as if he's in some kind of pain, though he has no wound. He hardly ever speaks, when he used to always have an opinion about *everything*, but he's so tender and gentle when he plays with his children, it scares me sometimes.

FRIDAY, DECEMBER 13
NIGHT

I'm writing this in Payne's old room, which is quiet, and warm because it's over the kitchen. The rest of the house is freezing. I can hear Pa, Regal, and some of the militia, talking and shouting in the big parlor. We go back to Nashville Monday.

I got Den to take me into town this afternoon to see Mrs. Johnson. It felt so strange, to have everyone ready to hang one another, over what used to be just politics. They're seriously talking about turning Mrs. Johnson, sick as she is, out of her house, in spite of her oldest son swearing the Loyalty Oath. Her daughter's husband swore the Oath only after they caught him leading a band of about four hundred armed Lincolnites to seize Rogersville. It sounds so insane! Men from the Confederate Army camp outside town have ambushed and beat up men, only for *speaking* out for the Union, not even for taking up arms.

It was Mrs. Johnson who told me, Justin Poole is leaving Tennessee. I will give him this letter tomorrow.

I wanted to send you this to say, *please* keep writing to me, even if my answers to you get lost. Everyone around me—Pa, and Julia, and the Elliotts back at the Academy—talk as if Secession and the

Confederacy and how terrible the Yankees are, are the *only* things that exist anymore: as if the world ends at the Mason-Dixon Line. I need you to keep reminding me that that isn't true.

Your friend,
Susanna

[N.B. Jefferson Davis ordered Southerners to boycott sales of cotton to Europe, as a demonstration of how much European nations needed the Confederacy—a policy which backfired rather severely.]

Susanna Ashford, Nashville Female Academy
Nashville, Tennessee
To
Cora Poole, Southeast Harbor
Deer Isle, Maine

TUESDAY, DECEMBER 17, 1861

Dear Cora,

I wasn't going to write again until I heard from you, but something has happened—or I *think* something has happened. You are the only person I would speak to of this; you are the only person who saw what happened at the depot, that day you and Emory left for Boston.

Saturday I got Den to ride up to the Holler with me, to hand your letter to Justin Poole. I hadn't seen him since that day at the depot. The whole house is in ruins now, not just the side he nailed up after his wife died. He and his dogs were waiting in the laurels, and because of what happened at the depot all those months ago, I didn't know what to say. He asked me, "Are you happy, Susie? Barrin' your grief." And I said, Yes, I am, because in a strange way it's true. Being at the Academy, and getting proper Art lessons, and being able to copy good paintings–knowing that I really am on the road that will take me to Philadelphia and beyond. It's as if nothing–not even the War–really matters, not deep down where the Real Me lives.

Mr. Poole said that he had a favor to ask of me, and we left Den at the Holler with the horses, and climbed part-way up the mountain to Skull Cave. (You remember, I took you there last March?) On the way he said he was sorry that he could do no more at Payne's funeral than stand in the church door, but I knew if he'd done that, he must have seen your Emory. And yet he did not mention it.

I asked him about what had happened to his wife. He told me that she'd run out of the cabin after they'd quarrelled, and when the storm came up he shut Emory (who was only three) into the cabin, and went looking for her. He found her broken body at the bottom of Spaniard's Leap, but the storm was too fierce then to get down the mountain. "I was no fit husband for her or any girl," he told me, and added with a little grin that's very like Emory's, "luckily for you, Miss. I know I was crazy, after. But I did all I was able, just then." I remember Mrs. Johnson telling me that her husband tried to take little Emory away from his father and that Justin drove him off with a shotgun.

There are all kinds of stories about Justin Poole's treasure, because he was the worst miser in five counties while Emory was growing up, saving the money to send him to Yale. But you'll never guess what's in the cave! It's even better than gold, Cora! Way down deep past where I took you, is the rest of his books. "I wanted somebody besides me to know where these were," he told me. I peered into one of the trunks and saw the *Inferno* and *Jane Eyre* and Marcus Aurelius's *Meditations* in Latin, and *all* Walter Scott's the Waverly novels, which I *desperately* wanted to take back with me to Nashville except I knew stupid Nora Vandyke would cut the pages out of them for curl-papers. "You'd think, in forty-five years, I'd have more to show," Justin said. I promised him that I'd come to check on them, every time I was back in Greene County. "You did ask Pa for my hand," I said, to make him smile. "Keeping these safe is the least I can do for you. Will you join the Army, when you get to Kentucky?"

"Not Kentucky," he said. "If I join there, Emory and I would meet, sure as death. I can't shed my son's blood." He said he'd go to his sister in Illinois, and join there. "And when the War is done," I asked, "will you be back?" He said, "I see it bringin' me nuthin' but pain," which made me feel strange, because everyone in the mountains swears Justin Poole has Second Sight. "When the War is done, you'll be gone," he went on, and put his hand to my cheek, the way he did in the depot, the day he went to watch his son get on the train with you as his new bride last April. "To Philadelphia, and Paris, and wherever artists must go." And just the way we did in the depot that day, I put my arms around him and we kissed, and if he'd asked me to go with him then, to Illinois or the Moon or back to the Holler to live the rest of our lives, I would have gone.

I thought that Art was the only thing I cared about, Cora, the only thing in the world for me: the road out of being the housekeeper at Bayberry all my life, the road out of the South, out of a world where everybody expects girls to marry and have babies when the only thing that makes me happy is drawing and painting. But with everything in me I also want to be with Justin. And I know I can't have both things. If I'm an artist, I would be a *terrible* wife, and a mother worse to my babies than Pa is to me. And I would hate them, and Justin, too. I can't be what *I* need, and what everybody else needs.

And I can't imagine living without either one.

I don't know whether to tear this letter up and throw it in the fire, or put it in an envelope and send it.

S

Susanna Ashford, Nashville Female
Academy
Nashville, Tennessee
To
Cora Poole, Southeast Harbor
Deer Isle, Maine

TUESDAY, DECEMBER 24, 1861

Dear Cora,

The Christmas present I most wanted (since it isn't likely anyone's going to give me a painting by Caravaggio); your letter from Deer Isle, about those awful ladies of the Southeast Harbor Reading Circle telling you that you must divorce your Emory. Being buried in snow like that with everything smelling like smoke sounds horrible, and it's hard to imagine how trapping *more* snow around the house is going to keep you any warmer. I love cheese-making but I'm afraid the only time I'm glad Pa is a slave-owner, is when it's time to make soap. But there's no cheese this fall because the militia has eaten most of the cows.

I've enclosed some of the drawings I made of one of the taverns on Spring Street. Use your best judgement about showing them to anyone. Nora and the other girls here all squeal when I paint things like old shoes and broken glass and ask, "Why do you always paint such ugly pictures?" *She* should talk! Her flowers all look like cauliflowers and her butterflies look like ducks. *Dead* ducks. I replied, "I don't know, Nora—why do *you* paint such ugly pictures?"

Most of the girls have gone home to their families, and the school halls echo strangely tonight. Mr. and Mrs. Elliot gave those few who are left here presents at supper. (New pen nibs! Heaven only knows how Mrs. E got them!) I will go to the Russells' tomorrow for dinner.

Wednesday, December 25

Well, everybody who said last spring, "The War will be over by Christmas" is wrong. Last Christmas was the last time I saw Payne. Now my dearest brother is gone, and Bayberry . . . isn't really Bayberry anymore. I hope and pray your brother Brock is well, and having a happy Christmas, wherever he is. I pray for Emory, and for you, buried under a hill of snow on Deer Isle.

Last night I pretended I was there with you in your snug bedroom behind the stairs; that we could whisper to each other the way Julia and I used to do. I pretended I still had all my brothers (even one whose wife would rather sew than read!) and a Papa to spend Christmas with, and a Mother who's strong and kind. Since I can't have those tonight, I'll settle for Athos, Porthos, Aramis, and d'Artagnan, savored secretly like candy in the stillness here that's broken only by the sounds of the troop trains.

Tuesday, December 31
Morning

I will send this off to Mrs. Johnson tomorrow, and hope she still "knows people who know people" (she should—her middle son is riding with the bush-whackers!). Mrs. Polk—widow of the President—gives a ball at her house. There is much dashing about the hallways and lending back and forth of gloves and laces, and you can smell burnt hair even downstairs in the parlor. Henriette's sisters will be there, but Julia begged Henriette to stay home with her. She would have begged me to stay home with her (she is due in March), except she and Henriette are trying desperately to marry me off. Both tell me I should change to second mourning for the occasion, to better my chances: Henriette's sister has a black-and-white that will fit me, they say, and hint that six weeks is "enough" for a brother. But I remember dancing with Payne, and in his honor will go to Mrs.

Polk's ball in my best black. Not that Payne would care, but I feel better so.

To be honest, I'd rather stay here at the Academy tonight reading *The Three Musketeers* . . . or better still, be magically transported to Maine, with a bottle of Mrs. Polk's blockade-run champagne in my hand, to toast in 1862–and all it may bring–with you!

A blessed Christmas, dearest Cora.
S

1862

Cora Poole, Southeast Harbor
Deer Isle, Maine
To
Susanna Ashford, Nashville Female
Academy
Nashville, Tennessee

THURSDAY, JANUARY 2, 1862

Dearest,

The same boat that brought Papa home to celebrate Christmas brought your letter of early November. I am so sorry, to hear about your brother–if there is anything that I can do, to help you or Julia, please let me know.

It feels strange to write that I'm glad you saw my darling Emory. Thank you for not upbraiding him on my behalf. You asked how you could make his departure more bearable for me, and you have done so already, in greeting him as a friend. Did he look well? Thank you, too, for that wondrous sketch in the margin, of him on the gravel of Bayberry's drive, wearing a borrowed black coat.

And thank you for the drawing of me in my room. I laughed at the portrayal of me reading that mammoth pile of newspapers in bed: would that there were so many available here! Yet more often–my preceptresses at Hartford Female Seminary would grieve to hear–bedtime finds me lost utterly in *Pride and Prejudice, Sense and Sensibility,* or the beguiling *Emma.* How often I have been told, *and have told others,* that the reading of novels "rotted" a girl's mind and rendered her unfit for "serious" mental effort. I suppose, if my mind is rotting this winter as a result of the contents of Mr. Poole's trunk, I would not be aware of it. Yet it is to Miss Austen–and to yourself, Susie–that I owed my ability to laugh and shake my head after my "speech" before the Southeast Harbor Ladies Reading Circle, rather than weeping with vexation and rage!

To give the Reading Circle its new and proper name: it is now the Daughters of the Union Propaganda Society. Do you have Propaganda Societies in the South? They have sprouted up over the East since the War began, to encourage recruitment and promote the purchase of government bonds to finance the War. I spoke of the people I met in Tennessee: said that many Southerners sincerely support the Union but favor slavery as well, that many are kind, good-hearted, Christian people who do not deserve to be judged by their leaders or by their neighbors. Of Emory I only said, "My husband made a hard choice, one with which I cannot agree. But he has not ceased to be my husband, before the eyes of God." This was when Elinor went to the melodeon and said, "Why don't we all sing 'May God Save the Union'?" The only person who spoke to me afterwards was Sukey Greenlaw. She said that her cousin is a lawyer in Portland and if I wished to divorce Emory for treason, her cousin would see to it at a quite nominal charge. When I crept to my bed that night, throbbing as if from a poisoned wound, I seemed to hear kindly Mr. Bennet say to his daughters, "For what do we live, but to make sport for our neighbors, and to laugh at them in our turn?" I managed one rich laugh, and slept.

I had been searching (vainly, alas) for another of Miss Austen's books in the trunk when I came on a slender volume by Mr. Dickens entitled *A Christmas Carol*, which moved me to tears. Surely you have read it? But Papa remonstrated, "Do you truly think any work of man is fitter to read on Christmas, than the tale embodied in the second chapter of the Books of Matthew and Luke?" And he is right of course. Yet on Christmas Eve, Ollie and Peggie and I huddled together in my room all under the same quilts, long after our parents were in bed, and I read Mr. Dickens's magical story to them. Knowing you were alone at the school that night, I pretended you were here with us, too. And I could just imagine how your eyes would sparkle when Bob Cratchit saw that Christmas turkey that was bigger than Tiny Tim!

When I say, by the way, that Papa was here to "celebrate Christmas," I must add that most of Deer Isle holds by the old New England habit. Here, Christmas *morning* is marked by church-going and prayer, but beyond that, it is a day like any other. We exchange little presents on New Year's Day, but that is all.

FRIDAY, JANUARY 3
MORNING

A quick word, to conclude. The weather has become threatening, and though we hoped that Papa might remain through Sunday, and return Monday to Yale when the students come back, it has been decided that he should leave today. There have been storms every week since I have been home, heavy snows followed by bitter "nor'-easters" as the fishermen call them. My fingers are always chapped and bleeding from the cold.

I see you in your curtained house, the grief of mourning, as if it were still going on today, this minute. But I look at your sketches and know that somehow, you will find a way.

I see Ollie bringing the sleigh around for Papa. I will write again very soon, Susie.

Yours,
C

Cora Poole, Southeast Harbor
Deer Isle, Maine
To
Susanna Ashford, Nashville Female Academy
Nashville, Tennessee

TUESDAY, JANUARY 14, 1862

Dearest Susanna,

Would I have gone on with my education, if women were allowed to go to college? I assume you mean a true college, with the same education as young men receive: in law, in medicine, in engineering, rather than the sterile piling-up of "accomplishments." There are, goodness knows, Female Academies and Colleges where one can progress quite far in the disciplines of history, languages, and such sciences as botany and mathematics: the Hartford Female Seminary, which I attended for four years, was one of them.

Yet at no time was there ever a discussion of what one *does* with one's education, if one is a woman. We–women–have come far, in that it is even possible to attend a Female Seminary these days at all. Forty years ago, the great discussion was, Should girls be taught to read? (They would, after all, only consume foolish novels like *Pride and Prejudice,* poor silly things.) All a young woman may qualify herself to do is teach–if she can find a school. And then, only very young children. I wish there were a way to send you my copy of Mrs. Wollstonecraft's astonishing book, *A Vindication of the Rights of Women*–since, rather to my surprise, a second copy of it lies in Mr. Poole's trunk: well-thumbed, imagine that! Find a copy, Susie, if you can. Read it, I beg you. It will open your eyes, as surely as mine were opened by *Uncle Tom's Cabin*!

It has been brought home to me how few places there are to go, if one is a woman, and with child. I am glad and grateful that my family has welcomed me, but I am aware–with the wave of patriotic feeling now sweeping the land–of how few here would welcome a

Rebel soldier's wife. I shiver to think of what my lot, and my child's, might so easily be! As I grow weary of pointing out to Peggie, when I married Emory he was *not* a Rebel soldier, nor did he have any intention of so being! On her most recent visit, Elinor did not scruple to repeat to me what Deborah said to her: *Every time I look into her* (that is, my) *face I wonder if she prayed this morning, that my Charles would be killed.* I cannot tell you, how ill this makes me feel. I could only be glad that a snowstorm prevented me from attending this month's meeting of the Daughters of the Union! I am grateful that by next month, snowstorm or not, I shall be too far advanced in my condition to be out in public.

Nor do I find comfort in the single newspaper that comes from the mainland once each week, with its squabbles over whether Southern slaves "deserve" freedom, and its dreadful cartoons of "Rebel ladies" collecting the skulls of slain Federal soldiers, and wearing shawls wrought of those soldiers' scalps and beards.

Mother counsels Bible reading, for she has never approved of my addiction to newspapers. I do find comfort in the Psalms, and the Book of Job. At least I am not the only person in the Universe, who has been *full of tossings to and fro, unto the dawning of the day.* Mother firmly agrees with the ancient destroyers of the Library of Alexandria: "Whatever was true in those books is also in the Scripture; whatever in them was not also in the Scripture, is better consigned to the flames." Yet my heart finds a gentler refuge in Mr. Dickens's *Bleak House.* And since I am not yet reduced to sitting on a dung-heap covered with sores, I find in its heroine's philosophy of helpful cheer a clearer road-map to guide me day to day, and, I blush to admit, in the horrendous Mr. Tulkinghorn an outlet for the pent-up malice in my soul: I can wish *him* all the ill in the world, and savagely rejoice when it finds him.

SATURDAY, JANUARY 18

Wash-day today. Please excuse the awkward penmanship. I managed to burn my hand, raking out the ashes from the stove. Because of the cold we only black-lead it once a week, early on Monday mornings, when it has been cold over Sunday. Raking of ashes on other days is a trick for which I never acquired the knack. The latest nor'-easter has at last ceased blowing. Yesterday was spent hauling snow and boiling water to soak everything overnight for washing today. Despite the bandage, my hand smarts from the lye, and I face a day of pouring yet more lye, hauling yet more snow, and boiling yet more water. We hope to have a few days' drying-time before another storm. With good reason do Deer Isle girls bring to their marriages wedding-chests brimming with sheets, chemises, towels, stockings to last through winter if possible. Since Peggie proves indeed to be with child, I can only contemplate what wash-days will be like next winter, with *two* infants in diapers under this roof.

All my affectionate wishes and prayers to your sister, who must be coming close to her own confinement.

NIGHT

I feel as if *I* had gone through the mangle, not the sheets. Yes, I long to see whatever drawings you care to send, Susie. Please send them, if you can. You are quite right, that no one in America paints like the Europeans—I *adore* Mrs. Acklen's little dog. I will not tell you of the little portfolio I've started of your sketches, lest you become conceited, but your sketches put me instantly at your side. If I cannot speak to you, I can see what you are seeing, and I treasure that.

Your friend,
Cora

Cora Poole, Southeast Harbor
Deer Isle, Maine
To
Susanna Ashford, Nashville Female
Academy
Nashville, Tennessee

THURSDAY, FEBRUARY 13, 1862

Dearest Susanna,

Is this how foxes feel, when hunters stop their burrows so that the wretched creatures can find no refuge? Though there can be little comparison, between the inconvenience of being whispered about by one's childhood friends as a potential traitor, and the frightening presence of armed and drunken men around one's house. I know your father and your brother Regal can be counted upon to keep Regal's men on their own side of what is proper, at least insofar as you young ladies are concerned, though I consider it criminally irresponsible, to say the least, not to speak out for his servants. I am so glad to hear you will be returning to Nashville soon!

At least my cousin Isaiah has come to replace our hired man. He and Oliver–

[letter discarded–not sent]

Cora Poole, Southeast Harbor
Deer Isle, Maine
To
Susanna Ashford, Nashville Female Academy
Nashville, Tennessee

TUESDAY, FEBRUARY 18, 1862

Dearest,

Are you all right? The most awful rumors have swept the island that Nashville is being evacuated ahead of Federal invasion and bombardment. It will be next week before we will even have a newspaper story, if then. Please, please, write to me, to let me know where you are, and that all is well.

Cora

Susanna Ashford, Nashville Female Academy
Nashville, Tennessee
To
Cora Poole, Southeast Harbor
Deer Isle, Maine

THURSDAY, FEBRUARY 13, 1862

Dearest Friend,

Rec'd your letter today–so little time to write! I have to hide your letters now, and mine to you.

My hand and arm are so cramped it's hard to hold a pen. The whole town is on tiptoe after the Yankee attack on the forts upriver.

Mrs. Elliott is on one of the hospital committees, and has the whole staff of the Academy and all the girls washing bandages. I didn't do badly, but the town girls who've never seen anything bigger than a chicken killed got pretty sick. It isn't just blood, the way it is with a deer or a pig.

Friday, Feb. 14

Terrible news coming down the river all day. Last night I got Mr. Cameron to escort me (capped and trousered as before) to the landing, to see the wounded from Fort Donelson brought ashore. At home I used to sketch pigs when they were hung to bleed out after slaughter. I didn't think this would be *so* different. If I am to be an artist—a true artist—I *have* to know. But it is different, and horrible, Cora! I didn't faint, but Mr. Cameron said, "I shouldn't have brought you." Still, I'm glad I know.

Later. Evening

More bandages. Raining on and off all day. Rumors everywhere, and no way of knowing which are true. People in the street just yell them up at the windows. Half the girls are weeping, and nobody is selling wood to do the washing with. I went to the attic to look for a basket for clean bandages and found Nora Vandyke up there, hiding. She called me all sorts of names and pulled my hair, but I got her downstairs somehow and put her right to work. If I can do it, she can. She's announced she'd rather kill herself than be "taken" by the Yankees and now about fifteen of the girls are all in a suicide pact.

Saturday, Feb. 15

Word just came down the river. The Yankees have been thrown back. Mrs. Polk is giving a ball tonight. Just about every house along the respectable end of Spring Street is illuminated in honor of the victory. Mr. Cameron says, you can drink yourself unconscious on champagne just walking three blocks. Nora's bragging how she knew all along the Yankees would retreat. Did I tell you she is engaged to three Captains and a Major?

In an hour Mrs. E is taking us up to the State House to hear the speeches of victory. Everyone is talking about the Battle of Marathon. All I can think about is Payne, and poor Gaius—who was killed with Jackson's men so near Winchester, Virginia, last month—and all those men they were bringing ashore yesterday. Is it over? Will Tom be able to be there when Julia's baby is born? Will Emory go back to Boston with you? Or will he be prosecuted as a traitor? Will Justin be able to come back, after all? And if so, what then? I thought I'd be glad when one side or the other won, but I just feel hollow, Cora, as if there's a hole blown in me and the wind's coming through.

Tuesday, Feb. 18
Bayberry Run

I just re-read what I wrote to you last week. It's as if it were somebody else writing about another world!

Late Saturday night, just hours after we got back from listening to the speeches of victory, word came that the Confederate Army was pulling out of Nashville and retreating south.

As soon as it was light I ran to the Russells' house. I found Henriette's mother and sisters packing to leave. They practically shoved Julia into my arms, to get rid of her. All Mr. Russell's money was invested in cotton and tobacco, and they've been living on almost nothing for months, so I can't really blame them for not wanting another mouth to feed. Julia just about swooned at the thought of setting foot outside the house, much less taking a train, in her "delicate" condition. But I asked her, who did she want to be seen by? Strangers in the depot when she's completely covered with a cloak? Or whoever was going to pull us out of the smoking rubble of the house if the Yankees *did* shell the town? There were mobs in the street, either trying to get to the depot and on a train, or taking carriages to loot the Army warehouses. Men and women–white and black–in rough, dirty clothes, were just walking around the streets watching to see who was loading up to abandon their houses: looters, waiting for people to flee. Of course the entire city police force joined the Army as it was pulling out. What a horrible feeling, knowing that if someone were to decide to kill Julia and me for our earbobs, nobody would stop running long enough to do anything about it!

Dr. Elliott somehow got the whole Academy down to the depot together. Half the girls were in hysterics the whole way. People were fighting to get tickets and cramming onto anything that moved. We got onto a train at about sunset, and reached Chattanooga just before nine. The self-respecting heroine of any novel would have gone into labor on the train, but for a wonder Julia didn't. In Chattanooga Mr. Cameron took us all to a hotel (one room, and glad to get *that*), where he'll stay with the girls and Mrs. Elliott until Dr. Elliott gets word to everybody's parents. But Julia and I went back to the depot first thing in the morning. After a lot of waiting, we got a train to Greeneville around noon.

That was yesterday. Julia and I didn't have a nickel between us when we arrived, but Charley Johnson was kind enough to drive us out to Bayberry Run.

Pa still isn't back from Richmond (not that he's written us, or anything like that) and most of the darkies have run off, and I can't blame them. The militia is still camped around the barn, but about thirty of them have now moved into our house. Regal wasn't here to order out the ones camped in our bedroom. Captain McCorkle (he wears spectacles and has an Adam's apple the size of a lime) got them to move finally, but the whole bedroom stinks—tobacco-spit, cigars, and plain dirtiness, a smell worse than any animal—and the bed and blankets are crawling with bedbugs and lice. So is the chair—I tried sleeping in that. The window is broken, so we needed to wrap up in the one remaining blanket, and we wouldn't have had *that* if Captain McCorkle hadn't been standing right there when the men got out of the room. We hugged each other to keep warm, and Julia wept all night (in between both of us scratching). She has been begging me for the last half-hour while I'm writing this to go downstairs and get Mammy Iris to come up with hot water to wash, and milk for her, and to have Cook boil up water to wash all the bedding.

Does she really think any of those women is still on the place?

LATER

Mammy Iris, Den, and a few others are still here!!! Cook ran off last week, after some of the men raped her and her daughter. Mammy looks at me like she hates me, Mammy who raised us all! The awful thing is I don't blame her.

LATER

It's almost too dark to write. I can hear the men downstairs, rough voices and things breaking. I don't really think they'd do anything to me with Captain McC in the house, but going out to use the out-house is truly terrifying. Julia and I pushed the bed up against the door.

WEDNESDAY, FEB. 19

Hunted the house top to bottom, for anything that can be sold. Hard to do that, with the men hanging around, chewing and smoking and playing cards. Pa had a couple of trunks full of Confederate bonds in the attic, but that's now a kind of dormitory. I didn't even dare go up there. Anyway, Captain McC says there's nothing left of value up there now.

EVENING

Got Captain McC to lend me "a couple of the boys" to ride into Greeneville, to see if there's a doctor there, and to see if anyone knows anything about the bank. Of course Regal's still gone, and there's no word from Pa. On the way into town, the Corporal in charge of my bodyguard scolded me about being brought to the plantation by Charley Johnson, a traitor from a family of traitors who all deserve hanging. "I hear tell you been sparkin' some Lincolnite hill-billy yourself," and gave me a look that made me think, *I'm out in the middle of the woods with four men I've never met before in my life.* I told the Corporal that I didn't think gentlemen discussed ladies behind their backs, and he snapped back, "They don't. But soldiers fighting to defend their country from invaders got the right to discuss if a she-traitor is likely to stab them from behind."

The bank in town was shuttered tight, and nobody knew anything about a doctor. Under pretext of looking for one, I got away from my bodyguard for an hour, and sneaked to the Johnson house, which is horribly broken-down now, with awful things written on it. Mrs. Johnson was thinner even than she was last spring, tho' she claims (to me) to be malingering so the local Confederate troops won't confiscate the house. I guess an Oath of Loyalty doesn't count if everybody "knows" you're a traitor in your heart. She asked very kindly after you, and offered Julia and myself sanctuary. I was hard put to find a way to say, *Oh, no, thank you, we couldn't inconvenience you* (as one is supposed to at least once for good manners) that wouldn't jeopardize the offer. She laughed at my expression and said we'd be doing her a favor, because the Confederacy would think twice about turning out the daughters of the most prominent Secesh in the county.

Well, I might just as well have saved myself the trouble of being polite. Because of course, Julia won't hear of it! She clung to the bedpost like she believed I'd drag her bodily out of the room, and said she refuses to have anything to do with a Yankee-loving traitor and her drunkard son (preferring I suppose the sober paragons of gentility in the next bedroom). "'This is my home, Susie! This is *our* home! Does that mean nothing to you?'"

This sounds terrible to say, but no, it doesn't. I try to joke about it, but I feel like I'm in a nightmare. I can't desert her—I could never face Pa, or Tom, or Emory, or myself in the mirror, if anything happened to Julia or her baby . . . But, Cora, I'm so scared I don't know what to do.

If you get this—*when* you get this—you'll know that everything turned out all right. But right now, tonight, it's dark, and I hear the men getting drunk again.

THURSDAY, FEBRUARY 20
GREENEVILLE
EVENING

Lincolnites attacked our home last night. They set fire to the tobacco-barn and the militia camp. I saw one man shot off his horse and dragged away screaming at a gallop with his foot caught in the stirrup-leather. I didn't see more because a bullet smashed the window beside me, and Julia went into hysterics. The men burst into the room, cursing us because we'd dragged the bed in front of the door again before going to sleep, and broke out the rest of the window to shoot at the riders down below. One of them yelled "Shut that bitch up!" and Julia screamed again, and I thought, *Oh, my God, she's going into labor!* But she wouldn't let go of me to let me look for a candle, and away from the firelight at the window it was too dark to see anything, and she kept screaming, "Don't leave me! Don't leave me!" It was Bedlam, Cora!

Even when the men ran out, and the barn-fire died down, she wouldn't let me go. It sounds gruesome, but I felt around her in the bed, and there didn't seem to be any blood. The shooting got less outside, and she finally fell asleep. I couldn't find the candle, and wasn't about to go out of the room, so I went to the shattered window. Standing there on the shards of glass, I saw the remains of our barn and the soldiers' encampment, glowing red-gold against the black night and the black trees. I guess that's what the Greek camp outside Troy looked like when Hector drove the Greeks back to their ships. Only when first light came and I could see Julia hadn't miscarried, could I breathe again. Outside, by the cut-off tree-stumps, six corpses were lined up on the ground.

I got dressed, and went downstairs and told Captain McCorkle in my most commanding tone that Julia and I would need an Army wagon, to take us into Eliza Johnson's in town.

And that's where we are, Cora. I don't know how long we'll be able to stay here, or what Pa will do with us when he gets back from Richmond, but at least we're safe and we've both *finally* had baths. I wasn't about to get undressed back at Bayberry even if we *could* have gotten water heated. By the time you get this, goodness knows where we'll be. Mrs. Johnson tells me that Nathan Forrest managed to get his men away from the Federals, and as of two days ago was holding Nashville. But nobody really knows what's happening.

I'm going to try to write to Dr. Elliott at the Academy, and to Mr. Cameron. I have no idea where Henriette is with her family and the children. I know they have family in Missouri, but what's going on there sounds even more frightening than what we've been through this week! I feel as if Julia and I have been washed overboard in some huge tempest, and are out in the middle of the ocean, clinging onto a plank. But right for now, we *do* have that plank, and from here at least there are people who can get letters across into Kentucky, and mail them to you. I keep your letters near me and re-read your last letter, and it's like looking through a window. Just because the room I'm in is pitch dark doesn't mean the sun has been snuffed out. I truly wish I was with you in your room with Peggie and Ollie, huddled under the covers listening to you read *A Christmas Carol*—or that I could go to one of those Daughters of the Union meetings and pull your friend Elinor's hair for you!

Your friend,
Susanna the She-Traitor

Cora Poole, Southeast Harbor
Deer Isle, Maine
To
Susanna Ashford,
c/o Mrs. Eliza Johnson
Greeneville, Tennessee

TUESDAY, FEBRUARY 25, 1862

My Dear Friend,

A letter from you—though of course it contains not one word of where you are now!

Weeks before I came around the corner of the station house to find you in Justin Poole's arms, I was aware of his love for you. Yet I had heard the dreadful stories of him, not from gossip or rumor, but from his own son, whom he neglected and suffered to grow up like a Red Indian in the woods. I know not what to say or advise. I trust your good sense, dearest Susie, yet I know how love intoxicates.

It surely was never possible for me to think clearly, when I was in Emory's arms.

Only remember that you do not have to decide anything now. You have no power over what will befall Justin, before you meet him again, nor over what will befall you. Use wisely the time that God has taken pains to interpose between you. Thus my advice is: to prepare yourself for the art academy in Philadelphia, when the opportunity shall present itself for you to go there. Such action will preclude no further decision—and the reverse cannot be said.

And please forgive me if I sound coarse, or prudish, or as if I mistrust your virtue—but if this man should by any chance return before the War's end, I beg of you, remember how easily a woman's freedom can be lost! Much as I adore my Darling-Who-Is-To-Be-Born, I know that, whatever happens to Emory in this war, I must now take Her into account, in what I myself can choose to do, henceforth and forever.

I should not say this. I should say instead, "All my hunger for a life of learning vanished like the dew when first I guessed I would be a mother." But it hasn't. Sometimes I feel that I have been cheated, tricked, led into a trap—a trap whose barbs are forged out of love, so that escaping would bring more pain than remaining in its meshes.

Is this, then, what it is to be educated, to be trained like athletes for a race we will never be allowed to run? Beware of your heart, Susie!

There! I have said what I think! It is snowing still, and the wind and the cold and the darkness in this house render me prey to morbid reflection.

THURSDAY, FEB. 27

It would help if I could believe spring would come soon. When I was at school, if there were no milk and no fresh vegetables—and we girls had been living on salt meat and salt fish and bread and corn mush for close to a month with no end in sight—at least we didn't have to go down to the cellar and see how low the supplies were getting. Such things could be readily bought. The Reach that separates Deer Isle from the mainland is frozen solid, the roads on the island impassable. There has been much sickness hereabouts, and many children have died. Few of Mother's friends can visit. I feel more isolated than ever.

Yet before dawn this morning, crossing to the barn in a luminous world of silence and starlight, I saw a fox making his way over deep snow smooth and white as marble, homeward bound to his den in the woods. God's creation, and innocent of human malice.

You will rejoice to hear that I have at last made the acquaintance of your friend Quasimodo the Hunchback, and Esmeralda the Gypsy, and all the others in that astonishing tale. They have helped me through many an endless night. Mother is right, when she says that in reading the Bible, one touches God's hand, and so cannot ever be lonely or afraid. But sometimes one needs to touch the hands of one's fellow humans. Since reading Mr. Dickens, and Miss Austen—and, I blush to report, Mrs. Radcliffe—now you know the depth of my depravity!—I have realized this about novels: they are like conversations, or acquaintanceships, that change us deeply by widening our experience. They are like *friends*. Naturally my father would warn me against unwholesome conversations, or against the sort of fascinating friends who would lead one into foolish acts by making them seem right and justified. Yet, to limit one's friendships to the narrowest of like-minded circles is to become provincial, perhaps self-righteous . . . like too many people on this island!

I will send this to Mrs. Johnson in the hopes that she will know where to send it on to you. But, as I read that her husband was so vociferous in his demands for the invasion of Tennessee, I fear that some retaliation may force her from her home.

I pray that it finds you safe.

Your friend,
C

Susanna Ashford,
c/o Eliza Johnson, Greeneville, Tennessee
To
Cora Poole, Southeast Harbor
Deer Isle, Maine

WEDNESDAY, FEBRUARY 26, 1862

Dear Cora,

Charley Johnson brought news that the Federal Army entered Nashville yesterday. What this will mean I haven't the least idea. Nor does anyone, really. Because the railroad doesn't run straight from Nashville to the eastern counties, the Federals can't push through to liberate us without taking Chattanooga first, and of course it's massively defended.

Regal (finally!) came here Saturday, with the regular CSA Commander from Knoxville, your compatriot, of all things, from Maine. Regal ordered Julia and me back to Bayberry. Since Bayberry gets raided once or twice a month by the Lincolnites and since the only Secesh boarding-house in Greeneville charges five dollars a week, it was eventually agreed that we two women would continue under "that skunk traitor Johnson's" unhallowed roof (only Regal didn't say *skunk*).

So here we are. For how long, no one knows. The rumor is that Senator Johnson will be named Military Governor of Tennessee, and I know it's only a matter of time before the Confederate States of America sequesters the house. Julia's baby is due in a few weeks. I asked Dolly (you remember Mrs. J's Dolly?) to tell me exactly what happens when a baby comes: what it looks like, what has to be done, what can go wrong, in case Julia should go into labor when there's nobody but me around. You'd have thought I'd asked her how to carve up and stew Baby Tommy (or Baby Aurora Victoria) (!) when little he-or-she arrives. It "wasn't fittin'" that a young girl (meaning a virgin, I guess) should know things like that.

But why *shouldn't* any girl who's old enough to have her monthlies know about babies, and how they're born, and where they come from? She's going to have to learn sometime!

SATURDAY, MARCH 8

It maddens me that a letter from you is probably lying in a Post Office in Nashville, undeliverable to the Academy or anywhere else. Or, worse, that *my* letters to *you* went to kindle some bush-whacker's cigar.

Julia keeps to her room. Dolly has found a black midwife in town. I help Dolly and her girls with the housekeeping, or help Mrs. Johnson tutor little Frank. Of course he's not able to go to school anymore, and Mrs. J is afraid that some Secesh in town is going to take out his politics on Senator Johnson's son. There was a time when I would have said, "Nobody would do that to a nine-year-old child!" but I honestly don't know anymore. In the evenings we lock the house up tight, and I read to Mrs. Johnson while she sews (or vice versa). Because of your letter, we're re-reading *Pride and Prejudice,* and it helps very much to occupy oneself with the Bennet girls' husband-hunt. But the threat that overhangs *them,* of being turned out of their home by Mr. Collins, cuts a little close to the bone—as does the realization of how helpless Julia and I would be, if that happened to our hostess.

I knew Pa hadn't paid my board bill at the Academy since the beginning of December, but there were several of us there in the same circumstance. And I knew Pa hadn't sent money to Mrs. Russell, either, one reason she treated Julia so shabbily. But going back to Bayberry, and trying to find out about the bank here in town, brings home to me that even tho' Pa still owns a plantation, we're poor. If someone were to come to me and say, "You can go to the Academy of Fine Art in Philadelphia tomorrow," Pa wouldn't be able to send me. Julia hasn't the least idea that we're now living on Mrs. J's charity. She still keeps calling her "that traitor"! With the field hands run off and the militia all over the property and the banks closed, there's nothing else for us to live on *but* charity.

It makes me turn hot all over to think of it, because I know Mrs. J can't afford two more mouths to feed. I don't know what to do, and until they get this war over I don't even know what I *can* do. I'll write to Pa in Richmond, but I know already he's just going to write back, "Of course you must leave That Traitor's house immediately and I'll take care of everything when I get back." But I know, too, he's not even going to write that, because Pa always finds some reason that he's too busy to write. I can just see him when he returns, pinching my chin and grinning, "I knew my Babygirl would take care of everything!" And giving me a new handkerchief that he bought for me in Richmond, and Julia a diamond necklace!

It makes me feel better to write this to you (and to draw the enclosed picture of Pa's triumphant return).

Monday, March 10

Having just re-read the above, I want to ask you, or tell you . . . I know you love your parents, and your home, and Elinor and Emory. I love Julia and Pa, and Tennessee. But sometimes I feel two things at once–like sincerely loving Justin with all my heart, and sincerely not wanting to marry him because it would mean not going to the Academy of Art. All my life, Julia's been telling me, "You can't be angry at Pa if you truly love him." Well, I truly love him, and I'm *furious* at him, Cora. And I'm furious that I'm not allowed to say so; that most people will say there's something wrong with me even for thinking, *He's acting like an irresponsible blackguard.*

Can we make an agreement, you and I, that whatever I write, you know that I'm not mad to love Pa, and Julia, and Justin, even though I may decide that I love Art even more?

I think that's one reason I love *David Copperfield* so much. Mr. Dickens touches it so *exactly.* It truly helps to know that I'm not insane for feeling two contradictory things with equal force. Is there a copy of it, by the way, in Mr. P's trunk? Mr. Dickens also talks, in *DC*, about what *I* do with books—put myself in those places, make up other adventures for those people. Mrs. Elliott would say, like your Father, that we should only read what improves the mind, but I don't think that's so. Sometimes we just need to rest our minds, to let our hearts sit quietly next to a warming fire until the chill abates. With dear friends, if our friends are near-by. But if they aren't, then with those other friends—Quasimodo and Eliza Bennet and Mr. Micawber, and all the rest.

Wednesday, March 12

Julia had her baby, a little boy. Thomas Jefferson Ramsay Balfour.

Wednesday night

Charley Johnson just brought word that his father has reached Nashville, to take over as Military Governor of the Union-held part of Tennessee.

Love,
S

Susanna Ashford,
c/o Eliza Johnson, Greeneville, Tennessee
To
Cora Poole, Southeast Harbor
Deer Isle, Maine

Saturday, March 15, 1862

Cora,

Your letter came yesterday, but I daren't pass your good wishes along to Julia. She hates the Yankees with a virulence equalled only by the Daughters of the Union for the South. I keep your letters hidden, and only read them when she's asleep.

Aunt Sally Bodmin came today. Ordinarily you couldn't get Aunt Sally into Senator Johnson's house at gunpoint. Since Mrs. J is supposed to be at death's door I went downstairs, to tell her we'd had to give Mrs. J Extreme Unction last night (even though she's a Methodist). But the minute I came into the parlor Aunt Sally demanded, "Has Julia had her baby yet?" which makes me laugh, Cora, because she'll slap my hands if I even *hint* that women *have* babies. So I said, Wednesday, and I couldn't help noticing that in spite of the Union blockade, Aunt Sally's hoopskirt, silk dress, bonnet-feathers, and lace all looked new. So did the coloring of her hair. She asked, "Can Eliza travel?" Meaning Mrs. J. When I shook my head she glared at me and asked, "If the house were burning down, could she flee?" With that she brushed past me and went upstairs to Mrs. J's room with the news that within a week Mrs. Johnson and Charley were going to be on their way to Libby Prison (and poor little Frank on his way to God knows where!) because Senator Johnson has arrested the entire city government of Nashville (*and* poor Dr. Elliott!) for refusing to swear the Loyalty Oath to the Union.

"And no more than that husband of yours deserves," snapped Aunt Sally. "But I pay my debts, Eliza. And I owe you this, for getting my nieces out of Bayberry when that cretin brother of mine lets militia white-trash camp in the house because they haven't the red blood in them to join the real Army and actually do some good against the Yankees." She'd talked to Pa in Richmond and didn't have a good word to say about him or President Davis or anybody on either side. "I'll send my coachman over on Thursday," she told Mrs. J, "and he'll escort you up to your daughter's place in the mountains. That part of the state is crawling with Tories like an old dog with fleas. You should be safe enough there."

I asked, What about us? and she looked down her nose at me, even though I'm seven inches taller than she is, and Julia who'd crept in very quietly, with tiny Baby Tommy in her arms. "Pa didn't say we have to go back to Bayberry, did he?"

"He did," Aunt Sally replied. "And I told him not to be stupid. You girls are coming with me to Vicksburg."

So that's where we'll be, Cora. It's far down the river enough to be out of the way of the Yankees, and so heavily fortified that even the Confederate High Command (Aunt Sally says) can't be idiots enough to let the Yankees take it.

Wednesday March 19

We leave in the morning. For days we've been smuggling things from the house to be stored all over Greeneville with other Unionists. Of course Julia thinks we should go back to Bayberry. I packed up my sketchbooks and pencils (which are all down to stubs), and all the remaining paper in Senator J's desk, and the precious pen nibs Mrs. E gave me for Christmas only three months ago. The Academy seems years in my past now. I just re-read your letter, the one that you wrote when Emory left: about pretending that it's years and years in the future. I pretend that I'm a little old white-haired lady, writing to you (from where? to where?) and saying, "Remember how scared I was, when there were bush-whackers and militia fighting all over Greene County, and Julia and I had to go live with dreadful Aunt Sally in Vicksburg?" And you'll write back, "And you see, honey, it all turned out all right." I want to reach into the future tonight and hold that letter from you in my hand.

I'll say special prayers for you the whole month of June, when Baby-Cora is going to be born. It's nearly midnight, and I'm downstairs in the parlor, where you and I first met, and the house is freezing. I feel like I'm sitting on a stage after the play is done, waiting for the stage-hands to come and strike the scenery. All the things that took place here—you and Mrs. J coaching me so I could go to the Academy; Mrs. J teaching Emory back when he was a boy—all those things are going to vanish when we walk out of this house tomorrow. After that, they'll only exist in our hearts.

Enclosed is a sketch of the room.

Love,
S

P.S. Write me care of Mrs. J care of her daughter Mary Stover in Elizabethton, Carter County, Tennessee. I guess the mountain folks have a regular service across the lines to Kentucky, which drives the Confederates just about crazy.

Cora Poole, Southeast Harbor
Deer Isle, Maine
To
Susanna Ashford, c/o Eliza Johnson
Greeneville, Tennessee

Tuesday, April 1, 1862

Dearest Susanna,

Thank God you are safe!

The stories I read of conditions in Nashville during the evacuation were dreadful, and I had great fear for Julia, knowing how far advanced her condition must be. The *Portland Transcript* speaks of a Federal Army of over fifty thousand men encamped in and around Nashville, and of more approaching it; of Rebel sympathizers jailed and sent to prison camps on the Michigan border for "aiding" an "enemy" which consists of their brothers and sons.

I received your letter with a sensation of reprieve as well as delight. At the same time I try to push from my mind the knowledge that by the time this reaches you, you and I may both be living in, as you say, "another world"—if they have not altered beyond recognition by the time *your* letter reaches *me*.

My mind pictures you and Julia clinging to your metaphorical plank in the ocean, and I marvel at your matter-of-fact courage. I marvel, too, at the fact that in retrospect, you can laugh. Marvel, and hope that by your example I'll one day be able to do the same.

I cannot help comparing this approach to life with the Gothic heroines whose lurid adventures I have lately begun to explore. For Emily St. Aubert and her spiritual sisters, terrible events have the character of falling over a bottomless precipice in the dark. But in truth—and in Miss Austen's tales—the cliff is not bottomless, however deep the chasm may be. One does not fall, but is only obliged to climb down, one painful but possible hand-hold at a time, until one reaches the bottom. One gropes one's way across the bottom, and climbs—one painful but possible hand-hold at a time—up the other side. Which is another way of saying, I suppose, Where there's Life, there's Hope.

I feel as if I am slightly less than half-way down, my friend. When I call out in the darkness, it is your voice that calls back to me. Though I cannot see you, I know we are both carefully descending the same cliff, and will meet on the other side.

I pray for your safety.

Elinor is the only one of the Reading Circle—the Daughters of the Union—who visits me now. Last week word came that Charles Grey—my friend Deborah's fiancé—was killed in battle at New Bern, North Carolina. At church Sunday Pastor Wainwright spoke of it as a "crime," as if men had broken into Charles's house and shot him.

After services I heard many denounce his "murderers." No one did so to my face. Even Mother's friends turned from me.

Charles and I played together as children. I feel that I *should* be angry at the men who killed him. When I realize that he *is* dead—and this realization returns to me many times a day, as fresh as if I had not heard it before—I am ill with anger. But I do not feel their personal rage. Is this because Emory is fighting on the Rebel side, not because he believes in slavery or States' Rights, but out of duty to his homeland? The same duty that moved Charles to fight? Or is it only because no lover, no husband, no brother of mine has been killed . . . *That I know of? Yet?* Whatever the reason, coming down the church steps, Charles's mother, and sisters, and Deborah looked at me as if they suspected I had myself loaded Emory's gun, to personally shoot the young man we all so loved.

Later. Evening

After bringing in wood, helping Mother take down the stiff-frozen laundry, and as you see by my writing I have burnt my finger in the stove again. Oliver, Isaiah, and Uncle Mordacai's hired man are tapping the maples tomorrow—we begin to boil the sap for sugar. I do little enough these days, being slow and clumsy now, and it irks me, to tire so easily. The world is a sodden morass of muddy snow that freezes hard each night, weakens to slush only for an hour mid-day. I dreamed last night about egg-custard, which I have not tasted in six months.

Thursday, April 3

Sugared all day yesterday, and again this morning. Icicles as long as my arm bar the eaves. Snow patches only in the woods, inviting

Oliver most reprehensibly to smack me with a snowball! I responded in kind–*far* beneath the dignity of people who shall both be parents one day soon!

Elinor visited this afternoon, to help sugar off. Elinor has borne two children, has walked the path on which my feet are irrevocably set, and has passed through that gate of pain that I myself face in less than ninety days. Peggie, looking to her own confinement only weeks beyond my own, will talk of nothing, as she and I sew in the evenings, but of how two of her aunts died in childbed, one of them in lingering agony which she does not hesitate to describe repeatedly and at length. To this, Mother invariably contributes, "If it is God's will that you give your life bringing forth a child into this world, remember that it was so ordained since the beginning of Time."

Susanna, I am frightened, terribly frightened. I try not to think about dying, and I try not to think about the pain. And all Elinor will talk about is how the town has voted to pay ten dollars per family, to any man who will enlist, and how towns all over Maine have been trying to wriggle out of paying the families of volunteers anything, and what a shocking thing this is, and what the Daughters of the Union must do about it. I try to remember that I am in God's hand, and that *this present moment*–Elinor's chatter, Peggie's wails, the marvelous smell of maple-sugar, and Mother's belief that saying "God knows the hour of your death" will comfort me–*all* this was formed by God, for my benefit, and is part of His ultimate intention for me.

Most of the time I do not succeed in this attempt. My child is due in the middle of June. If this is the only letter from me that reaches you, pray for me in that week. May God have mercy on my beautiful child.

And may God bless Mr. Poole, whatever his sins, for providing a trunk-full of comfort, of distraction, of amusement secretly imbibed, to lift my heart and dispel my fears. With my confinement approaching I should read nothing that does not calm and inspire, yet I find myself gorging on Mr. Poe's macabre tales. Black cats–give me a sack-full! Gruesome resurrections? The more shocking, the better! Frightful revenge? I revel in each detail!

Can this be akin to my periodic, overwhelming cravings for pickles and crab?

Or is it only because these absurd horrors banish true fear?

May God bless you, my friend. Keep you safe.

Love,
Cora

P.S. I am more sorry than I can say to hear of your brother Gaius's death, and the bereavement of poor Henriette, who was so hospitable (was it only March?) although I'm sure she quite agreed with your Aunt Sally about my Yankee barbarity. Please let me know, when you hear that she and her children came to safety. Let me know, too, if you have news of what became of your dear friend Mr. Cameron after seeing the Academy students safely to Chattanooga–and whether Mrs. Acklen's art gallery suffered during the looting in Nashville.

C.

[forwarded to Vicksburg–reached Vicksburg end of May]

Cora Poole, Southeast Harbor
Deer Isle, Maine
To
Susanna Ashford, c/o Eliza Johnson
Greeneville, Tennessee

WEDNESDAY, APRIL 9, 1862

Dearest,

News of horrendous battle in Tennessee, casualties almost unbelievable: nearly one man in five. Though as far as I can make out,

Shiloh is far from Greeneville (the nearest atlas belongs to Elinor), I have heard fearful stories of conditions in the east of Tennessee. I fear for you and your sister, though I know, even as I write these words, that I am powerless to help or even to know what is taking place there at this minute. And when you read them, the situation will have improved or worsened, but will not be the same situation. What manner of world do we live in, Susie?

Saturday, April 12
Evening

Snow is flying, just when it looked to be spring at last. Papa is expected but has not yet arrived. Ollie is carrying in extra wood. He and Papa were to have cleared away the boughs from around the house this afternoon. Yet another week of darkness and snowshoes . . .

Wednesday, April 16

Still snowing. Sugared off four times. How I wish I could send you a cake of it!

Tuesday, April 22

Your letter. A prayer of thanks, that Julia's child is safe born! It gives me hope for my own. I feel such fear, and then the child moves within me, and all the world transforms to joy.

And you, my dear, have a wicked, wicked pen! And yet, like Miss Austen's books, your drawing of your Pa's triumphant homecoming disarms my rage at the man, for reducing the two of you—the *three* of you, now, counting Baby Tommy—to living on charity.

And yes, charity or not, poverty or not, you *will* find a way to get into the art academy. And then you can put your Pa's face in paintings, say, of King Charles the Simple being forced to give up his land to the Normans, or of Nero falling off his couch in an orgy while good Christians sneer at him from the doorway. Please paint me in as a Christian.

Yes, a thousand times, and thank you, a thousand times: there will be a pact between us, that no matter what anger either of us expresses, it is understood that I love Elinor, and Emory, that you love Julia and your Pa. We feel what we feel, and pretending otherwise can only lead us—and the people around us—to grief. But, we are responsible for what we do, and for what we say in public. We can change the focus of our thoughts, until our feelings cool, or change, or pass.

This is the magic that I have discovered this winter: the secret blessing of being buried under a mountain of snow with a trunk full of forbidden novels.

LATER

You are quite right. My mother always cautioned me that it was improper to consider the physical relations between husband and wife. Only in reading of the natural rights of women have I come to the belief that it is not only a young woman's right to know the workings of her own body, it is her duty. Surely to let her remain in ignorance is like sending a young soldier into battle only half-armed? I thank Heaven for my sister-in-law Betsy, who, as soon as I knew I was with child, explained to me exactly what I would have to face, and how best to get through it.

THURSDAY, APRIL 24

Sunlight at last! The snow has melted from the ground. The early saxifrages have bloomed in the woods—in a week, the world will be carpeted in flowers.

We begin spring-cleaning tomorrow—such a relief, to finally scrub away the greasy soot of winter, throw open every window to the air, to beat every rug and re-stuff every bed-tick and wash every curtain in the house! When Papa comes on Saturday, we will begin our garden. The fishing-fleet has gone out, and Ollie and Isaiah have just come home, with two weaner pigs whose bacon and hams will see us through next winter's dreary cold.

All my love,
C

Susanna Ashford, Vicksburg, Mississippi
To
Cora Poole, Deer Isle, Maine
c/o Eliza Johnson, Elizabethton, Tennessee

FRIDAY, APRIL 4, 1862

Dearest Cora,

This is in the nature of a trial-balloon, sent up to see if Eliza is in fact able to get letters to "people who know people" and so across to where they can be mailed to you. I understand there is a woman in Sullivan County who operates a regular mail-service via the bush-whackers: every week she goes about to all her Unionist friends with a mail-pouch of letters from their husbands and sons in the Federal ranks.

Aunt Sally ordered us to dress in our best on Sunday, and took us visiting to all her friends, to introduce us to Polite Society here.

Julia agreed earnestly with everyone we took tea with, that in fact there are *not* hundreds of men fleeing Tennessee rather than fight for the Confederacy, but "only a few white-trash troublemakers." I keep my mouth shut like the she-traitor spy that I am, firstly because these are Aunt Sally's friends and I am Aunt Sally's guest and secondly, because disagreeing wouldn't change their opinions one whit! When I confront Julia with the fact that she *knows* that thousands in our State are riding in arms against Confederate rule, she widens her eyes at me and scolds, "Now, you know that isn't true, Babygirl." In any case, she is so taken up with Baby Tommy that it's difficult to converse with her about any subject but how many times Tommy has needed his diaper changed today. I think Aunt Sally would have left Tommy under a bench in the depot if she thought she could get away with it.

Aunt Sally's house is on China Street, at the top of a hill. In addition to being set on the bluffs above the river, Vicksburg is all hills, worse than Greeneville. From the one called Sky Parlor–if you climb it up either a switchbacked zig-zag path, or a long flight of wooden steps–or from the cupola of the Court-House, you can see miles up and down the Mississippi. It's a breathtaking sight, Cora. Vicksburg lies just south of a sharp hook in the river around DeSoto Point. North of town the land flattens into a swampland of bayous around the Yazoo River, and across the Mississippi from us the land is flat, too: the best cotton land in the world, Aunt Sally says, though it floods in winter. You can see all the little houses of DeSoto, where the railroad comes in from the west, and where the ferry crosses to town. The house is large and luxurious, since Aunt Sally's most recent husband was a wealthy merchant here, and has a garden where I draw most afternoons. Her second husband made the Grand Tour and she has three Italian and two French paintings here in the house for me to copy, in oil, if I can get any. Mr. Cameron set out a program of drawing-practice for me, to follow if I cannot get regular lessons. One thing that reconciles me to Sunday calls with Aunt Sally is, to see who has decent paintings in their houses. I am currently making plans to ingratiate myself with them all!

She also has her third husband's whole library! Including *all* Jane Austen's novels (including *Northanger Abbey,* which I've never read!), and Sir Walter Scott's *Paradise*!

The paintings are: *Bacchus Comforting Ariadne* (by Vernet); a *Portrait of the Artist's Sweetheart in Gypsy Costume with a Suit of Armor* (it isn't called that, but that's what it is); a *splendid Rape of Lucrece* (which I think she purchased because she likes to gaze upon the semi-draped Adonis the artist got to model Tarquin); Samson grinding grain (ditto ditto the model for Samson); and *A Mother Displays Her Daughter to a Wealthy Suitor.* The Wealthy Suitor has a scrawny neck and squinty pale eyes, exactly like Captain McCorkle, only without the spectacles.

MONDAY, APRIL 7

Unspeakable fighting at Shiloh. I remember the wounded being carried ashore at Nashville back in February, after the fighting at Fort Donelson—when I got Mr. Cameron to take me down to the landing—and I am filled with rage, at the lives so casually blotted out.

TUESDAY, APRIL 8
LATE NIGHT

~~*[I dreamed about Payne, and Gaius: an awful dream in which they came back to Bayberry, Payne carrying his right arm in his left hand like a stick, Gaius with his lungs in a basket and a hole through his chest you could see daylight through. Bayberry was the way it is now, trees cut down, rugs torn up by the militiamen. When the boys smiled at me, their mouths were full of flies*~~—entire paragraph heavily crossed out]

Please be there to get this letter, Cora.

Love,
Susanna

Susanna Ashford, Vicksburg, Mississippi
To
Cora Poole, Deer Isle, Maine
c/o Eliza Johnson, Elizabethton, Tennessee

FRIDAY, MAY 30, 1862

Dearest Cora,

Two letters!!! How strange to read of icicles and snow still on the ground in April!, then go down to the river landing, where the air is hot and close as steamed towels. Reading your letter made me wish again that I could go there and pull Elinor's hair for her. When Payne was killed, I know Regal and Julia both felt angry at President Lincoln, *personally;* at Senator Johnson, *personally;* at Justin, *personally,* as if everyone who favored the Union had conspired to murder our brother. Sometimes I find myself wanting to blame someone, for the fact that I'll never see Payne again, and I'll never see Gaius again, but there's never anybody really to blame. I go calling with Aunt Sally, and everyone sounds the same. Hating the Yankees. Wishing every one of them would die, and that they could watch it happen.

Your other precious letter was the one you wrote back in February, about Justin Poole. Thank you for not being horrified. Or for not saying so, if you were. When Justin took me in his arms at the depot I didn't know what to think myself. It was the first time that I thought that I might not *want* to leave Greeneville—only I knew I really *did.* (You're absolutely right about not being able to think clearly.)

". . . . the time that God has taken pains to interpose between you." I remember when I was a little girl, Mammy used to tell me: "In front of every door that it's best you don't walk through, God has placed an angel with a flaming sword." Needless to say, I did *not* appreciate this piece of advice! But hearing it again, now, like Elizabeth Bennet re-reading Mr. Darcy's letter several times, I see what it actually says. Thank you.

And of course I don't think you're being "coarse" for telling me not to let Justin seduce me if he gets the chance. I have never understood why "nice" ladies don't talk about how babies get born. I helped Cook with the accounts in the kitchen since I was a little girl. What I *didn't* learn listening to her and Mammy Iris, when they forgot I was there, talking about Pa and the housemaids, could be written on the back of a visiting-card. It always sounded sort of silly to me. Mammy slapped me for asking about it, but Payne and I used to hide and watch when Den would put one of Pa's stallions to the mares. Obviously, God invented this means of producing colts. It can't be *that* different for human beings.

And I will say, that when Justin took me in his arms in the cave, suddenly I *did* understand why girls let themselves be seduced. (And suddenly a lot of novels make a lot more sense.)

Saturday, May 31

The night before Julia and I left Greeneville, I asked Mrs. Johnson about Patsy Poole. She told me that the night of the storm, when Justin brought Patsy back to the cabin, it was to find that Emory had gotten out of the cabin and into the woods. It was looking for him, that delayed Justin taking his wife down the mountain, until the road washed out.

While the battle was going on at Shiloh, I thought about Justin a lot. If he were killed, I'm not even sure who his commander would tell. I got a letter—with a beautiful little drawing—from Mr. Cameron in Virginia. He was drafted, as little and as sick as he is. The draft was suspended in Tennessee because *so* many men were sneaking across the border, that there was no one to raise crops, but the other States made such a fuss they may put it back.

The blockade has everyone grumpy and on edge, because it's very hard to get coffee or tea or wine or PAPER! This is the last of the precious, precious cache from Aunt Sally's first husband's desk. You *must* find, and read, *Northanger Abbey,* whose heroine keeps thinking she is in a book by Mrs. Radcliffe instead of by Miss Austen. If that does not make you laugh, nothing will.

EVENING

Every morning and every night, dearest Cora, I pray for you when your baby comes. I wish I could pull Peggie's hair, too, or at least tie a gag in her mouth. I promise you, everything Dolly and the midwife told me about childbearing sounded awful, but *not something that you couldn't get through.* (I don't know why I'm writing this: by the time you get this letter, your Little-Miss-Fidgets will have been born and probably be heaps prettier than Tommy. Aunt Sally says he looks like a jack hare).

Even though Aunt Sally's right and Tommy does look like a hare, I'm making a chalk portrait of him and Julia. I wish I could be there, to make a portrait of your child. One day I will.

Love,
Susanna

Susanna Ashford, Vicksburg, Mississippi
To
Cora Poole, Deer Isle, Maine
c/o Eliza Johnson, Elizabethton, Tennessee

WEDNESDAY, JUNE 18, 1862
JULIA'S BIRTHDAY

Dear Cora,

Julia turned twenty-one today. I gave her a portrait of herself and Tommy, and reaped unexpected dividends in the form of three (!!!)

commissions to do portraits of other people's children. And, Aunt Sally's best friend Mrs. Bell (her dear departed was some relation to one of Aunt Sally's early husbands) has given me a *carte de visite* of one of her nephews now serving in Virginia, with the request, would I do a portrait? The photograph on it isn't very good, but I'll try.

All this is because, tho' as usual no one will admit there's anything wrong, a number of people are sending their children elsewhere if they can. A few weeks ago, ships from the Federal fleet put in just beyond the town landing, and the Union Commander Farragut demanded that Vicksburg be surrendered. Gen'l Smith, who's in charge of the town, told the Yankees to take a long walk off a short pier (or words to that effect). Now from Sky Parlor Hill you can look down-river and see the Federal fleet, just out of range of our guns. More troops are pouring into town every day. The labor of every field hand for miles has been requisitioned to dig breastworks, rifle-pits, and gun-emplacements.

Wednesday, June 25

Got your letter! You wrote it to me care of Mrs. J in Greeneville, but the "postman" in Kentucky knew by the time it reached him that she had gone to Carter County, and had it taken to her there. A miracle!

Still snowing on the sixteenth of April!! You must be going insane, cooped up all those months! And yes, I will definitely paint Pa into a historical panorama, tho' now I'm inclined to do something like *The Discovery of Writing*, with Pa as one of the skin-clad barbarians goggling in amazement at whatever monk it was who first wielded quill and ink. "What are those little squiggles? I don't believe it! You tell me a man can actually *inform* his daughters who are about to be attacked by our Nation's Foes when he's going to come visit them? *Never!* The thought is too fantastical!"

Like you, I was always told that it wasn't "nice" to talk or even think about "unladylike things," that is, where babies or for that matter kittens and puppies come from. But nobody could ever explain to me *why* it isn't "nice." The ancient Greeks and Romans thought statues of people without clothes on were "nice." Mrs. Acklen had some in that style, and I've never seen anything so beautiful in my life! Even Mr. Cameron had me draw statues ("semi-draped"), while any boy art student would have already started on models. I am eternally grateful to Mr. Cameron for taking me "down the line" so I could actually see what goes on there. The way "young ladies" whisper and giggle and pretend not to see things—like their fathers and brothers treating the parlor-maids exactly like prostitutes—makes me wonder who started all this "don't look it isn't nice" business. And *why*.

I am glad and grateful that your sister-in-law in Boston could at least give you some accurate information.

Your baby has to have been born by this time. That's so strange to think about. I wait EAGERLY for your next letter!!

THURSDAY, JUNE 26

Woke this morning to the pounding of guns. Federal mortar-boats had come down-river overnight, and started shelling the shore batteries. I'm writing this in the cellar, which has a tiny window looking out the back where the hillside slopes away towards Adams Street. You can feel the impact through the ground every time a shell hits a few streets away. Julia is huddled in a corner, with Tommy wrapped in a quilt, Julia rocking and sobbing while the wet-nurse attempts to comfort her. Aunt Sally is upstairs doing the accounts. I should be helping her, except that Julia clings to my arm, screaming, "Don't leave me! Don't leave me!" which sets Tommy off. It waxed pretty dramatic.

Aunt Sally just sent down lunch.

Later. Evening.

The shelling quit when evening fell. The whole town smells of churned-up dirt, Cora, and smoke, tho' the breeze off the river cleared most of the dust. Aunt Sally and I walked to the bluff's edge, and in the very last of the evening light, we could see the dark shapes of the Federal boats, dozens of them on the shining water, both north and south of town. The sight made me feel queer, and very angry. I keep thinking there should be some better way of ending this Secession problem, without destroying the homes and lives of innocent people.

Would women run the country any better, if *we* had the vote? Or would Julia just vote the way Pa tells her to? And that would give Pa two votes instead of one.

On the way home we walked past Mrs. Bell's house, and that of the Petrie Sisters (other "nice folks," married to two brothers, both in the Army), to make sure they're all right. Both are close enough to the river to be in peril. Shell fragments had torn huge holes in the street a few dozen yards from the Petrie house, and Mrs. Bell was just coming home, with her servants and her Persian cat Mithridates tucked into a picnic-basket with his tail hanging out the back (see sketch). She'd taken the whole household to visit friends at the back of town, above the ravines where the troops are digging rifle-pits.

Friday, June 27

Shelling all day. Aunt Sally asked Mrs. Bell and her household to visit, as if the house is merely being painted!

SATURDAY, JUNE 28

Shelling continued last night after dark. So of course Julia refused to leave the cellar, and refused to let *me* leave. About two a.m., after she fell asleep, I went upstairs. I found Aunt Sally in the parlor still, though Mrs. Bell and her servants had long gone to bed. We could hear other noises from the river, shots and explosions, and together we went up to the top of the house, and looked out the attic windows. The whole Yankee fleet was coming up-river in two columns—you could see the glow of their smokestacks.

The boats traded shots—muzzle-flashes, like volcanoes in the dark—with the shore batteries for the rest of the night, until dawn. Aunt Sally sent me downstairs to wake Cook and get us some coffee; of course Cook and the others were all wide awake and at their work, like nothing was going on. The batteries sank three Union boats, but the rest got past.

When we walked Mrs. Bell home we found a shell had torn clear through her house, punched a succession of holes through the parlor window, the dining-room door, the rear wall of the dining-room, and a corner of the pantry, lined up as if someone had hit the house with a ramrod. Mrs. Lillard's house on the next street had the parlor chimney shot off, so that daylight and squirrels come right in. Nobody's been hurt up here—yet.

Seeing these things—knowing how little money the Petrie Sisters have—I'm angry all over again. Mrs. Lillard served us tea (or what was supposed to be tea) and the ladies all joked about it, as if all this stupid damage had been done by some malicious child. I think about what it will take to bring Bayberry back to production, even if we can get hands to work the land again, and I had to bite my tongue not to say, "The politicians who got us into this mess are idiots! This should never have happened!"

I don't tell Aunt Sally this. She'll talk about things nobody else will, like babies, and who in town drinks, and how to run a plantation—not just the bookkeeping, the way I did, but marketing crops and getting loans from Northern banks. But she is a true daughter of the Rebellion. However, she is also my best hope to pay for me going to the Pennsylvania Academy of Art when this is all done, so I'm working extremely hard to stay on her good side.

Sunday, June 29

Dressing for the Great Round of Calls after church and dinner with Dr. Driscoll, who is 70 years old and jokes that he means to marry me. Aunt Sally is resolved to "make a lady" of me and get me a husband, so her maid Nellie has the fire lit in here to heat irons to curl my hair, and the room is hot as a stove. I'll mail this tomorrow, care of Mrs. Johnson. After the noise of the shelling and battle, the silence feels so ominous, dearest Cora. Everyone's saying, "Whew, that's over," but it's not. It will come again, and worse. They're organizing hospital committees, as they had in Nashville.

I wish there were some way to talk to you, face to face, even for five oh-so-precious minutes. I feel as if I'm in a trap, when I look down-river and see Yankee boats, but it's considered almost treason to admit the Yankees are anything but a silly nuisance that will be swatted away very shortly.

It's *got* to be summer on your island by this time, so you—and your beautiful baby—can have milk and eggs. You can finally get your egg-custard! Tell me how you are, and who you would like me to kill in trade for your cake of sugar. How is your mother, and Ollie, and even Peggie? Your father will be home from Yale, to be with you all summer and get the harvest in. I envy you so much.

Love,
Susanna

Cora Poole, Deer Isle, Maine
To
Susanna Ashford, Vicksburg, Mississippi
c/o Mrs. Eliza Johnson, Elizabethton, Tennessee

MONDAY, JUNE 23, 1862

Dear Susanna,

Little Mercy Susanna Poole asks me to send you her regards, and her abject apologies at not being able to take pen in hand herself! But, she says, she is feeling quite well. Needless to say, she is the most beautiful girl in the world. She is three days old, today.

I, too, am feeling well. It is like falling in love a second time, differently. The world looked different, the morning after my wedding to Emory. It is more profoundly altered now, with my child in my arms. With *his* child in my arms. She was born Friday afternoon, at about three o'clock, after a very short travail. Mother and Aunt Hester were present, with Ollie, Peggie, Papa, and Uncle Mordacai exiled to the parlor. I'm sorry to say Peggie was deeply upset by the whole proceeding, and has clung all the more closely to her husband ever since. Her own child is expected in five or six weeks, and Mother and I are doing what we can to bolster her spirits.

I cannot wait, to be up and helping Papa in the garden.

Your "trial-balloon" arrived from Vicksburg only a few days before Mercy's birth. I cannot express my relief and gladness, to hear from you. Only days before that, a letter reached me from Mr. Poole, now in camp in Jackson, Tennessee. I will write to him of the birth of his granddaughter, and give him the news of your whereabouts and safety.

Tuesday, June 24

Elinor called upon us yesterday. She said that Charles Grey's things had arrived, sent back by his commander from New Bern, North Carolina. With them in the box was the bullet that killed him! Elinor showed it to me—a chunk of lead as big as a quince. They intend to display it to the Daughters of the Union at their meeting tomorrow night.

Wednesday, June 25

Papa is to go to Northwest Harbor in quest of another hired man, Isaiah having joined the fishing-fleet with his father. I will end this note, and send it on with him. I sat in the summer kitchen this morning, with Mercy in my arms, while Mother churned the butter and spoke at length of Herod's slaughter of the Innocents at Bethlehem, and what a good thing this was for those murdered babies. I should not laugh at her, not even within my secret heart, for she means well with her tales of Biblical horror. My little treasure I named for the sister who was born when I was seven, and lived barely two weeks. Of course Mother seeks to steel my heart against such a loss, in the only way she knew how to armor her own. For an encore she treated me to the tale of the Biblical hero Jephtha. He, it seems, slaughtered his little daughter in fulfilment of a vow too rashly made to God. Mother is nothing if not thorough.

It is as if winter never existed, nor ever could again. On this June morning I love all the world.

Love,
C
and M

Cora Poole, Deer Isle, Maine
To
Susanna Ashford, Vicksburg, Mississippi
c/o Mrs. Eliza Johnson, Elizabethton, Tennessee

SATURDAY, JULY 5, 1862

Dear Susanna,

I am so angry, and so troubled in my heart, I do not even know if this letter will make sense. Yet I must tell someone of what happened yesterday. The Union is the only hope of true human freedom in this world: this I truly believe. And, I believe that its preservation takes precedence over—I know I should write the word "everything" and I can not. But I do not know what to write instead.

Oliver has joined the Army. Recruiters came to the island's Fourth of July Fair and Celebration yesterday, giving away free liquor and accompanied by a small company of soldiers doing very smart drill in their wool uniforms in spite of punishing heat. The Captain engaged Ollie in talk, saying, I'm sorry to hear you have a broken leg—or is it the consumption, that's keeping you from joining up? Or is it only that your "wifey-ifey won't wet her 'ittle man go?" Will Kydd, who fetches the mail from Belfast every Monday, tried to answer back, but the Captain dismissed him as "one of those men who'd rather see himself walking around safe, and his nation crippled." At length Oliver, in a burst of pride, signed the recruiting papers, before I could get to him.

Elinor assures me that Peggie "would rather die in childbed" than be "married to a coward"—which, in fact, I don't think is the case. She further assures me that it's only a three-month enlistment—until apple-picking time—and pressed into my hand one of her Propaganda Society pamphlets, the verse enclosed. Yet, even if Ollie only goes to Virginia for that short while, it does not lessen the danger while he is there. Through the wall that separates my room from theirs I could hear Peggie crying, all night.

I am still angry today. Should I be angry with myself, for feeling as I do? Is it evil to love my brother *[~~more than~~*–crossed out] *[~~as much as~~*–crossed out]? Is it wrong of me even to write these questions to you, who have lost two precious brothers and the home you loved?

Remembering your letter, I went to the attic and searched out *David Copperfield,* which I knew I had seen in Mr. Poole's trunk: seeking proof I suppose that I am not insane or wicked to feel, at the same time, genuine love and blinding rage. Bless you for not holding me to any of what I have said above.

MONDAY, JULY 7
EVENING

Your letter came like an answer to the thoughts tearing at my heart. *Everyone sounds the same. Hating the Yankees. Wishing every one of them would die.* I cannot say the relief it brings me, to read that you don't hate *me,* or wish my family impoverished or my house burned, in revenge for your brothers' deaths. Sometimes I feel as if I were surrounded by strangers, who only *look* like the people I used to know . . . *as if everyone who favored the Union had conspired to murder our brother.* Like Mother, I suppose, telling me horrible tales of children's deaths, to lessen the hurt she still carries for the little girl she lost.

LATER

I take back what I've said about Elinor. I suppose it just shows how mixed are the elements of the soul. That was she who came to the door of the summer kitchen just now, with the news from her father, a selectman of the island, that I've been offered the position as schoolmistress on Isle au Haut. Among the men who volunteered along with Ollie was Peletiah Small, the Isle au Haut schoolteacher. The town is now offering a bounty of a hundred dollars for enlistment, but hired men are dearly expensive now, if they can be found at all. I think this is Elinor's way of making good this loss.

Tuesday, July 8

Laundry; a task infinitely easier in summertime when it can be done every two weeks instead of every six or eight. I still feel as if *I*, rather than the sheets, had been boiled in a tub. Ironing tomorrow, nearly all day, and picking the first of the cucumbers and stoning cherries for Mother to put up. How I love the feel of garden-earth between my fingers! The sky holds light until ten or ten-thirty at night. We all live in the summer kitchen, as late into the evening as we can stand the mosquitoes, which seem to be insatiable. I am generally the last one left, and sometimes write with a pillow-slip draped over my head like a hood, in which ridiculous attitude I sit now, dear, dear Susie, aching shoulders and all.

The cod-fleet has gone out again, and Papa has not found a man yet. I wanted solitude, and quiet, to re-read what you wrote of my father-in-law, and the death of my husband's mother. I will admit that Mr. Poole's letter surprised me, in both its erudition (for in person he makes a Spartan look like a chatterbox) and in its kindliness. Even as I write those words, I remember how difficult Elizabeth Bennet finds it, to reconcile Mr. Darcy's cold haughtiness—or Mr. Wickham's facile charm—with the truth, until more information is received. This gives me pause with regard to my father-in-law, and his estrangement from his son. As Miss Bennet did *not* do—to her sorrow—I will withhold my judgement, and wait upon events. I will say, things seem to be much simpler in the Bible, where men are good or bad, than in one of Miss Austen's novels!

WEDNESDAY, JULY 9

Oliver has gone. It is the time of year when the girls go over to Isle au Haut "a-plummin'"—that is, gathering blackberries, a task with which I will not be able to help, nor with the making of the jam. Tomorrow I begin my career as a teacher. Isle au Haut stands six miles farther out to sea than Deer Isle, and is so primitive as to make Deer Isle appear cosmopolitan. I'll cross back and forth every day with Will Kydd ("If you can stand the thought of sailing with a Copperhead," sneers Elinor). Elinor, who is still nursing Columbia, promises she will look after sweet little Mercy Susanna, as well. I've always gotten on well with Will Kydd, and I would rather that arrangement, than board on the island five days a week, and only see my beloved treasure Saturday evenings and Sundays. Before last Friday, I have not been away from Mercy for more than a few minutes at a time. There is no pleasure on Earth comparable to holding her in my arms, to bathing her, changing her (now you know I have gone insane!), touching her tiny hands and feet. And yet, I find the thought of going off to work each day—of earning money to help my family—fills me with an unladylike relish that is almost savage.

Thank you, dearest friend, for your kind thoughts, and your words of encouragement about my darling's birth. Yes, I fully expect a portrait of her—in oils!—one day . . . if you can make time among your other commissions.

I will refrain from writing to inform Mr. Poole of your new suitor. The prospect of a duel between two gentlemen of such venerable years can cause nothing but revulsion to ladies so refined as ourselves!!!

Love,
Cora

[enclosure—clipping from propaganda pamphlet]

"Don't stop for a moment to think, John–
Your country calls, then go;
Don't think of me or the children,
I'll care for them, you know."

Susanna Ashford, Vicksburg, Mississippi
To
Cora Poole, Deer Isle, Maine
c/o Eliza Johnson, Elizabethton, Tennessee

THURSDAY, JULY 17, 1862

[lost]

Cora Poole, Deer Isle, Maine
To
Susanna Ashford, Vicksburg, Mississippi
c/o Mrs. Eliza Johnson, Elizabethton,
Tennessee

SATURDAY, AUGUST 2, 1862

My darling Susanna,

A hundred times in the past three weeks I've thought –*Susie needs to know about this!* And by the time I finish cleaning the school-house, and step off the *Lady Anne* at Green's Landing, and walk, through peaceful summer woods at twilight, the mile and a half to Elinor's to get Mercy and then another mile and a half home, and feed Mercy, and help Mother with supper, and tell Papa about teaching (there are youngsters in my class under the impression that all United States Presidents are lineally descended from George Washington), and—and—and . . . it is ten o'clock, with dawn, breakfast, and the walk to Green's Landing again all due at five.

I must and will write, though once again it is nearly ten, with the prospect of even-yet-earlier awakening tomorrow. Uncle Mordacai is taking Mother, Elinor, and myself to the mainland, to deliver the news to Ollie of the birth of his beautiful son Oliver Lincoln Smith, who is wailing fretfully in the next room. Mercy, very much set up in her own opinion of herself as *far* too adult to give way to bouts of babyish weeping, sleeps like a furled rose-bud in her basket, hung over with cheesecloth to keep the mosquitoes away.

You need to see all the thousand tiny islets of Merchant Row in morning's first light—tabletops of granite each with its little tuft of pine-trees—garlanded about with diamond waves breaking, wreathed in crying gulls. You need to see the lobster-boats going out of Green's Landing when the *Lady Anne* sets forth, the air chill enough to require a shawl and the smell of the sea filling the whole of the world. You need to know what a deck feels like underfoot when the wind takes the sails and the sloop surges forward like a team of matched horses settling to gallop. I'd so love to see you sketching all this!

Dearest friend, I read the news of gunboat battles near Vicksburg, and huge Confederate raids in Kentucky, and I pray that you are safe.

Sunday, August 3
Visit to Sixteenth Maine Regiment, in camp at Augusta, Maine

Uncle Mordacai took us across to the mainland in the *Gull:* Mother, Elinor, and myself. Recruits are still coming in, and the rows of little shelter-tents along the Kennebec look sloppy and half-finished, little more than strips of muslin draped in an inverted V over a pole about three feet from the ground, open to the elements at both ends. The men of Company B—Ollie's company—haven't gotten their shelter-tents yet. They share a single marquee, sleeping on bare ground. The men crowded around us, clasped our hands, stammered greetings, even men from other parts of Maine, men we had never met before. Someone gave Mother half a barrel to sit on, and I was handed a visibly unwashed tin cup full of the sort of coffee the Devil must brew in Hell. Mother gave Ollie the molasses-cookies she'd baked and he promptly distributed them among his mess-mates. Looking at their faces, as Mother told him the news of Peggie's safe delivery, I realized that Mother wasn't just Ollie's mother now, but the mother each of them left back in Kittery or Bangor or Portland. I was the sister each of them grew up with. The news of little Nollie's birth was to each man tidings of the birth of his own son, the safety of his own wife.

The men shouted congratulations and thumped Oliver on the back, but I wondered if he was ill, for he was curiously silent, and he looked so much thinner than when he'd left home three weeks ago. But only when he walked with us back to the train-station in the late afternoon, did he break the news to us: his Colonel had that day informed him that his enlistment was for three *years,* not three months as he had originally supposed when he joined!

Elinor of course put her arms around my waist and Mother's, and declared stoutly, "Three years or three months, Ollie, does that change your country's need? You know Peggie will understand." But Peggie wept until she was sick, when she heard the news upon our return, and could not nurse poor tiny Nollie. Between doing double duty, and comforting her, I was not in bed until long past midnight.

Thursday, August 7

One of the lobstermen who's been over to Belfast says, Word is that the Rebels have attacked Baton Rouge. To the best of our knowledge, the Thirteenth (Brock's regiment), though in Louisiana, is not at Baton Rouge . . . or wasn't, as of his last letter. But Elinor's Nathan is in the Fourteenth, as is John Henderson, whose brother Alex—in the same company—died of fever in New Orleans only weeks ago. Papa is still not yet back from Northwest Harbor (it is nine now, and growing dark) where he walked to learn more, if he can.

Friday, August 8
Night

Bless Will Kydd! Though he greatly objects to the War, he crossed to Belfast last night, the moon being nearly full, to fetch what news he could. With it, he fetched your letter. (With all this, he remembered to ask the postmaster if there was something for me!) He vows he will cross again tonight.

The whole island holds its breath. Almost fifty island men are in the Fourteenth, a great many of them married men with families. Those who aren't thinking of Charles Grey and Alex Henderson, surely cannot keep from their minds poor Charlie Noyes, and George Herrick and Billy Dunbar, who were returned alive but will never be anything but charges upon their families for the remainder of their lives.

It is as though the Angel of Death passes over the island this night: *There was a great cry in Egypt, for there was not a house where there was not one dead.* Would that we could avert it, by prayer, or obedience, or blood smeared on the lintels of our doors!

I read that the shelling has ceased at Vicksburg, at least for the time being. By the time tonight's words reach you, Susie, tonight's fears will be part of the past. Yet in my heart I see you hiding in the cellar with Julia, I smell the churned earth and see the ruined homes of your friends, as if those events took place just today. Would matters be different, if women could vote? I don't know. Elinor's devotion to the cause of the War—and the equal devotion of your Aunt Sally's friends—makes me doubt it. Would matters be different, if women could go out and get work, and support themselves and their families? If we were equals in the sight of Mammon as well as of God? I would like to think so. At least then we would not be waiting upon the choices of others, to learn how we must live the rest of our lives.

TUESDAY, AUGUST 12
NIGHT AGAIN

Sunday Ollie, and half a dozen others, had leave to come from camp: his first sight of his son and it now appears his last for some time. All leaves have been cancelled. The Sixteenth marches in a week, to Virginia.

Through my bedroom wall I hear Peggie sobbing again. Nollie is in here with Mercy and me, sleeping the sleep of exhaustion, for Peggie's weeping kept him awake, and she is again unable to feed him. First cock-crow is only an hour away. Exhausted as I am, I find rest in reading even a page or two from *David Copperfield.* There is a comfort in knowing you're probably doing the same. Like you, I long for only a five-minute conversation with you, face to face, now in the present, to see what is taking place around you by moonlight on the twelfth of August, not two months ago or two months hence. I am not a Spy in Enemy Territory, but a Sinner in the Land of the Righteous. My doubt is sin, but I doubt all the same. I am as unable to alter my doubts as I am unable to wish away my love for Emory.

MONDAY, AUGUST 18

When I knocked at the back door of Elinor's house this evening my darling Mercy was brought out by Katie, with the curt information that Elinor "can't look after her anymore." Mercy was crying wretchedly, exhausted as if she'd been crying for hours, and had been neither changed nor fed. Inside I could hear both Columbia and Ned howling. I stared at Katie, mouth half-open that anyone would leave a two-month-old infant in such a state, and Katie said, "Nathan is dead," and closed the door on me.

When I reached home, Mother told me that Nathan, and Otis Greenlaw from Southeast Harbor, were wounded in the Baton Rouge fighting, and sent down-river to New Orleans on a steamboat to be taken care of. The steamboat hit an underwater snag, and tore out her bottom. The boat sank, and all the wounded on-board, trapped within, were drowned.

I have written Elinor a letter, offering my condolence and whatever help she shall need, but I know it will go unanswered. Mother has been feeding wee Nollie cow's milk, as Peggie's milk has dried. He does well enough, but I will take Mercy with me tomorrow across to Isle au Haut, and see how that answers. Will, whose mother and grandmother are midwives, at least will have no objection to an infant's presence on-board the *Lady Anne.*

My heart aches tonight, for Elinor, and Nate, and Peggie, and Ollie asleep on the ground with his head on his pack, ready to march away tomorrow. May morning bring hope with its light.

Love,
C

Susanna Ashford, Vicksburg, Mississippi
To
Cora Poole, Deer Isle, Maine
c/o Eliza Johnson, Elizabethton, Tennessee

Thursday, Sept. 4

Dearest Cora,

Hurrah and welcome to the lovely Miss Mercy Poole! Of course she's the most beautiful baby in the world—she's *your* daughter! And thank you for sending me news of Justin. I enclose a letter for him, if you would be so good as to forward it. I have thought a great deal about what you said in your letter: that we can not know what will befall either of us, before the War's end. As you know, I'm something of a Pagan (particularly in comparison with your mother), and I fear I grow more Pagan every time the Reverend Crouch edifies us with Sunday sermons about how God is going to send every Yankee straight to Hell. Yet, there is a great deal of comfort in your faith, that all things—even the horrible ones, like losing Payne, and hiding in the cellar last June with shells landing three streets away—are the work of God, designed for His own Purposes that we do not understand. I do wish He would explain them just a little more clearly, though!!!

I laughed to read your Mother's version of Nursery Tales For Little Ones. But, I am astonished she missed the one about the little children who mocked the prophet Elisha's bald head. As I recall, Elisha called two she-bears out of the woods *(are* there woods in the Holy Land?) and they proceeded to tear those bad children to pieces. It's in Second Kings Chapter Two. Every time Tommy has the colic I can tell it's one of Aunt Sally's favorites.

It's ironing-day here. I've left Julia my share of the mending (I would rather muck out stables than sew!), and will spend the afternoon in the kitchen with Cookie and Nellie, hearing all the gossip that nobody talks about in parlors. In every town of any size below the Mason-Dixon Line there are really two separate towns: the free blacks and the house servants of everybody in town all know each other, the way the "quality" whites all do. Cookie doesn't mind me helping because I won't tell Aunt Sally, if Cookie spits on the iron to test it.

That Night

With the doors and windows all thrown open, and the river breeze coming through, the kitchen isn't really bad to be in, even with the stove going for the irons. And I love the way the clean, warm linen smells! Still, I'm glad ironing-day's over for another two weeks.

The moon is almost full, setting over the river. I've heard nothing yet of where Henriette or her children might be, though that just may be because she's as bad about writing as Pa. Still, having lost Gaius, every time I see Tommy I feel a sadness, at having now lost Gaius's children, as well.

Monday, September 8

Yet another letter from you! Enclosed in one from Mrs. Johnson, who seems to be moving here and there among her relatives in the mountains. But, it made me so angry my ears got hot. It's one thing for my brother Payne to go to war when he was eighteen—he'd been a cadet in the Military Academy, and everybody knew he wanted to be a soldier. But for someone to shame and coerce your brother to abandon his wife—even if it's only until apple-picking time—is inexcusable. *And* Elinor can keep her silly verse.

Would you have married Emory, if you had the choice to be or do something different? At least, if you'd had a profession, you could be following it in Boston, instead of being stuck on Deer Isle in the snow with the Daughters of the Union telling you you should divorce Emory because of his politics!

What I'm saying is, I'm delighted you have the chance to teach school. I take back what I thought about Elinor. I'd almost take back what I said about Ollie joining the Army (since his doing so opened this door for you) . . . but not quite.

THURSDAY, SEPTEMBER 11

It's funny, Cora: I usually *hate* making jelly, because it's always the hottest day of the year, and I burn my hands and get smoke in my eyes and every fly in Mississippi comes to watch . . . But there's that moment when the jelly "sets up" and I feel as pleased as if I'd just finished building the Great Pyramid of Egypt, all by myself. I burned my wrist so I can not hold the pen properly—and it's a quill pen, too, since there isn't a nib to be had anywhere in town for any money.

[~~Damn~~—heavily crossed out]

Curse the blockade.

With regard to Mr. P, thank you for reminding me of Elizabeth Bennet, and how we need to reserve judgement, even though we *think* we know we're right about a person. But the other thing *P&P* taught me (and *Persuasion* even more) is, that people's hearts can change. That *people* can change. In the meantime we can only, like the heroine of *Bleak House,* keep ourselves cheerful and useful, no matter how many evil lawyers all around us get shot or wicked rag-and-bone dealers burst into spontaneous flames . . .

Yes, you are absolutely insane for taking pleasure in changing your beautiful daughter's diapers. I love Tommy, but there are limits and that quite lies beyond them!!!

I suppose it is my destiny to love insane people.

Your own,
Susie

P.S. *I* become insane contemplating what's going on at Bayberry, because I'll bet my last three sheets of drawing-paper that Regal never got even a corn-crop in the ground, much less tobacco. If my brother manages, on top of everything else, to lose the plantation because he can't pay the mortgage, I'll—I don't even know what I'll do. Go on living on charity, I suppose.

S

Cora Poole, Deer Isle, Maine
To
Susanna Ashford, Vicksburg, Mississippi
c/o Eliza Johnson, Elizabethton, Tennessee

Saturday, September 20, 1862

Susanna,

Devastating battle news. Wednesday evening the lobstermen all saying there were rumors on the mainland about fighting in Virginia; dead and wounded in numbers so high I can not believe they are not exaggerated. Oliver is there, and twenty other island men. Papa came back from Yale. So much work to do, to get the apples in, and the cider made, and start on the cheeses, with only Peggie to help, and me only from sunup today until it was too dark to see: with this standing beside us, an invisible spectre, like the terrible Ghost of Christmas Yet to Come. At night Papa and Mother sit quietly in the kitchen, reading the Bible to one another: *Be strong and of good courage, neither be thou dismayed: for the Lord thy God is with thee, withersoever thou goest.* Their courage shames me.

Tuesday, September 23

News like a blaze of light in darkness. Will met me at the wharf this afternoon with news that's up and down the wires all over the country: that in the wake of our victory in Virginia (if so ghastly a massacre can be so called), President Lincoln has issued a Proclamation, freeing the slaves in the South. As I stood open-mouthed, amazed, that after all these years that horror and disgrace on our nation—on *humanity!*—has been finally struck down, Will added, "But, 'tis only in the South, not in the States that stayed loyal to the Union. And only in those Rebel States that *don't* give up and re-join the Union by January first."

I felt shocked, angry, and furious with President Lincoln. How *dare* he treat the freedom of hundreds of thousands of human beings like a parlor-trick, to threaten the Rebels with? What is in your heart about this, Susanna? What is in your thoughts? I asked you once before—how long ago that seems!—about slavery, and *Uncle Tom's Cabin.* What do the people around you in Vicksburg—both black and white—think of this? As I walked home, with Mercy riding in the little sling I've made for her, I passed Elinor's house, as the sun was going down. It stands back from the road, on the tall hill above Green's Landing. I paused by the gate and could see from there two men stacking cordwood—her father's employees, from the store or the marine-yard—and a woman dressed in deepest mourning. I remembered how Elinor and I had sat on her bed with our hair down our backs, talking of *Uncle Tom's Cabin,* and slavery, and our duty to see that somehow, the wretched slaves would be freed, until past midnight.

I think if Nathan had not been so lately dead, I would have let myself through the gate and walked up to speak to her. To cry, *We did it! We did it!* Maybe Will is right, and this "Proclamation" of Mr. Lincoln's is just a "smart" move by a politician who cannot win a military victory. But it is the small end of the wedge. On that foundation, freedom can and will be built.

But I walked on.

Monday, September 29

And just as well that I did. At church yesterday Pastor Wainwright preached a sermon of thankfulness for the Proclamation. As we were leaving, I heard Elinor scolding him for the praise he'd given to a "half-hearted piece of politics" that would "disgrace a common pickpocket."

But to make up for that, this afternoon when I came down to the wharf at the Town Landing to come home, Will met me with a letter from Ollie, which he'd gone all the way to Belfast on purpose to fetch. My brother is well, for his regiment was held in reserve, and did not see battle. Still no letter from you. I have gone back to *David Copperfield*, with its gentle reassurance that people come and go in our lives, and return again in time. Haying is done, and gathered into the barn. Apple-picking time has come and gone.

Your friend,
Cora

Susanna Ashford, Vicksburg, Mississippi
To
Cora Poole, Deer Isle, Maine
c/o Eliza Johnson, Elizabethton, Tennessee

SUNDAY, OCTOBER 5, 1862

[lost]

Cora Poole, Deer Isle, Maine
To
Susanna Ashford, Vicksburg, Mississippi
c/o Eliza Johnson, Elizabethton, Tennessee

TUESDAY, OCTOBER 28, 1862

[lost]

Susanna Ashford, Vicksburg, Mississippi
To
Cora Poole, Deer Isle, Maine

[not sent]

MONDAY, OCTOBER 20, 1862

Dearest Cora,

Your letter reached me today, What do I think about Mr. Lincoln's Proclamation of Emancipation? Everyone here says this is his malicious way of inciting slave revolt, but not a servant in this household—or anywhere in Vicksburg, so far as I can tell—is thinking about revolt. The ones who don't like being slaves (and there are quite a lot that don't mind it: they have food and clothing and a roof over their heads, and trust their masters—and apparently their masters' heirs!—not to sell them) are all thinking about running away, because now they have someplace to go.

All my life I've heard Pa's friends, and my brothers, fretting about slave revolt, and I've always thought: *If they weren't slaves, they wouldn't revolt, would they?*

But the other thing that reached me today is the news that Mrs. J and her family have been forced to flee from Carter County. So there is no way I can send you this just now. I will continue to write—and to make drawings for you—and send it all when I can.

At least I won't run out of paper. The attic here is chock-a-block with old magazines and sheet-music, some of them dating back to the twenties, and as you'll soon see (this is my last sheet of Husband #3's stationery) there are plenty of blank inside-covers and spaces. I've been drawing on them for weeks already. We still get firewood and coal by railroad from Jackson, but they're shockingly expensive—over thirty dollars a cord! That's Confederate dollars, but even so!

As late in the year as it is, I still haven't had a bedroom fire, though I notice Aunt Sally always has one. We can't get black lead, either, so it takes more scouring and fussing to get the grates clean and they always look rusty and dingy. At least, even though we can't get carborundum powder, either, we can still use brick-dust to clean the knives.

I remember how horrified I was last year to pay a dollar a yard for plain calico. Most ladies in town would scalp for a chance to get it for that little now. Aunt Sally, of course, always manages to "get" bolts of new and quite good muslin and calico as presents from the Generals here and in Jackson, all of whom are her dear good friends. As a result, Julia and I are suddenly the two best-dressed young ladies in Vicksburg. Everyone else's dresses have all been turned once and some of them twice, and I'm told people in the country are setting up looms to weave their own cloth.

I still haven't managed to find a copy of Mrs. Wollstonecraft's *Vindication.* But, stowed away on a top shelf I found a marvelous book by her daughter. It's about a doctor who creates a human being out of pieces of dead bodies, and by scientific means endows it with life . . . and having done so, refuses to take further responsibility for it, because it is misshapen and ugly. I have never read anything remotely like it, and *could not* put it down. I was totally enthralled. I suspect your Father would say it is completely morally unedifying, and yet—why is the story of a creature who is assumed to be evil because of his ugliness, different from that of one who is deemed unfit for a place in society because he, or she, is black? Or a woman?

Sunday, October 26
Night

No letter from you, and who knows how long, before I get one again? I pretend I can post this tomorrow, and in time get one back from you, reminding and reassuring me that . . . Well. Out calling today (with a two-inch burn on my temple from the curling-irons!), there were several young artillery officers at Mrs. Lillard's, one of whom—Captain F—seemed to think I would be enthralled to hear about his family, and his three plantations, and how he'd moved all his slaves except his valet down to Alabama where they'd be "safe." I kept getting up to get tea (or whatever it was) or bread-and-butter for Julia so I could change my seat, and Captain F kept moving to wherever I was sitting, and on the way home Julia told me that he was clearly in love with me.

She sounded so *gleeful*, fussing with my hair and tweaking my lace, and I just stared at her: "Oh, Susie, you're going to be the belle of Vicksburg!" And Aunt Sally, when we got home, took me aside and had a great deal to say about F's family's investments in France and Mexico and in New York banks—which is where *her* investments are. Both gave me much solid advice about how to "attach" a man.

And I'm ashamed to say my first thought was, "Gosh, if I *did* hook him, I'd get him to send me to the art academy in Philadelphia!" Please write me and remind me how stupid this is.

Mrs. Lillard has not been able to get her chimney repaired, and during tea, squirrels kept coming up to the hole and looking in, impatiently, as if they wished everyone would leave so they could get at the bread-and-butter. No fire can be made in that fireplace, of course, and you must imagine all the above scene of courtship with everyone muffled up in scarves and coats.

The newest Bennet Sister,
Susie

P.S. Actually, I know how stupid it is, because "hooking" Captain F would almost certainly involve kissing him, and he has flabby lips. (Tho' Miss Austen does not say so, I feel sure Mr. Collins in *P&P* has flabby lips, too.)

Cora Poole, Deer Isle, Maine
To
Susanna Ashford, Vicksburg, Mississippi

[not sent]

WEDNESDAY, NOVEMBER 5, 1862

My dearest Susie,

Monday a letter reached me, not from you, but from Eliza Johnson, who is now safe in Nashville after a horrifying journey across enemy lines. I rejoice to hear she and her family are out of danger, and re-united with the Senator; yet, my heart sinks as I realize that for a time, I will be unable to hear from you.

For a year now, I have thought of you as a friend, and more than a friend. It is not simply that you are on the same "side" as my husband, as some Daughters of the Union deride. The tide of patriotism runs so strongly over all the North that it has swept before it any possibility of regard for opinion different than that of the majority: one must be very, very careful now what one says. Yet in the night, between sleeping and waking, I still dream that I feel your hand gripping mine, though I can no longer hear your voice. As I am re-reading *David Copperfield,* I ask your forgiveness, if for a time you join the company of those friends he speaks of: present, close, treasured yet untouchable, whose invisible presence has become a lifeline which sustains my soul—the Bennet Sisters, Miss Summerson, the sturdy and faithful Quasimodo. All souls need friendship, even, I am convinced, the cats whom I see lying snug together in the loft, and the cows who seek one another out, with all the pasture's acres to choose from. What is this human capacity, to keep flame burning for years without tangible fuel? Where does the line lie, between great distance and sheer fancy?

The school term is drawing to a close on Isle au Haut. I grieve its loss, for the fisher-folk of the island—whose soil is too thin and stony to permit much in the way of farming—though they regard me as a "foreigner," are less inclined to suspect me of treason. Yesterday I helped Mrs. Barter, who operates the general store at the Town Landing, to air and turn the bedding of the family rooms behind the store, in preparation for winter, she having scalded her hand severely at pig-killing. The moon is young and thin, setting just at twilight, or I would have stayed to help her with the second, and worse, part of the task: painting the mattress-seams with camphor and turpentine, against the inevitable winter live-stock of bedbugs and fleas. I returned home to find a similar scene in progress, Mother instructing Peggie in the art of applying the camphor with a feather, Peggie's own family having been, I am sorry to say, entirely ignorant of the art.

We have had hard freezes these past four nights. Saturday, when Papa comes, we will spend the day at Uncle M's butchering. All week, my students have been erratic in their attendance, from their families being themselves so engaged.

Your friend always,
Cora

Susanna Ashford, Vicksburg, Mississippi
To
Cora Poole, Deer Isle, Maine

[not sent]

MONDAY, NOVEMBER 10, 1862
TWO A.M.

Dear Cora,

As you can see by the sketches, I'm writing this in the maids' room in the attic. Nellie is down with pneumonia. Cook will be up to relieve me at four. Nellie was off her head with fever earlier this evening, which was quite terrifying. Julia has taken it into *her* head that Nellie has either scarlet fever or the Black Death, and forbade me to help nurse her because I'd transmit it to Little Tommy. I've been doing all the doctor said to keep the fever down, wrapping Nellie in a cool-water pack, and she seems to be sleeping a little easier now. I brought a book with me, but have discovered that *Frankenstein* is not something you want to read at two in the morning when the house is so silent you can hear the rats discussing politics in the main attic.

Speaking of books, someone (and I can guess who!) evidently whispered to Captain F that I "read books," because he offered me a *tremendous* bribe for my affection—Charles Dickens's newest, which I understand is an historical novel set in the French Revolution! Captain F himself finds Dickens "common" and "sensationalistic." (I'll bet he's never read him, or anything else, ever.) I am in agonies. I conjure your response, in your fine Italianate handwriting, before me on my lap-desk:

My darling Susie—Why expend ink (at $2.50 per bottle) discussing such callow perfidy? I know you will spurn such offers with the contempt they deserve, without the slightest prompting from me. You are destined for Art: never waver in your pursuit of your chosen Star. Moreover, I have written to Mr. Dickens in London and he adds his encouragement to mine. He intends to base the villain of his next novel (Phineas Slunchbug) upon F. Mr. Slunchbug will be transported to Australia and then struck by lightning upon arrival. Your own, Cora.

I miss you.

Tuesday, November 11

Nellie is no better. She keeps calling out for her mother, and crying; she is no older than I. When I was little, and Payne and I both had scarlet fever, Julia nursed me; our Stepmother had us both put out into the overseer's house, so *she* wouldn't catch it.

I kept falling asleep all day, when I should have been helping Cook do the lamps.

Friday, November 14

It's three in the morning again and Nellie has just drifted off to sleep. The stillness is frightening. Every time I doze, I wake up trembling, thinking I hear Regal's militiamen stumbling and cursing in the hall, or trying the bedroom door. How long does it take to forget something like that? I have a book with me—*Persuasion,* NOT *Frankenstein*!—but am far too weary to make sense of words on the page.

Sunday, November 16

Dr. Driscoll says, Nellie might very well have died, if she hadn't been nursed as she was, for which Cook deserves far more credit than I. Last night was my first good night's sleep, and I slept most of the morning. All the strange dreams I had, half-sleeping up in the attic, seem to have shrunken back down to little things, memories of something that happened to me once.

I will seal this up, and drop it into the imaginary post-box, and imagine that you unfold it on Deer Isle on some snowy afternoon. I pretend I can look forward to hearing from you, about your Mother, and the lovely Miss Mercy, making cheeses and cider, and setting forth across the glittering sea to earn your own keep.

All my love,
Susanna

Cora Poole, Deer Isle, Maine
To
Susanna Ashford, Vicksburg, Mississippi

[not sent]

THURSDAY, NOVEMBER 27, 1862

Dearest,

Winter closes in. Icy winds and sleet for weeks now, while like squirrels Mother, Peggie, and I try to outrace them: making head-cheese and sausage, feeding the slow-burning fire in the smoke-house, digging potatoes, patiently rubbing butter over the newly-pressed cheeses: big cow-cheeses, small strong-smelling goat cheeses. Uncle M sent one of his sailors to bring wood into the shed and the summer kitchen, cut boughs to bank the house, and sharpen all the tools, Papa being disastrously unhandy with edged metal. The house is dark, and it has begun to snow, which I fear means Papa will not be able to come from New Haven this Saturday.

Having added you, for the moment, to those friends who exist only on paper, I have come to meditate on friendship, its nature, and its comforts. As I re-read my way slowly through this precious hoard of volumes, this is what I see: Who in these tales are friends with who, what they do for their friends, and what they ask of them. Coming new to novels, I find that those which seem to me the most convincing are those in which the heroes and heroines are loyal friends, as well as ardent lovers or passionate martyrs. It interests me that the villainous Montonis and Ambrosios, and even the Tulkinghorns and Heeps, have Evil Henchmen, but not a single friend. Perhaps I only see this because I am quite desperately lonely myself. Isn't it curious how few sets of friends one finds in the Bible? David and Jonathan; Ruth and Naomi; Paul and Luke; Jesus and his Apostles; Job's four unhelpful "comforters." Fitting, I suppose, in a book whose purpose is to define Man's relationship with God, and only secondarily with Mankind.

Tell me what you think of this, my own dear friend.

Monday, December 1
Early morning

Six inches of snow, and a hush upon the world, as if somewhere, someone has pricked her finger on the spindle of a spinning-wheel, and all the world lapsed into slumber. Going into the barn to milk, all the cats were curled up tight next to Mrs. Brown, the matriarch of our little herd—Mother does not believe in fanciful names for animals—like six hats dropped down in a row. Such peace, gold eyes blinking at me in the lantern-light.

I miss you.
Cora

Susanna Ashford, Vicksburg, Mississippi
To
Cora Poole, Deer Isle, Maine

[not sent]

Sunday, November 30, 1862

Dearest Cora,

I forgot to mention, during Nellie's illness, that I got a commission for a full-sized portrait! (In colored chalks, for there are of course no oils to be had in the town!) The subject is Mrs. R, who is the head of the Episcopal Church Hospital Committee and runs the lives of half the people in Vicksburg, and can get Aunt Sally invited to her reception when President Davis comes to town next month. Mrs. R also promised me all the paper in her husband's desk, and all the pen nibs and ink. As you can see, I'm still writing—and drawing!—with a quill, and making ink out of lampblack and elderberry juice.

I had to do the portrait twice, because Aunt Sally took one look at the first one, and cried, "Good heavens, girl, you can't show that to Cecelia!" I guess Aunt Sally thought it was a little too much like her—it *did* capture her nasty little sidelong smile. My second attempt devotes a great deal of detail to the lace on her collar and the way her hair is done (thicker and browner than it is in real life). I'm actually glad I had to re-do it, because the second portrait gave me better practice in lighting and composition. I suppose court painters in Europe have to do this kind of thing all the time. Do you think making Life prettier than it is is a painter's vocation? We are going there to dinner this afternoon, to ceremonially present it, and I *know* Aunt Sally will make me sit next to the obnoxious F.

Later that night

Captain F formally requested permission of Aunt Sally to "pay his addresses" to me. Julia is beside herself with delight. I try to regard all of this in a comical light (and have so far steadfastly refused the proffered copy of *A Tale of Two Cities*!). In fact, Captain F—like Captain McC and even his poisonous "boys" back in Greene County—aren't the real villains of the story, any more than Mr. Tulkinghorn or Mr. Smallweed are the real villains of *Bleak House*. They are minions of an evil that has no shape, and is everywhere, devouring lives and turning friends Pa used to argue politics with into men who'd think nothing of lying in wait in the woods to shoot him dead—or girls you grew up with, into women who don't understand why you haven't stopped loving a man of whose politics they disapprove.

Wednesday, December 3

Curses! Aunt Sally did indeed secure invitations to that wretched reception! She has informed Julia and myself that we are also expected to attend–in new dresses for which she has obtained the silk through Heaven only knows what channels! Three weeks of sewing and fittings! And, worse, three weeks of listening to Julia *talk* about sewing and fittings and how to fix my hair! Death, where is thy sting?

The Belle of Vicksburg,
Susie

P.S. That's F in the margin, eating cream cake at tea at Mrs. Bell's. The other drawing is Mrs. Bell's house with the hole shot through it.

Cora Poole, Deer Isle, Maine
To
Susanna Ashford, Vicksburg, Mississippi

[not sent]

MONDAY, DECEMBER 8, 1862

Dearest,

Monday is Will Kydd's day to get mail from the mainland. Even knowing there will be nothing from you, still I cannot suppress that little spurt of anticipation in my heart. An additional cause for gratitude on waking this morning: the blizzard that blew in Sunday has finally blown itself out, and when I crossed to do the milking about an hour before daylight, I could feel that the day would be warm—warm for December in Maine, in any case. Saturday night we had rain rather than snow. By noon the world will be awash in slush, it means we can get laundry done.

THAT EVENING

There! An afternoon of lugging in wood to the kitchen fire to heat the soak-water, of filling tubs with garments—incredible numbers of rinsed and rough-dried diapers—to soak overnight. The whole kitchen is a fog of baby-smelling steam! Mother, Peggie, and I laughed and sang sea-chanties. Then a sadness: just as dusk was falling, Will knocked on the door, with a letter from Brock, in Louisiana, telling Mother that our cousin, Farnum Haskell, has died of fever in New Orleans. Cousin Farnum had joined the Thirteenth Maine just before I came home, so the last I saw him was at my wedding, dancing with his tiny daughter Susan, who was standing on top of his boots. Only a few weeks ago, when we travelled to Northwest Harbor to church, I looked across the street to his sail-loft by the mill-dam, and wondered, When would Cousin Farnum be home? Now I know.

Sorrowfully,
Cora

Susanna Ashford, Vicksburg, Mississippi
To
Cora Poole, Deer Isle, Maine

[not sent]

TUESDAY, DECEMBER 9, 1862
NIGHT

Dearest Cora,

Well, as you can see, the Awful Mrs. R came through and I now have actual writing-paper again, and real ink, and nibs. That drawing at the top of the page is how she actually looks: rather like Lady Southdown in *Vanity Fair,* don't you think? Julia and I have been cutting and sewing and fitting and sticking pins in our fingers for weeks, since we will need not only one new dress apiece, but *two.* Tho' the Awful Mrs. R is having a reception for President Davis, Aunt Sally has scored over her because *we* are having His Excellency (or whatever the proper term is–His Confederacy????) for dinner (as a guest, that is–judging by his pictures he would make a rather scraggy entrée).

Between making two dresses, and turning out the *best* good china that Husband #2 brought from France, and Nellie still being very weak (tho' Julia says, like Pa, that she's just lazy), I have little time to either draw or read. At night I've been reading my way through *Waverley* and all its sequels, like a rat going through cheese.

WEDNESDAY, DECEMBER 10

You spoke of carrying Baby Mercy back and forth to Isle au Haut on Mr. Kydd's boat; how did that answer? Does she like the sea? What does she look like now? Is her hair golden like Emory's, or that lovely flax-straw color like yours? Are her eyes as beautiful as yours? Is she big or little for her age? I wish, *wish,* you could tell me what Isle au Haut is like, for I need to picture you there!

Here I conjure your reply:

My dearest Susie–The inhabitants of Isle au Haut dwell in caves, dress in skins (tho' quite warmly and decently), and live chiefly upon raw sea-gull. I have introduced them to the works of Miss Austen, having first taught them the alphabet for that purpose. Your affectionate, Cora.

Saturday, December 13
Night

News of the battle in Fredericksburg, Virginia. Even first reports sound hideous, and I pray, pray, that your brother isn't there, Cora. Curse this distance between us! Curse that I can't fly there to be with you and little Mercy until it's done and you know he is safe. I pretend you'll get this and I pretend I'll get one from you but sometimes it comes back to me that I won't know, I won't be able to give you any comfort—and I don't know, if he's killed, if you'll come to hate me.

Wednesday, December 17

As we were coming out of headquarters today, I heard my name called and turned around and saw—*Emory*! I stood quite foolishly open-mouthed, and then in spite of all Aunt Sally's instruction about good manners, flung myself into his arms. He looks well, Cora, and extremely handsome in his uniform (even if it is the wrong color). He embraced me so that he almost swept me from my feet, to hear that he has a daughter, that I had heard from you as late as October, that you still loved him and were true to him, despite the disapprobation of your friends. I told him what you had said, to the Daughters of the Union: That your loyalty to the Union, and your love for him, are alike unaltered, and he laughed and kissed me and pulled my hair the way Payne used to. He is an aide to General Pemberton, and on the train home I wrought upon Aunt Sally, to invite him, and Tom (who is in the same regiment), for Christmas, if they can get furlough from their duties.

How I wish this was a real letter, so that I could really tell you that he is well!

Your friend,
Susie

P.S. Here's a sketch of Emory, kneeling in the street to kiss Aunt Sally's hand.

Cora Poole, Deer Isle, Maine
To
Susanna Ashford, Vicksburg, Mississippi

[not sent]

FRIDAY, DECEMBER 12, 1862

Dearest Susanna,

So much for the week's warm weather! Wild wind bringing down snow; I hope the storm was bad enough in New Haven, to discourage Papa from setting forth, for there is little hope he will be able to cross the Reach tomorrow. But we are well for diapers, for many weeks to come. As I direct these letters to you, and drop them one by one into the "post-box"—an old candle-box tucked into a corner of Mr. Poole's trunk—I imagine them flying straight to you, now freed of the tedious process of being carried across to Belfast, and delivered to some horny-handed bush-whacker in Kentucky, to be passed on to Eliza's guerilla son and thence to Eliza . . .

And all, all to tell you, that we are well-stocked for diapers! I picture you reeling under the impact of this revelation. Yet could I get a note in your hand, recounting who said what at your Aunt Sally's Sunday tea—or a scribble from Emory telling me how many thousands in Confederate money he has won on the cockroach races—I would rejoice in them. Perhaps, as Dora Copperfield says, it is better to be stupid than uncomfortable. Forgive your silly friend.

Saturday, December 13

More steam, more fogs: baths in the kitchen, with the wind howling dimly on the other side of cushioning snow. I write this in bed, tucked to my chin in feather-ticks, Mercy curled sleeping at my side. It is the New England way, to bathe on Saturdays as if in expectation of being able to attend services, and to dress in our best on the Sabbath, and spend the day in quiet sitting and reading the Bible in the parlor, where a fire has been laid ready—the only day of the week, in winter, that it is so.

A family of mice has taken up residence in one of my dresser drawers. I have put out flour mixed with plaster, and a vessel of water, yet have found no corpses yet.

Thursday, December 18

Newspapers at last! And, God bless Will Kydd, he has brought me the *New York World,* the *Chicago Tribune,* as well as the usual paper from Portland. The storm did not abate until yesterday, and like a cold shadow on the island, worse than any storm, came news of the bloodshed in Virginia. Only preliminary reports, but the Sixteenth was engaged. Peggie huddles weeping in a corner of the kitchen, "I know he's dead! I know he's dead!" and I struggle not to shout at her. Does she think Mother loves Ollie—her baby and her favorite—less than she? This evening, after supper, I read aloud the Psalms of hope, and the Acts of the Apostles—tales of faith and courage, whose end we know was good. But alone here in my room, with Nollie as well as Mercy at my side, I weep.

SATURDAY, DECEMBER 20

Why do I think it more likely that Ollie will be killed in battle, than that Brock will take sick with fever in Louisiana? Brock has written many times of the poisonous heat there, the deadly fevers that have felled one man in four in their camp, and have killed already seven of our island men in the Thirteenth. Little comfort to tell myself that tonight—Saturday—the battle is over and done, one way or the other, because I know Ollie may in fact be wounded unto death.

How does the imagination produce so many ways of tormenting oneself? God gave us the capacity to dream into the future, and the gift of faith, double-edged swords that can tear as well as mend. Yet these are the angel elements of our nature, for I feel certain that Mrs. Brown and her bovine sisters in the barn feel no anxiety about the quality of their fodder next Tuesday. Or perhaps they do—I can hear you saying, "How do *we* know?" How indeed, my dear friend?

You have passed before me along this road. I will take courage from your cheer.

Your own,
Cora

P.S. One mouse dead at least—and a great deal of flour and plaster dust tracked about my room.

Cora Poole, Deer Isle, Maine
To
Susanna Ashford, Vicksburg, Mississippi

[not sent]

MONDAY, DECEMBER 22, 1862
NIGHT

Susanna,

Though the moon is new and the clear night moonless, still Will Kydd snowshoed to our door, to give us Ollie's letter. He is safe, Susie!

THURSDAY, DECEMBER 25
NIGHT

Papa arrived yesterday, and this morning the six of us traversed the marble-white world to Northwest Harbor to church in Uncle M's sleigh. Only one brief service: there are chores to be done, wood to be cut and sawed, diapers—*how* many diapers!—to be rinsed and stacked in the corner of the summer kitchen, where they will freeze solid until next laundry-day. Still, for all the disapprobation of Pastor Wainwright and Uncle M and Mother, Christmas is *not* a day quite like other days. I can see it in Papa's face as he plays with his grandchildren in the parlor. A rare fire has been kindled there, to the indignant horror of the spiders in the chimney.

Peggie declined my invitation, to read *A Christmas Carol* together as we did last year. So I have lain here, huddled under all my quilts, reading it to myself, sometimes aloud to my precious Mercy, who seems fascinated at my attempts to give different voices to Scrooge, and the Ghosts, and Mr. Cratchit, and Tiny Tim. At least she does not yet say, "Oh, Mama, you're doing it all wrong!" as I'm sure she one day will.

I hope your Christmas is as kindly, my friend. I hope your New Year will be as blessed.

Love,
Cora

Susanna Ashford, Vicksburg, Mississippi
To
Cora Poole, Deer Isle, Maine

[not sent]

MONDAY, DECEMBER 22, 1862

Dear Cora,

With every good intention in the world, to write at least a line to you last night, I couldn't do it. Here is an advantage to not being able to post these letters at all: I can pretend that as I write them, you will receive them the very next day, and know about Emory already, and the dinner for President Davis.

The dinner went astonishingly well. You will have heard that there are terrible shortages of food in the Confederacy: well, you could not have told it last night. Nellie, tho' still not at all well, worked like a hero in the kitchen, setting tiny paper-lace crowns around each crawfish and wrapping chicken-livers in strips of bacon. While Julia wrote out place-cards and menus (my handwriting being insufficiently elegant) I polished silver, twenty place-settings of it all covered with curliques which had to be cleaned with an old tooth-brush, and by naked extortion and scouring the countryside, Aunt Sally was able to field eight full courses, including turkeys, chicken vol-au-vents, duck à l'orange, and a cream soup in spite of the fact that nearly every cow in the countryside has vanished into the maw of the Army. *And* coffee. *And wine.* The butler, and Zed the stableman, both looked strikingly impressive in livery.

Julia, who has been nearly distracted since Friday, when we heard that yes, Emory and Tom got twenty-four-hour furloughs to spend Christmas Day here, flirted outrageously with every man at the table (and there were twenty of them, just about all of the President's staff, and every single one of them needed a fish-fork *and* a cheese-fork). I pretended to be a Spy in Enemy Territory again and managed a five-minute chat with President Davis about *Waverley* (which his wife is currently reading aloud to him when he has headaches, which he has just about every night, and no wonder). I asked him about Pa. The President says, Pa is making himself extremely useful in the government and waiting for a "good position" to "materialize." I wanted to ask him, Has Pa got a ladyfriend yet? but didn't know how to phrase it politely. After everyone left I got unlaced, put on my oldest dress, and helped Nellie clean the knives.

Thursday, December 25
Night

And now the house is still again. I wish you were here. Selfishly, because I miss you, but also, because Emory is asleep in the room across the hall: I know you'd want to be with him there!!!

Last Christmas I was in Nashville at the Academy; the Christmas the War was supposed to be over by. Bayberry was still a little bit the same as the place I remember growing up in. I think of the Dashwood sisters, and the Bennet girls, and saintly Amelia Sedley, who all face being put out of their homes quite penniless; is that why we find those books so appealing? Because when I read them I can say, the Dashwood sisters survived the loss of the place which brought them close to their childhood: so can I? As you wrote to me, "One small and possible hand-hold at a time." Even those lurid tales where the heroine is kidnapped and put in dungeons and pursued across the moors in rainstorms at midnight clad only in her night-gown: in most instances (except for poor Esmeralda), she emerges without even catching cold! Reading them, I can think, If Emily or Isabella got through it all right, I will be all right, too.

But I'm beginning to notice that they all involve marrying a man, and him being amazingly rich. And the women who want something else in their lives turn out to be wicked harlots. Or comic figures like Betsy Trotwood, or sinister mad ones like Miss Havisham.

I'm sorry I'm the one under the same roof with Emory tonight, and not you: that you're buried under snow by this time on Deer Isle, with pine-boughs like a nest all around your home, and a tempest blowing outside. I hope your Papa was able to come home for Christmas, and that Ollie came safely through the battle and both your brothers got furloughs. I hope that you were able to be happy on your daughter's first Christmas in this baffling world.

Thinking of you,
Susanna

P.S. Friday, December 26

A Yankee expedition under General Sherman has landed at Steele's Bayou, ten miles north of town.

[sketches]

1863

Susanna Ashford, Vicksburg, Mississippi
To
Cora Poole, Deer Isle, Maine

[not sent]

FRIDAY, JANUARY 2, 1863

Dear Cora,

It is bitterly cold this afternoon, the wind sweeping down the river straight from the North Pole, it feels like, and cord-wood up to *forty dollars*! I'm in the attic above the kitchen, where it's warm. There's a gable behind me facing west, and I get a good strong light for about three hours a day. Mr. Cameron told me to draw something every day, even if it's only old shoes or old gloves. As you can see by the margins of this page, there are plenty of those up here. Sometimes if we don't have company for the evening, I'll creep back here after supper with a couple of candles and read. Nellie will come and say good-night, on her way in to her room on the other side of the attic, and tell me stories her Mama told her, about how you shouldn't sleep under trees near the crossroad because the witches will ride you. You have witches in New England, don't you? What tales do people tell? Is that particular shade of blue ("hai'nt blue" Cook calls it) proof against Maine devils the way it is against African ones?

Captain F to dinner tonight. Aunt Sally is more determined than ever to marry me off. When I try to speak to her about why women aren't allowed to be doctors or lawyers or engineers (or even artists), she looks at me as if I were speaking Ethiopian. "Women just don't have the capacity, dear." She says this after sending off letters diligently to her business agents in France, New York, and three South American countries.

My friends here—only they're the kind of friends Miss Austen talks of in *Northanger Abbey,* that are your friends because you happen to all be in the same place at the same time—have even less of an idea of doing anything *but* getting married and raising children. Lately I find myself two different people: who I am with them, and who I am really. We have a reading-group here—and at last! Somebody has acquired a copy of *A Tale of Two Cities* and we start on that in February!—and we're getting together to put on "Scenes From Shakespeare" at next month's Musicale to raise money for the local hospitals. And most of them are mostly interested in trading excerpts from letters from beaux in the Army, or talking about what kind of dresses they'll make the minute the blockade is "over." Like Lady Middleton in *S&S,* they suspect me of being "satirical" because I read, without quite knowing what "satirical" is.

Much of the time I feel very strange and alone.

Later. Night

Whew! Every time I think F can not get more boring, he proves me wrong. A surprise guest at dinner—can you guess? Emory came—on errand from Gen'l Pemberton, and Aunt Sally ordered him to remain, and the Gen'l can make the best of it for all she cares. Lottery-tickets and a game of Speculation in the parlor. You will be quite delighted to hear, Emory cleaned F out of his tokens like a picked carcass. Julia played the piano and sang, and Emory reduced her to blushes by recounting how Pa threw him off Bayberry, back in the days when he was courting her.

Sunday, January 4

Back from Sunday calls, in *freezing* wind. Barely any cream in the not-quite-tea, and that had been watered and mixed with chalk,

I think, so it wouldn't look thin. Would *much* rather have stayed home in the warm kitchen and helped Cook and Nellie do the lamps. Despite the terrifying cost of oil these days, Aunt Sallie *insists* on using at least some lamps, just to prove the Yankees aren't really a problem. And poor Mrs. Bell's house, though she's had some of the shell damage repaired, is like sitting on a particularly drafty iceberg. Such a relief to return to the attic and re-read your letters. Sometimes when I read a book I know you've read—*P&P,* or *Bleak House*—I feel as if I'm in that same place—in London, or Meryton, or even Otrano's accursed castle—and am likely to come around a corner and see you. And if we do not have time to talk that particular day, at least I know that you are well.

I am well, too, and ever,

Your own,
Susanna

[sketches]

Cora Poole, Deer Isle, Maine
To
Susanna Ashford, Vicksburg, Mississippi

[not sent]

FRIDAY, JANUARY 2, 1863

Dearest Susie,

Happy 1863—and may it be happy, and bring us actual letters from one another again!

A strange New Year. The weather has been warm—twenty degrees or more nearly every day—and no snow lies on the ground. Nevertheless the well is frozen, and the thick ice must be broken several times a day by dropping the bucket down weighted with stones. Mother made the most of the fair weather by doing laundry, a blessing with two infants in the house, and we saw Papa off this morning without last year's fear of his being caught by a storm in crossing the Reach. I shall miss his conversation sorely. He has never come to approve of my novel-reading, yet he is the only person with whom I can speak now about Shakespeare's plays, and *The Iliad,* which I have come to see in a different light since my acquaintance with such heroines as the Bennet Sisters—of whom I am sure Mr. S would have approved—and poor mad Don Quixote. Papa and I took many long walks together—such a luxury in winter!—sometimes with Mercy on my back in what Papa calls my *papoose.* Mother is certain that there is something "heathenish" in carrying one's child about so. Though the ground is dry—and the house looks a little foolish, banked deep in boughs and not an atom of snow in sight—the island is strangely silent without its birds, the woods queer and naked-looking, full of pale winter light. Even far inland at the end of the pond, I can sometimes hear the sea.

Darkness comes early. We return home, Papa and I—or I alone, today—in good time to help Mother with dinner in a kitchen lit by tallow candles and reeking of their scent. No matter how much we rinse and soak, the taste of salt clings to everything. This whole week, we have had fires in the parlor, and by them, chess or dominoes. Tonight it is only we five again: three mothers, two babies, in the kitchen, the rest of the house cold and dark. What a comfort to know that you are somewhere, on the other side of that darkness. What a comfort to have, at least, those friends between the covers of books: to know that such a powerful barrier exists against loneliness!

Your friend,
Cora

Cora Poole, Deer Isle, Maine
To
Susanna Ashford, Vicksburg, Mississippi

[not sent]

MONDAY, JANUARY 12, 1863

Dearest,

The unseasonal warm weather continues. Every road on the island is a foot deep in mire, and we are as trapped on the farm, as if snow heaped our walls. Moreover, the shutters remain closed and the walls banked deep in boughs, for not one of us is such a fool as to believe that this situation will continue until spring. Still, my joy at long walks in the woods is rivalled by the pleasure of short dashes to the privy, rather than the blizzard expedient of emptying chamber pots into buckets in the summer kitchen. You wrote to me of what I as a New Englander knew nothing of—the lively second world of black families, black gossip, black friendships in any Southern town—so now I return the favor upon you, who surely have no experience of being trapped by snow and wind within the walls of a six-room farmhouse for days on end. What a pity we have not a third friend—indifferent to both South and North—living on the islands of Hawaii! She could no doubt tell us unimaginable commonplaces of her existence that would leave us both bemused!

I re-read the novels I read last winter, encountering new things even in such completely unedifying works as *The Mysteries of Udolpho* and *Fantomina, or Love in a Maze.* (If Mr. Poole permitted you to read that last one as a girl, he should be ashamed of himself!) It is as if new chapters grew in them while I wasn't looking. Perhaps, in my feverish haste to discover the nature of Valmont's Dreadful Disease, or to learn the ultimate fate of Trooper George, I skimmed past these secluded groves and vistas like the passenger on a speeding train. I commenced the winter bemoaning the fact that I have only the same seventy-eight volumes as I did twelve months ago. Now I see the treasure God has designed for me this winter: that deeper acquaintance, the chance to see both pleasures and lessons missed before. That is, I assume it to be God, though I'm sure Papa would give me an argument about *Fantomina.*

It is hard not to have someone to talk to of this. What was difficult last winter seems yet more so now, perhaps because all summer I have had the teaching of my little scholars. I have acquired the habit of facile conversation with Peggie, though her spirits are easily depressed and she frets herself endlessly over Oliver. This is understandable, but painful to herself and frightening, I think, to her tiny son.

We are both much engaged in sewing after dinner has been made, eaten, and cleaned up after in a great sloshing of water and scratching of scouring-sand. I am making new dresses for Mercy, who rapidly outgrows her old ones; Peggie is picking apart and turning her own frocks, for even homely calico is four or five dollars a yard at Lufkin's store. Nollie will inherit Mercy's dresses, though he is so tiny yet that the garments that fit her at four months swallow him up, like a corn-cob dropped into a pillow-case. Other prices are high, too. With the cutting and hauling of wood to be hired, and money set aside for spring plowing, Mother must budget Papa's salary very carefully, until school resumes in June.

I try to keep Peggie's fears from kindling anxieties in my own heart–things I can not even know, much less remedy. Is Emory well? Is he even alive? I find it easier not to think of my husband at all, than to go through the pain of uncertainty: of wondering what my life–our lives–will be, when the fighting ends. Yet in the evenings his face, and his voice, return to me . . . as do yours, my dearest friend. I will close this letter, and pinch out my candle, with a prayer that you are well.

Love,
Cora

Susanna Ashford, Vicksburg, Mississippi
To
Cora Poole, Deer Isle, Maine

[not sent]

Saturday, January 17, 1863

Dearest Cora,

At last, a letter from Pa. (Is there a mark that conveys non-excitement, as a ! denotes delight?) He complains bitterly of the food in Richmond, and hints that much money can be made there, so he'll stay, and maybe bring us out to join him. I'll believe that when I see train tickets in the envelope! Elsewhere he spoke of coming back to Greeneville to take over command of our militia. Why are we so disappointed when those we love behave precisely like themselves? He concluded with, "I will be sending you money shortly." O be still my heart. But, it was good to hear he is well, and Julia—of course—wept as she read and re-read his words.

Aunt Sally and I took the ferry across to De Soto to meet the trains when they come in from Texas, and buy flour, cornmeal, molasses, etc. Neither coffee nor tea to be had. Nor paper—as you see I'm writing this on the back cover of "Rosalie, the Prairie Flower" (with titles of additional songs available appended). This expedition took half the day.

In the reading group we're reading *Persuasion,* yet, no one seems to see beyond the simple actions of the characters: *Will* Anne be united with Frederick? Will she lose him to the machinations of the dreadful Musgrove Sisters? My mind keeps going to what you wrote: *Would the world be different, if we could be equals to our husbands in the eyes of Mammon as well as God?* I keep wanting to ask, How does it come about, that Anne Elliott, and the Bennet girls, and all those others including myself and Julia, are bound in the ropes spun by their fathers' improvidence, and dependent upon the next generation of potential fathers for their liberation? And for that matter, Where are Napoleon and his armies, while all this romantic heart-rending is going on in Bath?

Tommy is teething: feverish, fussy, crying. Julia accuses the nurse of dosing him with opium (she isn't–I searched the nursery), yet orders her quite crossly to keep him quiet. She made Aunt Sally give her half of *my* paper, so she can write Tom seven-page letters about how much she loves him and Tommy and what she wore Sunday to go visiting. It is a comfort to know Tom will be able to get his camp-fires lit without trouble for a while.

Your friend,
Susanna the Spy

[sketches]

Susanna Ashford, Vicksburg, Mississippi
To
Cora Poole, Deer Isle, Maine

[not sent]

TUESDAY, FEBRUARY 3, 1863

Dearest Cora,

Great excitement here yesterday: the Union ram *Queen of the West* rammed a Confederate steamer practically under the Vicksburg guns. Everyone in town crowded the windows that overlook the river to see. The *Queen* is a huge ironclad double side-wheeler, easy to pick out even miles away from the lookout on Sky Parlor. The sound of the guns shook our walls. Because Aunt Sally was having–

Later—after dark

The guns started up again as I was writing. This time for propriety's sake I got Nellie and Aunt Sally's good Swiss field-glasses, and almost ran all the way up the zig-zag wooden steps to the top of Sky Parlor. A dozen people were there already. We could see the *Queen* below, guns blazing and smoke everywhere from the shore battery. She drove three of our steamers ashore, one after the other. Old Dr. Driscoll lent me his spyglass when I was letting Nellie use the field-glasses, and he walked us home. I asked, did he think the *Queen*'s guns could get up as far as the town? He said, "I guess we'll find that out."

[sketches]

Wednesday, February 4

Of course, nobody in the reading-circle wanted to read. There are six of us—seven, before Selina Boyette dropped out when her husband was killed last September at Antietam—and they only wanted to talk about the Union ships on the river, and how quickly our Army will sweep them away. That, and what new dresses everyone would make if it weren't for the blockade. I said I had a headache, and excused myself, and walked home alone.

I wish there were enough light to draw. I'd dearly love to work the sketches I made from Sky Parlor into real drawings. Before everyone started talking about the attack, I read the first paragraph of *Tale of Two Cities,* and it comes back to me now: *It was the best of times, it was the worst of times, it was the age of wisdom, it was the age of foolishness . . . we had everything before us, we had nothing before us . . .*

And we have no way of telling right now which it is. I will seek refuge for a while in the sixteenth century, Cora, where one has only to worry about what lurks behind the Black Veil, or whether a mysterious monk will emerge through the wall of your room at night by means of a magic branch . . .

Your friend,
Susanna

[sketches]

Cora Poole, Deer Isle, Maine
To
Susanna Ashford, Vicksburg, Mississippi

[not sent]

THURSDAY, FEBRUARY 5, 1863

Dear Susanna,

Still no snow. Still the hard bright sunlight, the slush-filled roads that keep us from even venturing to Northwest Harbor to church. This is just as well, for I understand from Will Kydd, whom I met at Green's Landing Saturday when Mother and I walked there to meet Papa, that half a dozen of the children there are down with the measles. Moreover, in the fine weather Army recruiters have been back to the island nearly every week. The town council has voted to borrow money in order to offer bounties to those who join. I can not say I am surprised that few men will enlist these terrible days. Of the sixty island men who have enlisted so far—including the five who believed themselves to be enlisting for three months only—eleven have been killed. A dozen returned home as invalids, some of them clearly crippled for life. Of these, the recruiters—and the Daughters of the Union—do not speak.

Will was delighted to see Miss Mercy again. He promised to convey my good wishes to all my dear students on Isle au Haut.

MONDAY, FEBRUARY 9

How strange still, not to hastily finish a letter on Saturday night, that Papa may take it to post in Belfast Monday morning. Dinner is done, the kitchen cleaned. It sounds so selfish to say, I miss my brothers intensely while cleaning the knives, for to get sufficient friction on the knife-board to remove all the stains is really beyond the strength of a woman's arm. It was Brock's chore before he went to college, and then Ollie's. The sharp smell of the cleaning-paste on the board seems to bring back the momentary expectation that I will see one of them or the other, coming into the room.

WEDNESDAY, FEBRUARY 11

In the early hours this morning I dreamed about being back in Mrs. Johnson's house in Greeneville. I was frantic with dread, as was the case then, that Emory would announce to me that he could not leave his home State, with the battle over Secession just beginning. If we missed the train that morning something else would happen later in the day that would demand that Emory remain in Tennessee, and I would be condemned to live, for who knew how many months, among strangers who regarded me as a hated Yankee alien; who would not even ask what my actual feelings on any subject were. In my dream I kept trying to pack my trunks, but someone had hidden all my things. I wandered upstairs and down, searching for Emory in growing terror. I called out for him, which woke me, and in that strange state between sleeping and waking—dreaming that I lay in my bed at home on Deer Isle, in the icy darkness of my shuttered room—I heard his voice very clearly speak my name.

Then I fully woke, and lay in the stillness for a time, knowing it had been a dream. I could hear Mother in the kitchen, so knew it was dawn or nearly so. I put on my shoes, and my robe, and my coat over all, and walked out, through the kitchen, through the dark summer kitchen, into the dawn world pink and gray and unbelievably cold, ground and dead grass bleached the color of sand. I went past the lines of frozen laundry, and the barn, and through the belt of woods to the pond, and walked along its iron edge until the sun came over the trees and glittered on the ice. The stillness helped me, as reading does. Yet, for a time I felt that I was the only person left alive, not only on the island, but in the whole of the world.

Always,
Cora

Susanna Ashford, Vicksburg, Mississippi
To
Cora Poole, Deer Isle, Maine

[not sent]

THURSDAY, FEBRUARY 19, 1863

My Dear Cora,

I'm troubled tonight, and missing your counsel. I tried to talk to Aunt Sally about Mr. Poole (Emory is coming to dinner Sunday), but the subject quickly turned to how I will never get a husband if I am "cold," which she declares I am. Yet, I now realize that for all her flirting and husbands, Aunt Sally is the coldest woman I know. She isn't shallow and she isn't stupid, but, to her, men are a crop to be harvested, and she goes about it carefully and deliberately. When last together you showed me how to fix my hair; it was (as you said) to show my respect for those around me, *not* to get men to fall in love with me so they'd do me favors or will their plantations to me when they die. Yet don't men look at women the same way? Will she be a good housekeeper? Will she bear me sons? Will she bring in a little money? It reminds me about how Pa used to talk about a new slave.

Nobody ever talks about this—I mean men, and money, and how we should live and what we should expect—at least not in the South. Everyone tells you, It's important to "get" a husband, and mocks you if you don't. If you even wonder if things *could* be different, you're "eccentric" or "queer." You learn never to speak of it—never to think of it. Is it different in the North? I think it must be—I take comfort in that fact.

Friday, February 27

More excitement. Last night the lookouts on the river set up the alarm as what looked like a *huge* vessel armed with cannon came out of the Federal fleet up-river. The night was overcast and the vessel bore no lights, so all that could be seen by the flashes of the battery guns was a shape. It didn't return fire, but bore down under fire on the *Indianola,* the big gunboat the Confederates captured last week from the Union fleet, so inexorably that the crew of the *Indianola* panicked, abandoned the ship (carefully taking with them all their liquor supplies), and blew it up so it wouldn't be re-taken. Daylight showed this mysterious monster vessel was actually an empty Union coal-barge fitted up with tree-trunks for guns. Aunt Sally remarked how much money it saved the Yankees, that instead of *them* fighting an expensive battle to blow up one of the best ships in our fleet, they got *us* to blow it up and save everyone a lot of trouble.

Aunt Sally is having Zed dig a bomb-proof shelter behind the house, where the hill slopes down sharply to China Street.

Thursday, March 5

This morning Julia demanded half of my remaining paper (I told her I hadn't any left) to write to Tom. "My husband could be dead this very minute, and I would know nothing of it!" she sobbed (in which case he wouldn't need to have a letter written to him, I *didn't* say). It crosses my mind that *you* could be dead, Cora, and I not know it . . . or precious Mercy, or your parents. You could have spent all Sunday grieving, thinking that Emory is dead, when he was in fact sitting across the dinner-table from me, flirting with Aunt Sally.

But, this is a line of thought productive of nothing but madness. We will become like those heroines imprisoned in dungeons, who pound on the stone walls and shriek "I am alive! I am alive!" (Or, "He is alive!" Whichever.) I can pretend that you are dead, or that Mercy is dead, or that Deer Isle has mysteriously sunk beneath the waters of the sea—or, I can pretend that you are safe and well (tho' still buried in snow) and have somehow acquired a copy of *Tale of Two Cities*. Curiously, I find it far easier to believe that something terrible has occurred. Do you?

Your fellow-prisoner,
S

[sketches]

Cora Poole, Deer Isle, Maine
To
Susanna Ashford, Vicksburg, Mississippi

[not sent]

SUNDAY, FEBRUARY 22, 1863

Dear Susanna,

Church in Northwest Harbor, for the first time in nearly a month. Friends crowded around Peggie and Nollie; Nollie fretted and cried through both services and the dinner-hour between them. Yet it was as if, like Scrooge, I had been rendered invisible and unheard.

Monday, February 23

A letter from Oliver. He will be home on furlough, in the second week of March.

Wednesday, February 25

Nollie feverish, wailing all night. Early this morning Mother and I started a regimen of cool baths for him. Mother brewed a willow-bark tea that Grandmother Howell used as a febrifuge. It is bitter, and poor Nollie spit most of it up. Brock's letters, and Ollie's too, speak of the sicknesses that race through the Army camps like grass-fire. I wonder if the recruiters—who were indeed at work before the church Sunday—bring in illness with them.

Monday, March 2

Snow yesterday, beginning shortly after Mother, Papa, Peggie left for church, six inches deep by the time they returned. Nollie seems better, though still sleepless, crying, thin as a bundle of sticks. My little Mercy ran a fever for a day or so, but not nearly as badly. Friday, when Nollie was at his worst, Peggie confessed to me that she was convinced they *both* would die: it was all I could do not to snap at her, and Mother of course was no help on the subject. You would not tell Julia such a thing about little Tommy, no matter how sick he might be! I try to tell myself that Peggie's fears for my brother run over into all her perceptions of the world, yet I find that knowing (or suspecting) the cause of her sensibility does not make me more forgiving of it.

This morning was much warmer, and we had no fears for Papa's safety, as Uncle M took him away again to Belfast in the *Gull.* Still no luck in finding a hired man. A girl to assist with household tasks would help also, but few will undertake the work for room and board only, as they used to.

Wednesday, March 4

One day I fear that I really will shout at that girl! Are all those sweet, calm heroines I read about complete figments of fantasy? Snow again today, and much colder, freezing yesterday's thaw to ice. Mother slipped, coming back from feeding the cows, and struck her head on the boot-scraper beside the back door. It was only a shallow cut, but it bled copiously. Peggie flew into such a panic that I had to order her outside to bring in snow to melt for wash-water. Both babies were wailing, but I didn't dare let her pick up either one. Mercy would probably survive being dropped on the kitchen floor, but poor little Nollie doesn't look like he could stand being so much as sneezed on! After that I turned Peggie out of the kitchen, in spite of the fact that as usual there was no fire anywhere else in the house. Now she is in a pout. Once I am a little calmer I will need to go in and apologize. How on earth did–and do–people manage, who are locked together with dozens of total strangers in prisons? Or crowded into the holds of emigrant ships? And why has no one written a novel about *that*?

Your crotchety friend,
Cora

Cora Poole, Deer Isle, Maine
To
Susanna Ashford, Vicksburg, Mississippi

[not sent]

FRIDAY, MARCH 13, 1863

Dearest Susanna,

A blustery morning, with threat of snow again by night. I am home with the two babies, the rest of the family having gone to Mount Adams cemetery, to the funeral of our cousin Farnum Haskell. His coffin arrived from Louisiana the day before yesterday. It was "thought better" that I do not go: "You know the funeral does not mean to her what it does to us," said Peggie, who has become very friendly with Elinor over the winter. I did not argue the point. The day is very cold, and Nollie is still quite weak.

Oliver has been home six days, and returns to camp Monday. All week I have not been able to dismiss from my mind your letter in which you spoke of your brother Gaius on his last furlough home: that he moved as if he were in pain, though he bore no wound. Oh, Susie, I read that same expression in Ollie's eyes! Last night he came to my room, where I sat up reading *Vanity Fair* long after the others had gone to bed, a spare quilt wrapped around his shouders: "I just want to hold him," he told me, because I had taken Nollie in with me for the night, as I often do. We sat silent for many minutes. Peggie has often pressed my brother for accounts of camp-life and battle this week, recollections he is loath to share. But last night he began quietly to volunteer pieces of information to me: how just before they go into battle, the men will throw away the cards and dice with which they entertain themselves in the camp, lest being killed, such things be found in their pockets, and reported to their parents. He showed me a scrap of paper, much stained with sweat and dirt, bearing his name, that he'd pinned inside his shirt before going into battle at Fredericksburg. "Sometimes the ambulance-men don't get to you for three days," he whispered. "It's hard to tell, then." I said, "Ollie, don't."

"I have to," he said. "Corrie, I have to tell." And then he told me: he is thinking about *deserting*. This is only partly, he says, because he is afraid: most of the men are afraid. It would not be so bad, he says, if they believed their officers knew what they were doing, but they don't. "They're politicians," he told me. "So many of them got commands because they got votes for Lincoln and his party. When we were kids playing soldier out by the pond, *we* knew better than to charge up-hill at other kids who were dug in behind a wall. I wouldn't mind–not so much–if I thought any of it was going to do any good. But it is senseless." He laid Nollie down again, and clasped my hands, and whispered, "If I decided to do it, Corrie, would you hide me?"

Susanna, what could I say? It shames me to relate, that among my first thoughts was, Elinor had told Peggie I was disloyal to the Union–that I would rejoice at any "true-hearted man" taken out of the lines–and she had told Ollie. And Ollie believed her, and so came to me. I was silent, struggling to find the right thing to say, and then I told him, "You could not come back here." Which is the truth. In Indiana, when citizens rioted to protect deserters from the Army authorities, both citizens and deserters were arrested. And, Mother would never permit it. Ollie has to know this. I stammered, "Papa is very proud of you," and Ollie turned his face away, knowing, as I know, that Papa would be flayed with shame. We held one another, and both wept. It is hard for me to know–

Later. Evening

I feel better. The interruption was Will Kydd. He had fetched kin of Farnum's from Isle au Haut for the funeral, yet knew himself, like me, to be *persona non grata* at the graveside. Driving back to Green's Landing to wait, he saw the smoke of our chimney. I asked him, *Did* the Copperheads go about trying to get men to desert, to weaken the Army? Before he replied, I reconsidered what I had asked, and asked instead, *Are* you a Copperhead, Will? Or is this only what Elinor says? There are, says Will, different degrees of Copperheadedness: from those who believe strongly in the principle of Union but do not approve of the actions of President Lincoln and Congress, all the way to men and women who are actually getting money from the Confederate government at Richmond, to interfere with our efforts to prosecute this War. These different groups are not under any central organization, any more than are the various denominations of the Christian church, nor the many organizations before the War that pursued freedom for black men and women. You remember how different they were: Immediate Abolitionists, Gradual Emancipationists, Immediate Emancipationists, and several species of mutually antipathetical Colonizers—and they would squabble amongst themselves like girls in a boarding-school. " 'Tis easy to say, *He who is not with us is against us,*" Will told me. "But 'tis hard to justify fighting for your homeland, if the fight will change that homeland into something it wasn't before."

He meant that Congress has approved a Conscription Act. Too few men are volunteering, and battle losses have been appallingly heavy. Mother quashed it as a topic of conversation this evening, but Will told me that the men of the island are outraged at the idea, particularly in light of the fact that any rich man may hire a substitute, or pay outright a sum of three hundred dollars to be excused.

Ollie has not spoken to me again of desertion. Forgive me for writing of this to you, Susanna, you who have lost two brothers, and your beloved home, as well. Even were it possible to do so, I might not even send this sheet to you, but might simply fold it away: send it only in thought, to that ideal Susanna of my imagination, that Dickens heroine whose superhuman compassion will effortlessly surmount her grief. Forgive me, for separating Her from the real You, human and in at least as much pain as I.

Your own,
Cora

Susanna Ashford, Vicksburg, Mississippi
To
Cora Poole, Deer Isle, Maine

[not sent]

TUESDAY, MARCH 17, 1863

Dear Cora,

Bandages to wash. Wounded flooding in, from the terrible fighting on Steele's Bayou. Unmarried girls to work among convalescents only—I can just hear Mrs. J's Dolly say it "isn't fittin'." Julia declared herself ready to die for Our Boys, and burst into tears: has been weeping since. This will prove a useful qualification in times of crisis. Unmarried or not, I long to work in the hospital, with Nellie. It doesn't seem to matter that *black* girls see white men naked. Steele's Bayou is ten miles north. From the window of my attic I can hear gunfire.

SUNDAY, MARCH 22

Asked Aunt Sally, Would it be safer to move to Jackson? She replied, Yankees would need to take Jackson before they could come here, because of the railroad. Confederate High Command all being imbeciles (she says) we might not defend Jackson; even imbeciles can see they *must* defend Vicksburg. After dinner, Emory playing with Tommy while Julia and Aunt Sally played duets, piano and harp: Dr. Driscoll took me aside, asked me quietly, Did I think I could work as assistant in an operating theater, if it came to that? I said yes immediately.

Wednesday, March 25
Night

Julia sent home from first day of hospital work. Between fainting and tears, she takes one or more other nurses from their work as well as not doing any herself. Nellie and men servants at hospital, so Julia and I clean house, wash dishes, chop kindling, air bed linen, get dinner ready with brief pause while I bandage up Julia's burned fingers (ref. dinner, above), do mending, search for Tommy (found playing in the "cave" Aunt Sally had Zed dig in case of further shelling), wash Tommy (a *lot*), and of course wash bandages. Julia faints at smell of bandages. Almost too tired to think now. I envy you, my friend, buried under mountain of snow in the dark with Mr. Poole's novels.

Thursday, April 2
Night

Drat it. I'm still experimenting with making ink, and as you can see, sometimes it works and sometimes it doesn't. I've been experimenting with different woods to make charcoal (when we heat water to wash bandages). Willow works well, and cane from the brakes down by the river is good also. Most of the men in the shore batteries aren't like Regal's militia. You have to have some education and training, to be in the artillery. Maybe they're just too tired to be nasty. Aunt Sally and Julia are up in arms, at the state my dress gets into. The lamp oil is gone. More can not be gotten anywhere, and even candles are getting woefully expensive. Aunt Sally of course refuses to even consider rush-lights.

FRIDAY, APRIL 17

Shelling last night. Julia woke me screaming, refused to go down to the shelter without me. When Nellie dragged her and Little Tommy away, I ran up to the attic. It was filled with the smell of powder-smoke and magnolias. Aunt Sally stood in the gable window, looking down over the river; red light, gold light coming up from below. Tar-barrels were burning all along the river's bank, dyeing the red-gold bluffs. Across the river, the whole town of DeSoto was in flames. Black masses of Union gunboats against the fire-glare on black water, and even from up in the attic I could hear the men shouting in the shore batteries, the clatter of hooves on China Street and the whistle of flying shells. I asked, Were they attacking? and Aunt Sally replied, "Just running the battery. Taking supplies down to Grant. He'll be getting ready to cross over to our side of the river." A shell hit near-by and shook the house, and she only remarked, "That'll be a Parrott. They're accurate over a mile. Damn Yankees. And Damn Jeff Davis for an imbecile." We both leaned our elbows on the sill and looked out and down, and after a time Aunt Sally said, "Even if they come ashore, they'll never get up the bluff. Our men can pick them off from above, every foot of the way."

"Like in the Middle Ages," I said. "We could pour boiling oil on them."

"Not with the cost of oil these days," remarked Aunt Sally. "Don't lean your elbows on the sill, girl, they'll be wrinkly as a camel's knees before you're twenty!"

I knew I should go down to be with Julia, but I had to keep looking, how the gunflashes reflected in the black water, and the glare of the fire on the banks outlined the boats. One of them was hit, and took fire. I could see little black figures running back and forth against the flames, like when the Tories burned the tobacco-barn a year ago. The boat turned as it blazed, and drifted with the current, falling behind the rest of the fleet. I could see it burning long after the others were out of sight, like a crimson star in the darkness.

Later. Evening

This afternoon after I wrote to you, I went up to Sky Parlor. The river's a half-mile wide here, but from Sky Parlor you can see across it, to where the Union soldiers were building concealed gun-emplacements. By daylight, with Doc Driscoll's spyglass, I could see the town of DeSoto, reduced to cinder and ash, the people who lived there—and Union soldiers—moving around in the ruins.

Always your friend,
Susie

[sketches]

Cora Poole, Deer Isle, Maine
To
Susanna Ashford, Vicksburg, Mississippi

[not sent]

Wednesday, March 18, 1863

Dear Susie,

Disquieting visit to Lufkin's store yesterday with Mother. Mother told me, troubled, on the way home that she had heard a shocking rumor about Will Kydd stealing parcels entrusted to him for transport about the islands. She rebuked the gossip with a suitable passage from Holy Writ, yet, she told me, with the cost of cloth, and molasses, and salt so high, surely a man so poor as Will would be tempted? Exasperatingly, a few miles farther, Mother turned to me and repeated the identical rumor, as if she had forgotten that she had already done so: a trick she has acquired since her fall two weeks ago. She tries to conceal it, but the blow on her head affected her memory a little. She let slip yesterday a remark that made me realize she has no recollection of the fall, nor how she came to have a healing cut and a clipped place in her hair, just above her left ear.

I wish, just for once, that Mr. Poole's trunk contained at least one medical book. Surely *Fantomina* could have been spared, to give it room?

Friday, March 20

Uncle M still down with *la grippe.* Will came to chop wood and sharpen the tools. I was talking with him at the wood-pile when Peggie came out and told him we didn't need the help of "such as he." Fortunately Will is the best-natured man on earth. He waited til Peggie went inside again—which she soon did, as it was terribly cold—and resumed chopping. Later in the afternoon she regaled me with her suspicion that Will is in league with the Confederate raiders, who have captured and burned so many coastal vessels and taken their crews prisoner. Why could he not, she demanded, only be waiting to deliver the whole island over to these pirates, to use as a permanent base?

I laughed at this, as I laugh now in retrospect. Yet this kind of hurtful rumor tells me the sort of thing that is probably being said about me, behind my back. *He who is not with us is against us.* Fear of the raiders makes even the most stupid innuendos seem likely. The wood stores are low, and we are down to the last few crocks of last fall's butter. Thank Heavens that the cows are freshening again, and will be in milk soon. I am grateful that Will has offered to cut wood, as neither Peggie nor I is strong enough to wield the broad-ax. Mother can cut logs into stove-billets, but this past week she has thrice dropped things in the kitchen—Mother, whom I have seldom seen drop anything in her life—and I do not like to see her, with an ax in her hand. You grew up in the country, dear friend, around work-crews engaged in heavy labor. Do you know how long it is, after a blow on the head like that, before its effects finally dwindle?

Perhaps you are right, and I should consult Dr. Ferguson in Northwest Harbor.

Your fellow Spy,
Cora

Cora Poole, Deer Isle, Maine
To
Susanna Ashford, Vicksburg, Mississippi

[not sent]

TUESDAY, MARCH 24, 1863

My dearest,

Troubling news in the papers, of fighting all around Vicksburg. I hope your Aunt has removed you from that town, since it now seems there will be a determined assault upon it. My heart hurts me, at this link with you severed: that I do not even know where you are now, or under what circumstances.

I refuse to believe that it is the last link. Wherever you are, I know that when it becomes possible, you will write to me again.

Love,
Cora

Cora Poole, Deer Isle, Maine
To
Susanna Ashford, Vicksburg, Mississippi

[not sent]

TUESDAY, APRIL 7, 1863

Dearest Susie,

Mother seems much better! Thank you for the kind note that I knew you would have sent, had you received my letters containing my concerns for her. And thank you for the sketches that would have been enclosed, of your errant Pa's adventures in Richmond. The snow is almost off the ground, reduced to three or four inches in the cold shadows of the woods, and in the brown, dispirited boughs that still heap the sides of our house and barn. We sugared off last week–twelve pounds of maple sugar, *plus* syrup! Men are readying the cod-fleet to go out, though Uncle M says the cost of rigging-line has quadrupled and the government is no longer paying bounties on fish. Although enlistments are at a standstill, with so many men gone–more than one man in three!–it is difficult for him to raise full crews, much less find a man to hire for the farm-work. He may only send out one boat this year.

For weeks I have not quit the farm, though I have received word that I will indeed teach this summer. This is a great relief, for those things that we can not raise, such as salt, lamp-oil, and garden-twine, are almost more than we can afford.

I have begun to re-read *The Iliad*–not one of Mr. Poole's, but my old copy Papa gave me–and having read *Don Quixote,* it has begun to occur to me to wonder: Was Homer being *sarcastic,* about his bronze-greaved Achaean heroes before the walls of Troy? Or have I had too many conversations with Will?

Three more men have come home disabled.

THURSDAY, APRIL 23

Spring Cleaning. *The Iliad* must be set aside. All Saturday Papa and I—and Mercy, who can now toddle and get herself unutterably filthy—dug in the new garden, while Mother and Peggie scrubbed floors, scrubbed walls, swept and black-leaded grates. The woods are a fairyland of early wildflowers: fragile trilliums and gaudy Devil's paintbrush, meadowsweet and steeplebush, each color like a note of music. I opened windows to let the wind blow through, carried furniture and mattress outdoors to air, beat carpets. The moon being a single day into its first quarter, Papa would not hear of planting potatoes, rhubarb, beets, or any other thing that grows beneath the ground. He left me with instructions for getting in the corn, pumpkins, squashes, etc. next week, as soon as the moon has waxed sufficiently not to have any danger of being termed New or Dark. Aunt Hester follows a still more Babylonian regimen: not only must crops that grow downward be planted in the waning of the moon, but they *must* be planted on the day of the month dominated by the proper Zodiacal sign as determined by the almanac. Papa shakes his head at this. Yet if word reached him that I planted the potatoes before the second of May, I'm certain it would give him sleepless nights!!!

Do these customs hold in Tennessee? Are they the same among the white farmers in the mountains like Mr. Poole, as among your Pa's Negroes? Or is there some African system that differs entirely? I know the fishermen have their own set of customs, which include casting silver overside when becalmed: "buying wind," it is called. Uncle M tells me of a man in the cod-fleet, who carries a dime wrapped in a rag and tied on the end of a cable, which he will throw into the sea in times of stillness, and haul back again if the desired result is not forthcoming. I suspect that the gods of Homer would have something to say about that!

The fleet has gone out. The nights are cold, but it is such a blessing, to go out to the milking in the flush of new light, when the world smells of pine and sea.

FRIDAY, MAY 1

I have not mentioned it before, but Mother has been sleeping later in the mornings, which is unlike her. I have told myself, she is fifty, and has not the energy of a girl. Yet this morning it was only with the greatest difficulty that I waked her at all, and for some minutes she seemed confused, as if she did not know me. When I spoke to her of it later, after we had set the milk-pans to separate, she did not remember the incident at all.

Tell me what you think of this, my friend. How I wish that you could!

Your friend,
Cora

Susanna Ashford, Vicksburg, Mississippi
To
Cora Poole, Deer Isle, Maine

[not sent]

TUESDAY, APRIL 28, 1863
NIGHT

Dear Cora,

I should be sleeping; I'm so tired I feel like I fell down a flight of stairs. Wounded coming in every hour, and in the heat the hospital is frightful. It's the old Washington Hotel; flies everywhere, and blood soaked into the lobby carpet so that it stinks. Sometimes they need help there, sometimes they don't, but there's *constant* laundry: bandages. Zed cuts wood and hauls water for it, first thing in the morning, then goes to the hospital to work himself.

Emory, in town with dispatches, told me Captain F was killed in a skirmish. I felt stricken with guilt—Why? He was boring and had no manners. Just now Nellie came up, saw my candle, asked me, What was wrong? I told her. And she said, "He used to grab at my pussy every time he pass me on the stairs." Maybe he still doesn't deserve to be dead, but suddenly I don't feel so bad.

Wednesday, April 29

People are fleeing town for Jackson. Emory to dinner. I asked him, Would we (meaning, little Tommy, really) be safer back at Bayberry? He said No, the whole section is in flames: militia of both sides, deserters of both sides, stripping the countryside bare. Even Seceshes are refugeeing to Nashville, where there's food. I wondered if Justin's books are all right, deep down in Skull Cave. Only later, did I wonder: Is Bayberry still standing? Did the Romans feel like this, when the bloodthirsty Goths came through?

[sketches]

Thursday, April 30

Floods of wounded. They say Grant is crossing the river. Sound of Union guns carries like thunder over the water.

Saturday, May 9
Late night

Emory came to the hospital. He brought word that Tom had both legs shattered by a minié ball. Julia there—too many wounded for anyone to stay home now—and fainted. He took her home. He is here still, and bids me send you his love.

Monday, May 11

Tom brought in—finally—today. Doc Driscoll said, "I wish I could spare you, Susie, but I can't," and I had to help him cut off Tom's legs. After two nights of no sleep, staying up with Julia, I didn't feel anything more than if I was helping Cook thigh a chicken. But I now know how kind God was, to Gaius and Payne.

Yours,
Susie

Cora Poole, Deer Isle, Maine
To
Susanna Ashford, Vicksburg, Mississippi

[not sent]

Tuesday, May 5, 1863

Dearest Susanna,

Newspapers—terrible fighting in Virginia, where I know Oliver is now. Nearly as bad is the account of the fighting all around

Vicksburg, where I fear—despite my efforts at optimism—that you still might be. I remind myself that your Aunt Sally did not appear to me to be a woman who would put up with seige conditions. I tell myself that it is foolish to torment myself over what I can not know, and can not help.

Sadness as well as fear: a letter from Mrs. Johnson, with news of the death of her son Charley, who once paid money from his own pocket to rent a buggy, to take you back to Bayberry. A fall from a horse, his mother wrote. God forgive me, my first thought—from my slim acquaintance with the man—was to wonder if he were sober.

Wednesday, May 13

Great worries and small. Blackfly season: swarming, pestiferous vermin. Do you have blackflies in Tennessee? When I read the tale of the Plagues of Egypt, that is what I see as the Plague of Flies. The days lengthen and warm, endless sweet twilights made hideous by the first mosquitoes. God created all living beings, including the mice that have returned to my dresser drawer.

I am beginning to be very uneasy about Mother, despite Dr. Ferguson's assurance that these symptoms are normal, in one who had what was almost certainly a mild concussion. Her fall was over two months ago. Surely the spells of forgetfulness, the abnormal clumsiness, should abate? Or at least, not become *more* frequent? For the most part I can not even speak to Peggie of my concern. As her friendship with Elinor has grown—she regularly attends the meetings of the Daughters of the Union—she avoids me with an air of uneasiness, as if she has been warned even against conversation. This room where I sit tonight has taken on something of the aspect of a sanctuary. It is the only place where I can feel safe, with the only company I can trust: yourself, Miss Mercy (who can now say Mama, G'amma, Eggie, Nollie, and One), and those dear fictional friends who meet perils and tribulations unknown to me, with courage, tenderness, and fortitude likewise worlds away from my own vexed strivings.

Every time I close the book—whatever book it be—I ask them, to give you my love, when they should meet you next.

Your friend,
Cora

Susanna Ashford, Vicksburg, Mississippi
To
Cora Poole, Deer Isle, Maine

[not sent]

FRIDAY, MAY 15, 1863
LATE NIGHT

Dear Cora,

This morning General Pemberton issued an order for all noncombatants to leave Vicksburg, while he still holds some part of the railroad. Jackson is in Union hands. Aunt Sally said that if the Army thought it could run *her* hospital without *mere women* cluttering things up, they certainly had *her* permission to try. She said she was taking me, Julia, and Tommy to Richmond. Julia clung on to Tom's hand (we were at the hospital—we finally got Tom a cot yesterday) and begged me not to leave her: "You can't take her from me, and you can't make me go!" And to me, "Susie, if you go I'll *die*!"

So I said I'd stay. Aunt Sally left this afternoon. She took Zed, Ruben the butler, and the nursemaid, leaving us with only Nellie and Cook. The house echoes queerly. I feel very strange, probably from lack of sleep, or not eating enough (there's no time, at the hospital). It's as if the Real Susanna—that little girl sitting on Justin's porch reading, who forged letters home for my roommate in the Nashville Academy—is sitting in a little room at the back of my brain, watching things and making drawings that I'll one day be able to put on paper. I don't think anyone would want to see them, tho'.

At the hospital I take care of Julia more than Tom, who hasn't really regained his senses since the amputation. I change the dressings on his stumps, and keep him as clean as I can, and give him water or broth if I can get it, and chase the rats away. I think every rat in town knows where the pile of amputated limbs is, and from there they swarm the rooms and the stairways where the men lie. Sometimes at night I'll hear a man screaming curses if vermin run across him or chew on his bandages. In between all that I help Doc Driscoll in the operating room (which was the dining-room—they had to get rid of the carpet there, too, because of maggots), and take water around to the men. Julia isn't much good for any of that, but won't leave Tom's side, like a sort of demented Mrs. Micawber. With hardly anybody to keep the men clean, I can't even tell you what it smells like. That's another reason I haven't eaten in days. When more men get brought in, Doc says, "Cut the arms and legs first. Head and belly, they won't live anyway." Part of my job in the operating room is just to keep the flies away from the open wounds long enough to clean and stitch.

I will confess to you, back when I got your letters, about first being on Deer Isle, and everyone hating you because of Emory, I was angry at Emory, angry that he'd do that to you, by making the choice he did. Cora, Emory has been like a brother to me and Julia, like a brother to poor Tom. He comes to the hospital whenever he's in town—muddy and tired and powder-burned—to sit beside Tom. You have married a good man, dearest Cora.

With love,
Susanna

Susanna Ashford, Vicksburg, Mississippi
To
Cora Poole, Deer Isle, Maine

[not sent]

SUNDAY, MAY 17, 1863

Dearest Cora,

Doc sent me home this morning, after I fell asleep in a corner of the operating room (which I don't remember, just being waked up by one of the orderlies). He said, "You go on home now, honey: that's not a request, that's an order. Grant's going to hit us with everything he's got, soon as he gets his men up. I'll need you then and I'll need you fresh. If you're not out of this building in five minutes I'll detail two men to take you home in handcuffs." I saluted and said, "Yes, sir," but instead of going home I walked to the top of Sky Parlor. The streets are filled with retreating soldiers, with wagons and ambulances. For a long time I stood at the top looking east and down, where Grant's men were coming up through the ravines, and the Confederates streaming back into town. It was like looking down on a very bright orange-and-green chessboard. Last night Pemberton ordered all the houses on those hills outside of town burned, to clear the line of fire.

I wondered if Justin were down there, and where he was.

Emory came up beside me, and walked me home.

Yours,
Susie

[sketch]

Susanna Ashford, Vicksburg, Mississippi
To
Cora Poole, Deer Isle, Maine

[not sent]

WEDNESDAY, MAY 27, 1863

Dear Cora,

I don't even know how to write about what's happened since my last letter to you. I should be sleeping, but I can't. At least I was able to wash, and rinse my hair. I think about how horrified I was the first time I got a louse in my hair, going down the line in Nashville, and I think, Who was that girl, and did she have nothing greater in her life, to earn her revulsion and alarm?

Grant attached the fortifications along the east of town a week ago yesterday. I think a week ago Monday night was the last time I slept in a bed. I suppose I ought to be glad the Union finally has two good Generals, but I find I'm not.

The land in back of town is all wooded gullies and ravines, where people used to pasture their cows. Gen'l Pemberton had rifle-pits and redoubts dug just beyond the last houses. The Federals had to attack up-hill. You don't have to be Julius Caesar to know that isn't a good idea. I was on my way to the Washington Hotel Hospital when the shelling started. I can't really describe the sound a shell makes. It's a sort of deafening rushing, like a waterfall or a train close-by. The first one hit a block from me, on Clay Street. Before I got to the hospital I could hear the cannons start up, east of town. While still outside the hospital door I could hear Julia screaming upstairs. I ran up, to find Tom awake for the first time since he'd been brought in, holding Julia in his arms. He looked at me as I came into the room and said, "Them's mortars." Something ran across my foot and I looked down and saw every rat in the building, high-tailing it for the cellar.

It's funny how quickly you learn to distinguish sounds during a shelling. I can tell the difference now between mortar-shells and Parrotts (the kind that explode in the air and shower the street with white-hot fragments of metal), and whether the shell is going to land in the next block, or the one where you're standing. Most people in town have dug some kind of shelter, like the "cave" at Aunt Sally's, which is where I am now. Zed worked on it on and off for weeks, in between Aunt Sally renting him out to dig other people's caves. It's about sixteen feet deep and has two rooms off it, and opens into China Street, which is a sort of deep cut where the land rises on both sides. I think it could not take a direct hit with a Parrott, but it's plenty of protection against fragments. I don't know if I've quit being scared, or if I'm just too tired to feel anything right now. Sometimes it feels like I was killed that first day, and so got it over with, and I'm fine, now. I wish I could talk to you.

It's blazing hot here, and worse inside the cave, which is airless and smells like dirt. Gen'l Pemberton pushed Grant back the first day, but the shelling didn't stop, and hasn't stopped: mortars from the river, and Parrotts and mortars from the other side of the ravines in the back of town. Doc and I worked for twenty hours straight in the operating theater that first day, with the whole building shaking and plaster fragments falling from the ceilings like snow. It was my job to hold a towel over the open wounds, to keep the plaster out of them. About three days later Grant brought up his whole army and hit the entire defensive line at once, on a three-mile curve. Emory swore nobody had seen anything like it. Just before that, we got Tom back to the house, Emory and Nellie and I carrying him in a litter and listening for when the shelling seemed to be moving our way. Bombs drop all day and entirely through the night, without stopping. They must be bringing them up via the railroad through Jackson, and working three shifts on the guns.

When the second attack was finally over, the Federals kept up firing across the battlefield, so no one could collect the wounded, not theirs nor ours. After two days, in heat like an oven, you could smell the battlefield from anywhere in town. I think fear of pestilence finally decided Grant. Monday, he silenced the guns long enough to get the wounded and the dead out of there. Doc said Grant didn't want to show weakness: that he was afraid of what the Northern newspapers would say about him.

I went with the orderlies and nurses, to bring in the wounded. In the silence you could hear them everywhere, lying in the gullies and under bushes, where they'd been for two days and nights without water or care. Their crying hung over the field, directionless, the way the sound of crickets fills a summer night. The flies were like black snow, and there were more ravens than I've ever seen in my life, and I could see the underbrush stirring with rats. The dead men were piled up on top of each other like a wall under the redoubt. It was two hundred yards down the hill before you could even see grass between the bodies. And way out on the other side of the field, I could see two dogs, trotting around among the wounded and the dead—not like they were looking for anyone, just out for a stroll the way dogs do—and I knew they were Sulla and Argus, Justin's dogs.

So he's here. (I looked at the dogs through Doc's spyglass, and it's them, all right.) He lived through the battle, and he's in the camp outside town. I haven't told Emory this, and I won't. Everyone says—Emory, and Tom, and Gaius the last time I saw him, and the men in the hospital—that if you think about anything in the battle, except exactly what you're doing at that moment, that's when you'll make a mistake that'll get you killed. If Emory learned his father was out there, he'd look for him, and might not pay attention to what he was doing. Yet, it feels so strange to know he's out there.

That's all the paper I have for now, my dear Cora. As you can see, I'm tearing the flyleaves and title-pages out of Husband #3's books, both to draw on, and to write to you. But, I wanted to write to you, wanted to let you know that I'm here, that I'm all right so far. Please don't let Justin know I'm here, or that Emory's here, because I don't want *him* looking for either of *us*. I have all your letters down here with me, and some of Aunt Sally's sheets and towels, to sleep on. Nellie and Emory made a sort of rough bedstead for Tom, to keep him off the ground, and one of Aunt Sally's trunks, with the lid taken off, as a bed for Tommy. When the shelling sounds like it's moved over a few streets away, Nellie and I run up to the house to get food, and sometimes we'll bring down things like dishes or even chairs. On the next trip, we're planning to get the parlor curtains, to close off the two rooms for privacy.

I will sleep now, before going to the hospital again. This is the first afternoon Doc has been able to spare me. Grant hasn't attacked again. But the shells keep falling.

Your friend,
Susie

[sketches]

Cora Poole, Deer Isle, Maine
To
Susanna Ashford

[not sent]

WEDNESDAY, JUNE 3, 1863

Dearest Susie,

My apologies for the delay. The moment wheat, corn, and gardens are in the ground, school starts, both here and on Isle au Haut, and though in the end Aunt H got us help with the plowing, Mother and I helped plant the corn. There are four "new babies" in my class this year, and the big boys of last year are out with their fathers in the fleet. As I walk up the hill to the school-house, I see my little scholars taking turns on the great boulder that stands near-by: "watching for pirates"—Confederate raiders—with spyglasses composed of their two curled hands.

Getting the garden in seemed harder this May, for I have formed the uneasy habit of keeping an eye on Mother. Will suggested I start a tally, of those moments of forgetfulness that are so unlike her, or of occasions when she seems clumsy as she was not before. For weeks she will be completely as she used to be before her fall . . . I *think.* Then last Friday morning I came into her room to wake her—which I never needed to do before—and found her standing in her night-gown, gazing before her at nothing like a revenant in one of Mr. Poe's tales. I called her name twice before she seemed to wake. I am grateful that Papa is now back for the summer. He is inclined to believe my fears groundless. He has heard of many such cases from members of the medical faculty at Yale, and reassures me that the effects will pass in time.

Friday, June 5

I *will* write you at least a few lines, before I sleep! I sit in the summer kitchen, last of all this household awake, wearing an old straw hat with cheesecloth veiling sewed around its brim, as protection against mosquitoes. Dishes washed, pots scoured, floor mopped, ashes hauled away, knives cleaned, while the last twilight dies softly in the doorway. Now beyond the glow of my lamp the room is still. The air is laden with the wondrous scent of the meadows and the pond.

Tuesday I had a letter from Justin, the first since March. He is indeed with Grant's army, camped before Vicksburg, and asks, Are you still in that town? The letter he encloses to you, Susie, is addressed to you there: *Please Forward.* Imagination, and hope, can only go so far, toward loosening the grip of fear.

Like the heroine of *Bleak House,* I try to make each day a bright stepping-stone through a world of dark surmise. Without my daily crossings to Isle au Haut, I would feel imprisoned indeed, like Robinson Crusoe: bounded within the narrow compass of what I can see. Mother asked me Sunday, with great concern, whether it is true that I am a Copperhead, of the sort they are arresting in New York. I can only surmise that she heard this at church in Northwest Harbor. Yet unlike the intrepid Mr. Crusoe, I am not alone.

Always your friend,
Cora

Susanna Ashford, Vicksburg, Mississippi
To
Cora Poole, Deer Isle, Maine

[not sent]

THURSDAY, JUNE 4, 1863

Dear Cora,

It's very strange, not having the slightest idea what's happening in the rest of the country, or the rest of the world, or even five miles away. Now that there aren't regiments of wounded coming in every day, I've gone around V'brg to see my friends and make sure everyone is all right so far. The Petrie Sisters and Mrs. Bell are sharing a cave over on Adams Street, and there's a huge cave, sheltering perhaps a hundred people, a few blocks farther on. Every day, there's somebody going someplace (usually looking for food), when the shells start to move from one block to the next (as they turn the guns, I guess). So there's always someone taking refuge here with us. Or, I'll miscalculate how long it will take me to get from one place to another, and have to duck into the nearest cellar or hole in the ground when the shelling moves my way. Some people are still living in their houses, because the caves are like ovens, not to speak of the wildlife that visits. At night we all sleep as close to the cave-mouth as we dare.

The first day I wasn't needed at the hospital, Nellie and I raced up to the house and took a count of the food left in the larder. Aunt Sally left us with half a wheel of cheese, three sacks of cornmeal, half a barrel of potatoes, most of a ham, and assorted preserves—we were due to start pickling cucumbers and bottling peaches in a few weeks, so supplies of those were low. We're moving those down to the cave a little at a time, because nobody knows how long it will be before the town is either relieved or surrenders. (*Nobody* admits there's any possibility of surrender, but President Davis would *never* make Lee leave Virginia to march here overland, the way everyone is saying he will and must.) In a way I'm glad Cookie ran away, the night Grant's men moved into position around the town, even if she did take all the sugar. I suspect we'll need all the food we can save.

After we move sacks and jars and dishes and bedding, I'll make one more trip—it takes twenty-three seconds to run from the mouth of the cave, up the bank, across the yard, and in the kitchen door—and run into the library and tear the flyleaves and end-papers out of as many books as I can in thirty seconds, then race back. Once, I got caught in the open, when the guns moved earlier than I expected and shells started landing in Aunt Sally's yard, but I threw myself down the bank and scrambled into the cave. At least we have plenty of water. Or we will unless a shell hits Aunt Sally's cistern, which stands in the back of the house. Emory tells us that there's no water to be had out at the rifle-pits, and in this heat the men are always desperate for it. I wonder if it's the same, on the other side of the lines?

Tuesday, June 9

Emory to dinner again—I say, "to dinner," as if we had something other than cornmeal mush, a sprinkle of cheese, and a few thinly-sliced potatoes, but he swears it's a thousand times better than they have at the rifle-pits. He says they have only a little bacon or salt beef (only it's probably not really beef), to last them a whole day's fighting, plus cornmeal and pea-meal, mixed. But, we now have the parlor table and three chairs, and plates and cups. Emory told us about the latest rumors, including a most pitiful story being circulated in the Northern newspapers, about Mrs. Pemberton, the Gen'l's wife, being killed in the bombardment. (She is perfectly safe in Mobile, and everyone in town knows it.) Where the rumors start, no one has any idea, but many are called across the lines from the Federals. Men come in from the lines all the time, for aside from the shelling—about which they can do nothing—and the shooting back and forth, they also have very little to do. Emory says it's like being trapped perpetually in a shooting-gallery, only the targets are shooting back *and* the building is on fire!

Considering how much danger we're in, the days drag fearfully. Emory carved a set of chess pieces out of spent minié balls, and I play with him when he's here. I think of you, Cora, shut into your house with darling Mercy for months on end in wintertime; sometimes this feels like a not-very-funny parody. We—Nellie and I—sweep the dirt floor, fetch water from the cistern, and count the hours until it's time to make a little mush for the five of us—or six, if Emory will be in from the lines. We are *always* hungry. Julia and I have had a dozen squabbles, for she cannot resist Tommy's pleas for food, and I say harshly, "Better he cries now than starves next week." She tells me—as Aunt Sally was always doing—that I am cold, and unwomanly, and selfish.

Today, before he went back to the lines, Emory helped me make a barrier out of a shed the Yankees obligingly blew up for us, to keep Tommy from wandering out of the cave when no one is watching.

Many afternoons, I read. I carried down books from the house—*Catherine de Medici* and *Rienzi* this week—but I have to keep an eye on them, and carry them back when I'm done, or Julia or Nellie will tear out pages to put on the fire, rather than go out searching for kindling. I cannot blame them, and yet, I cannot see it done. Rather, I always select some awful tome or collection of sermons to bring down, as well. Sometimes I read aloud to poor Tom, who drifts in and out of sleep—for he is in the most awful pain. Mostly, I just read. It's better than thinking, sometimes.

Yours from the Seige of Troy,
Susanna

[sketches]

Cora Poole, Deer Isle, Maine
To
Susanna Ashford

[not sent]

TUESDAY, JUNE 16, 1863

Dearest,

A confusion of rumor, spreading fast over the island as the lobstermen come in from the mainland. A Confederate army has invaded Pennsylvania, and is en route to Washington. No one would speak to Will at Green's Landing, but when I stopped at Uncle M's on the way home, Aunt Hester said that some of the men had gone across to Portland to get news if there was any. The moon is new, and they will not be back tonight.

WEDNESDAY, JUNE 17

I try to imagine you across the table from me; yet tonight I feel more alone than I have, perhaps in my life. The rumor is indeed true that the North has been invaded in force, and we know that Oliver's regiment is in the army that was sent to intercept the invaders. But there is a deeper trouble here. Papa met me on the road, and said, Mother did not come back in from evening milking. When he went out to see what delayed her, he found her sitting on the milking-stool staring before her, and she did not seem to hear him when he spoke her name. He led her into the house and laid her down on the bed, where she fell at once asleep. Yet, when I went in with him and shook her, she at once woke up, and was herself, complaining only of a headache. Papa tries to be cheerful, and to act as if this is but a normal consequence of her fall in March. Yet last night I came into the kitchen, and surprised him watching her with such a look of fearful helplessness in his eyes as I have never seen. He knows no more of how to help her than I do, Susie!

Thursday, June 18

And on top of great disasters come petty annoyances, like biting gnats! As if doing so would shield Oliver from danger, Peggie has taken to leaving pamphlets from the New England Propaganda Society on my pillow, or tucked beneath the sheets of my bed. *Execrable* verse—one can not call it poetry. I would laugh, but for my own terrible anxiety for my brother's sake.

Mother, at least, seems better today. Rain is falling, and fills the summer kitchen with the scent of the woods, mercifully keeping both mosquitoes and blackflies away. The whole night whispers with it.

My compliments to Julia on her twenty-second birthday. Please forward to her my sincere hopes for her health and happiness.

Saturday, June 20
Mercy's birthday tomorrow

Thank you for the kind letter you would have sent my daughter! I hope and pray that all is well with you and yours, my dear Susie, wherever you are.

All my love,
Cora

Susanna Ashford, Vicksburg, Mississippi
To
Cora Poole, Deer Isle, Maine

[not sent]

Sunday, June 21, 1863

Dearest Cora,

Wish your daughter happy birthday for me. The enclosed sketch is for her. The roses are real, and still blooming madly in the bottom corner of Aunt Sally's yard. The cat is from memory: between the shelling, and no food in the town, and the possibility of being eaten themselves, I don't think there's a cat this side of the Union lines.

We're just about out of cornmeal and all our flour is gone, so Wednesday I went down to the cane-brakes at the bottom of the bluff, to dig up the cane-shoots, which you can boil for food. It's funny, to meet there some of the ladies I used to go take Sunday tea with, on the same errands. Emory says there are Louisiana men in the lines catching rats, and they swear they cook up just fine. None for me, thanks. Friday he brought us some mule-meat, which was ghastly. Julia gives most of her food to Tommy, and she grows pitifully thinner and more ethereal-looking by the day. She has this look of martyred intenseness in her eyes, as if she expects every second to be her last and is determined to give her life for the South. Tom is fading, too, feverish and weak, and she is so patient with him, so loving, as if nothing existed but him and their son. Sometimes when the bombs are falling close, she sings. It is hard to imagine such love. Thursday was her twenty-second birthday.

[sketches]

THURSDAY, JUNE 25

Dearest Cora,

I'm sorry. I'm so sorry. Please forgive me.

Good-by,
Susanna

Cora Poole, Deer Isle, Maine
To
Susanna Ashford

[not sent]

MONDAY, JUNE 29, 1863

Dearest,

As I came down to the wharf at Town Landing this afternoon, I saw the men gathered around talking wildly and feared that the lobstermen had brought news of battle before Washington. But the men said a Confederate Navy schooner had sailed into the harbor at Portland, a few hours' sailing west of here, and attacked a Federal revenue cutter as it lay at anchor.

The island is aflame with suspicion of "Copperheads" and "traitors." Anyone who does not cry *hip-hurrah!* at the sight of a bunch of red, white, and blue ribbons on a hat is automatically suspect.

My hands ache tonight, as you can see from my writing: an exhausting Saturday of hoeing, weeding, picking cherries, cucumbers, peaches! A Heaven of scent and sunshine! As a child I accepted without question the astounding bounty produced by a single plant or tree. As I grow older, I look upon this generosity with wonder. All day until darkness spent in the summer kitchen, making pickles and preserves. I told Mother I wished particularly for this to be done of a Saturday, so that I might help, having left so much of the pig-killing and soap-boiling to Peggie last fall while teaching. But in truth, I wanted it so because I was not easy with the thought of Mother working so close to a blazing fire and vats of boiling vinegar.

I moved about the schoolroom like an old lady today!

Your decrepit,
C

Cora Poole, Deer Isle, Maine
To
Susanna Ashford

[not sent]

MONDAY, JULY 6, 1863

Dearest,

I wish—*how* I wish—I knew where you were, and under what circumstances. Papa says Pastor Wainwright offered up a prayer of thanks at church yesterday, and that everyone on the island says that now the fighting will soon be done. Yet at what cost, Susie! Three days of fighting at Gettysburg, from dawn to the late fall of summer darkness! The whole island holds its breath, waiting for the casualty-lists. Peggie is distracted–

Tuesday, July 7

Twenty-four hours. I recall how you wrote, after the fall of Nashville, that sentences penned only days before seemed to speak of another world. I speak calmly to Papa, and firmly to Peggie, and cross to Isle au Haut to explain to my students the six-times-tables, and behave just as if I were one of those perfect sweet courageous heroines in all of Mr. Poole's books. Only on the way back across the Bay this afternoon did I weep a little, for sheer terror and grief.

Last night I was brought running from the summer kitchen into the parlor by Mercy's screams and the smell of smoke. Mother was standing in the middle of the room. The sleeve of her dress was on fire. She stared fixedly at the flames without making a move to help herself; Peggie pressed in a corner, clutching Nollie, in frozen panic. I slapped out the fire–it was from her bedroom-candle, fallen on the floor where it thankfully went out–and turned to see Papa standing in the door of the bedroom in his nightshirt, hands over his mouth and panic stamped upon his face. Then Mother began to struggle and sob in pain, and Papa ran to hold her, and all was confusion, but it was clear that Mother had no recollection of brushing against the candle, nor of her dress taking fire. We bandaged her arm, made her drink a little brandy-and-water as a composer, and I made Papa drink some, too, for he was shaking as badly as she, dropping the glass and the water-pitcher and his glasses. Though it was nearly midnight I took the lantern and walked the four miles into Northwest Harbor to fetch Dr. Ferguson. The moon is in its last quarter and the night overcast, and it would not have been safe to take the horse. When I returned with the doctor I took Papa aside, and said, "Is there anyone that you know at Yale, who is a specialist in injuries of the brain?" He said yes; and, he would write in the morning, asking a recommendation, of who Mother must see.

I have just now been in her room. How much she has changed over the summer! It has been some weeks now, since I have seen her accustomed sharpness. I do not know what to do, except to follow the example and precept of those impossibly courageous, impossibly good young ladies—and to follow your example, my friend. Wherever you are, I know you have passed through horrors: getting your sister out of Nashville, coming home to find the world you knew laid waste. And those are only the ones that I know about. Please hold my hand through this time.

Wednesday, July 8

Oliver is dead. Of his regiment, only fifteen men and two officers survived. Will told me this when I came down to the Town Landing to return home this afternoon. When I got home at twilight I found Papa sitting on the boulder by our gate, alone. He said he had brought the news to Mother, and they and Peggie had wept together. Yet he said, a little later in the day, Mother had come in from the garden and asked, Was there any letter from Ollie? Peggie had sobbed out that he was dead in the battle, and both wept again, as if it were the first time of hearing it—but, Papa said, it had just now happened a third time, that Mother had no remembrance of the news, nor even that a battle had been fought. Peggie had told her, he said, and again it was as if she were hearing it for the first time, and he could not endure it.

I walked him up to the house, and took Peggie aside, and begged her, to be brave for Mother's sake. She struck my hands aside and told me, it was well for me to say, for it was *my* traitorous husband who had murdered *hers*. At this I caught her by the hair, and said, You may think whatever you please, but if you trouble Mother with that or with any mention of Ollie's death, I will pull all your hair out by the roots.

It is now three in the morning. Through the wall of my bedroom I can hear Peggie crying, and Nollie wailing feebly. Papa stays with Mother, who is in great pain. Peggie refused to let me bring Nollie in here with Mercy and me. I can not believe that at this time yesterday morning, I did not know my brother was dead; and I can not believe that I will never see Ollie again. I have prayed, and found a little quiet. You have walked this road before me, my friend, and it is as if I can see your lantern ahead of me in the distance.

Always your friend,
Cora

[N.B. The Battle of Gettysburg was fought July 1–3, 1863.]

Cora Poole, Deer Isle, Maine
To
Susanna Ashford

[not sent]

FRIDAY, JULY 10, 1863

Dearest Friend,

An appointment has been made with a Dr. Hazelitt, a brain specialist, in New York City, for Tuesday next. Will has offered himself as escort for Mother and me. Though it is nearly two days' travel by train, I have decided to take my Mercy, as well. She is a sturdy girl and not at all shy of strangers. To you only will I confide the ugliness that with long ostracism has taken root in my soul, like fungus in the dark: I do not *honestly* suspect that Peggie, or Elinor, or any Daughter of the Union would knowingly do harm to my child–

Emory's child. I have not read so many novels as *that.* Yet I know that for a one-year-old girl, adventuresome and newly adept at walking, neglect is enough to place her in danger. Papa is so distraught that he sometimes barely knows where he himself is, much less his granddaughter.

Perhaps I *have* read too many novels, or found too many pamphlets tucked under my pillow, lauding the burning of "Rebel" houses, the thrusting of daggers into Rebel hearts. Perhaps, like Papa and poor Peggie, I am also a little bit insane with grief, and as unaware of it as Mother is unaware that she is not as she was.

SATURDAY, JULY 11

If I cannot speak to you, my friend, or hold your hand, I have at least the acquaintance of the intrepid Miss Dashwood, to remind me that one is not necessarily flinty of soul—or a traitor to the Union—to be thinking. We must put up the cucumbers and the peaches, *now,* if we are to have them to eat in the dead of winter, whether Ollie is dead or not. With prices as they are, and—God forgive me for even thinking this—without Ollie's pay, this winter we will be able to buy almost nothing at the store. Peggie sees nothing amiss with "borrowing" what we need from Uncle M, and refuses to see that my Uncle is not a rich man: everyone more wealthy than her indigent father, to her mind, "can afford to help us." On my way home from the Landing yesterevening I stopped and spoke to Aunt Hester, who says, she will put up our vegetables with her own, if Papa will bring them to her. I think he will be fit, to do that.

Ollie loved preserved peaches. I will think of that, as Mother and I—Mother thank Heavens kept from work near the stove, by her burnt arm—labor through this hot, heavy day peeling, slicing, boiling syrup, and melting wax. Each jar will be for him. I will send a jar with this letter. If it can magically find its way to you, surely I can enclose two jars of peaches.

MONDAY, JULY 13

I had meant to write to you from New York City, informing you of our safe arrival. Instead I take up my pen in the summer kitchen again, exhausted and troubled at heart. Papa drove us to Green's Landing as soon as I set the milk-pans in the cellar, with Mother protesting all the way that her headaches are not so bad that she needs to see any doctor about them. Yet news of the rioting in New York turned us back when we stepped off the *Lady Anne* at Portland. Mother declared, "'That's ridiculous. It is the Copperheads, that are inciting those wicked foreigners to riot." Yet Will, Uncle M, and Papa have said that all over Deer Isle one hears the same angry muttering, that the government may as well ask three million dollars to buy one-self out of the draft, as three hundred, a sum that no poor man has.

Mother twice asked me, Why were we wearing black? I said gently that I would tell her later, but as we were returning, she began to weep softly, and said "Ollie—my Ollie is dead." Yet by the time we reached home, she seemed to have forgotten again. As I had arranged to recess school until Thursday, because of our journey, I spent the remainder of the day hunting eggs and putting them down in brine for the winter and churning butter. As with the peaches, I can only keep at these homely chores by telling myself, how much Ollie en-joyed having egg-custard now and then in the winter, and butter.

I do not know what else I can do.

Cora

Cora Poole, Deer Isle, Maine
To
Susanna Ashford

[not sent]

THURSDAY, JULY 30, 1863

Dearest Susanna,

Night, and peace, and the smell of cut hay heavy in the darkness. I am re-reading *Vanity Fair,* taking refuge in Mr. Thackeray's astringent amusement. He reminds me to have patience with those former friends who speak coldly to me, and whisper amongst themselves the moment I turn away. Or if I can not pity, at least I can laugh at their ways, and so dissolve my anger before it begins to corrode my heart. Right now, I find in this greater comfort than in those Psalms that urge God to break the teeth of the wicked in their mouths, or rejoice that the righteous will be able to wash their feet in their enemies' blood.

I seldom leave the farm now, remaining here on Sundays when Papa and Peggie take Mother to church. This is the only time that Peggie emerges from the house; almost the only time she emerges from her room. Hard labor tomorrow, for we have moved wash-day to Saturday, so that I can help. Thus, when I come home tomorrow from teaching, it will be the work of hauling and boiling water to soak the clothes and sheets overnight. Mother finds it ridiculous that these precautions are taken, but finally admits that her headaches render her too tired to do as much as she used to. Thank Heavens the evening light lingers until past ten.

Is all well with you, in Richmond, or Atlanta, or wherever it is that you and Julia have taken refuge? How I look forward to the day when the post will bring me once more a letter full of your drawings, bearing the longed-for word that you are safe.

SATURDAY, AUGUST 1

Nollie's birthday. We had a picnic at the edge of the woods close by the house, for the poor little fellow, but Peggie was so overcome with recollection, that she would not leave her room. Mother asked her, what was wrong . . . and so, learned of her son's death, yet again. Well that you wrote me, my dear friend, your letter about feeling two things with equal strength at the same time, though they be contradictory: else I would be hard put to explain the intensity of my desire to shake Peggie senseless. God knows the bottommost fathom of our hearts.

THURSDAY, AUGUST 6

Aunt Hester tells me that her friend Mrs. Eaton, whose husband died in camp of wounds after the battle at Gettysburg, is to marry again, and has sent her four children away to other homes, as her new husband cannot support them.

MONDAY, AUGUST 10

Selectmen went about the island today, summoning men for the draft. Many are out with the cod-fleet still. Many more say that the government has no right to take a man from the support of his wife and children, if he does not wish to go. Others ask why, if we were victorious at Gettysburg and have taken Vicksburg, is this War not over yet? As if every man in the Confederacy would cry in chorus, "Oh, we are beaten, hard luck!" and throw down their rifles. Sometimes I wonder if people listen to what they themselves are saying?!!

Papa has not been sleeping, so shaken is he still by the news of the Draft Riots in New York. Over a thousand people killed or injured, during the three days that the mobs controlled the city. Some of the papers say that it was the Copperheads who incited the Irish and German laborers to riot, but others–and Will still brings me half a dozen, both for and against the War– say that there was no need for outsiders to inflame poor men forced to risk their lives, when rich ones can buy their way free. When he read how the mob burned the black children's orphanage, and murdered one of the little girls there–how they lynched or drowned free black shopkeepers and laborers whenever they could catch them–poor Papa wept. For a time he even talked wildly of enlisting himself, though he is sixty.

Aunt Hester and the youth who works for her and Uncle M, named Jared Dow, walk over to help with the farm tasks nearly every day, for Mother has headaches two or three times a week now. The pain is so agonizing that Papa must remain at her side. With all else that is taking place, it is wicked for me to worry about the wood not being cut for the winter to come.

Dr. Hazelitt has not returned any of Papa's inquiries, and we can only assume that he left New York on account of the rioting. Papa has found no other recommendation yet.

Forgive me, friend, if I am too tired these summer nights, to write to you. When I come home I scrub the casks for the cider and vinegar, come September; often I must scald all the milk-pails and pans as well, if Peggie has left that task undone. I know you understand–not because you are one of those sweet, ideal heroines, but because you are my friend.

Your friend,
Cora

Susanna Ashford, Bayberry Run Plantation
Greene County, Tennessee
To
Cora Poole

[not sent]

Monday, August 17, 1863

Dearest Cora,

Please forgive me. You will wonder, I know, why I no longer write to you. Even when the War is over, why I won't and can't, not ever again. And it tears me to pieces, not to be able to explain. But I can't.

Yet I need to write. Not to tell you what happened, but only because there is no one else to whom I can say, I'm lonely, and I'm so afraid. When I was a child, I used to make up new adventures for people I love in my books: other things Gringoire and Quasimodo and the Beggar King did in Paris, that Mr. Hugo didn't write about (including how they rescued Quentin Durward from a sorcerer—I hope you've been able to make Quentin's acquaintance by this time, somehow?). They were real to me, like the fairies in the woods were real.

I know you're there in Maine, on your island, with your parents and Peggie and babies Mercy and Nollie, that it's beautiful there, and safe, and you have enough to eat and aren't afraid. Is it all right, if I pretend now that you're someone who lives in Paris in 1483, or that you're one of the fairies who live in the laurel hell on Scanlon's Mountain? Who I can write to, and not have to explain what happened?

As you can see, we're back on Bayberry Run. The day they hoisted the flag of truce, for Gen'l Pemberton to go across the lines and meet Grant, Emory brought, of all people—Pa. Pa all decked out in a new Confederate uniform with gold lace on his sleeves nearly up to his shoulders, and a black plume in his hat. Pa practically fluffing and crowing, as if he was the only person who'd ever sneaked across the Federal lines into town (which he wasn't, by a long chalk); Pa full of how this friend in Richmond had said this, and that friend in Richmond had promised him that, and how he'd gotten a horse and a wagon and papers signed by General McPherson, USA, himself, to get us across the lines. "I'm going to do for my girls what I should have done long ago!" he announced, posing for a statue of himself in the door of the cave. "I'm taking you back *home*."

We left V'brg the next day, passing lines–*rivers!*–of Federal troops, all marching into the town. I thought they'd look well-fed and smart in new uniforms (well, newer than the Confederates have, anyway) but they didn't. They weren't as gaunt as our men, but they were just as caked with red-gold mud, dusty and bearded and *tired.* They barely glanced at Emory, riding beside our wagon with a slouch hat on and one arm tied to his body underneath his shirt, so it would look like he'd lost it, and a patch over one eye. Tom lay in the back of the wagon, muttering now and then–he'd had a fever for days–with his head in Julia's lap. I kept looking along the lines of men, wondering if I'd see Justin Poole. There seemed no end to them, trudging past us, miles of them. The dust trampled up from their boots dyed the air yellow. And after them, wagonloads of provisions, and cows and sheep they'd lifted from farms between Jackson and here, and then like a second straggly army, hundreds of prostitutes and *thousands* of runaway slaves, men and women and even little children, sticking to the Army for dear life.

But what would I have done, if I'd seen Justin? Jumped out and gone with him? Yet I kept thinking, *He's here. I know he's here.*

I didn't see him. The men kept marching by, as many as trees in a forest, except each with his own face, his own eyes. At the end of one of the Illinois regiments I saw Justin's dogs again, trotting along in the yellow dust with their tongues hanging out. I don't know if Emory saw them or not.

It took us about two weeks to get here. Nellie ran off from us the second night, after Pa tried to get in her blanket with her. I was so mad I could have screamed, because Nellie was truly loyal to us, but Julia said, how ungrateful Nellie was, and told me not to have a "base mind." It's just as well Nellie did go, because Regal's militia is still here. The only servants left on Bayberry were Den and Mammy Iris and Den's brother Joey, living in one of the tobacco-sheds about a mile from the house. They grew the only corn on the place and just about in the county, and sold it to the militia. But a week after we returned, Regal's Corporal Lyle Gilkerson got drunk and shot Joey for being uppity, and Den and Mammy and their children left that night. With the Federals coming into the east of the State now, and Emory's experience in battle (which most of the militia don't have—not real battle), tho' Pa has taken over command from Regal, it's Emory who's really running the troop. All summer they didn't fight anybody, just "collected supplies." That means they rode around the county stealing whatever they could, from whoever they could. It's what we've been eating: Julia, Pa, Tom, Tommy, and me.

Now that the Federals are closing in on Knoxville, we're getting Federal corn and Federal beef, and most of Emory's men ride horses with *U.S.* branded on their hips. Once they even hit Greeneville, and hanged two men whose sons had gone to fight for the Union.

I kept up the corn-patch Den and Mammy started, and in the full of the moon would sneak ears out, and hide them in the rafters of their old house. It was pretty scary, because there's no way of knowing who's riding around the countryside at night, but I was lucky; I got about three bushels up there before the nights got too dark to see my way. Good thing I did, too, because Pa took and handed all the rest of the crop over to the militia. Emory is teaching me to set trap-lines and dead-falls in the woods, and I'm pretty careful only to bring home part of what I catch. This takes up the greater part of my day.

I long for Justin's books, up in Skull Cave. I've been up there three times, to make sure they're safe, and it's hard not to bring them back. I'm so desperate to read something—anything. So desperate to have company other than Julia, who goes cheerfully about her housework, singing. Sometimes I'll go in and talk to Tom, but between the pain and the moonshine the boys trade for him—it's the only painkiller he has—he has little to say. Alone in the dark of my room these moonless nights, I listen to the voices of the men downstairs. I know any book I brought would end up kindling the fires. I'm sure they'd read it first—but it would end up in the fire in the end.

What are you reading now? Do you still take Miss Mercy across to Isle au Haut?

Kiss her for me.

Love always,
Susie

Cora Poole, Deer Isle, Maine
To
Susanna Ashford

[not sent]

TUESDAY, AUGUST 25, 1863

Dearest Susanna,

If I can not take comfort in reading these days—and how sorely I miss the disreputable Becky's quest for gentility!—at least all the simple summer labors have the effect of quieting my heart. And, too, I find—set into my grief like jewels in sand—moments of beauty and peace: two yellow-winged butterflies playing over the long grass at the pond's edge; the taste of *perfect* blackberry jam. Peggie is still listless, and of little help to Papa, when Mother has one of her headaches. But, at least both are able—and Mother, too, often—to cut apples to dry, to thread miles of beans, to braid onion-tops, and churn butter. Like squirrels, we line our nest. All of my salary has gone to paying a man to cut the winter's wood, and now he is gone.

A hundred and seven men crossed to Belfast last week. Draftees—to be examined for entry into the Army: one island man in five. A further forty were drafted, but vanished into the woods or took refuge on the myriad hundreds of islands that dot our Bay. Every man owns a boat, even if just a little pea-pod for trapping lobsters. Almost thirty men were able to raise the three hundred dollars needed to buy their way out, including Mother's friend Jem Duffy, who mortgaged his house and farm to do so.

Tuesday, September 8

Papa returned to New Haven yesterday. I wish I could have crossed with him, and not simply walked him down to Green's Landing. But every dollar counts now, and I could not spare the days from my work, nor he from his. He has lost flesh this summer, and looked so tired, bidding good-by to Peggie and Mother in the dark kitchen. Will has said he will make sure the rest of the wood gets in and stacked.

Friday, September 11

Home with the twilight, which falls earlier now, to find the laundry yet needing to be soaked for tomorrow's washing, and the butter needing to be churned. It is midnight now, the kitchen full of softly-steaming wash-tubs, and this dark will not have passed when I must wake again for the milking.

MONDAY, SEPTEMBER 14

A curious circumstance. Coming to the Town Landing this afternoon, and finding Will absent, I went aboard the *Lady Anne,* to put Mercy in the little pen Will made for her out of two lobster-traps. My daughter seems determined to grow up to be the heroine of a Shakespeare play, or of a novel by Fenimore Cooper—or if possible, the heroine's intrepid companion, who actually does all the firing of pistols and climbing down ivy and riding sixty miles *à l'Amazone* in a night—rather than the more demure maiden of Miss Emily St. Aubert's cut! Thus, she requires confinement while on-board, to her great disgruntlement.

In quest of the water-jar, I looked into the little "cabin," a sort of rabbit-hutch on the deck, and saw, among the packages that Will takes for delivery, one wrapped in a shirt made of faded red calico, as if someone had cut up a worn dress. I knew the dress. I've seen its wearer about Green's Landing all summer, and only last week saw her two children in shirts of the identical cloth. Wrapped in that shirt were two loaves of bread, a paper screw containing salt and another of bird-shot, a chunk of cheese and a package of fish-hooks; information which I put together with my knowledge that this woman's husband was one of those who had disappeared after being drafted. There was no address at all in the package—few packages that Will delivers contain them, for he knows everyone on the islands, even as he knows every islet and rock-ledge of Merchant Row and the Bay beyond. By which I cleverly deduce that Will is the one taking provision to the forty-some men who have chosen to leave their families and go into hiding, rather than be drafted.

Your fellow Spy,
Cora

Susanna Ashford, Bayberry Run Plantation
Greene County, Tennessee
To
Cora Poole

[not sent]

SATURDAY, SEPTEMBER 5, 1863

Dear Cora,

Sometimes I pretend I've just gotten a letter from you! Sometimes I pretend that one day I will, or could. Thank you for the kind words you would have sent, and that long list of books you've read. When I go to bed at night now, I'll take one down off that imaginary list, and start to read it through, starting with Chapter One. Last night I got up to Mr. Collins asking Elizabeth Bennet to marry him, and her father telling her, "I'm afraid you must inevitably lose one of your parents; for if you do not marry him, your mother says she will never speak to you again, and if you *do* marry him, *I* will never speak to you . . ." Or words to that effect. Looking back, I realize how much Mr. Bennet is like Pa: funny and charming. And never there when you really need him.

Pa is gone again. I could see it coming, ever since Regal was killed, two weeks ago. Even before Regal's death, I could see Pa was getting bored. But of course he said that "Someone has to represent this section where his voice will be heard, and if I do say so myself, I'm a sort of unofficial advisor to old Jeff . . ." Which is not what Aunt Sally wrote, back in July. Julia fainted (need I say it?) and there was tumult, as you can see from my sketch. I hope you like the other sketches. I still try to keep up with Mr. Cameron's instruction, and your own urging, to keep myself prepared to go to the art academy, though it seems very far away now. I can't see how I'll manage—though once the War is over, I *know* I'll be able to figure something out. Right now I simply feel trapped in a box, and waiting, and praying I don't starve to death before everyone gets tired of fighting.

In the meantime, berries are ripe all through the woods, and I gather nuts to beat any squirrel in the county. I have about six places in the woods—cabins and farmhouses mostly, where people have been driven out, and tiny clearings in the laurel hells where I've got the berries laid out to dry—where with luck the bush-whackers won't stumble across them. They know the houses are empty, so don't go through them again. I've been watching for chickens and pigs, too, that got away from foragers on both sides. I've seen tracks, and have found several nests, but haven't caught anything yet.

Sometimes it's pretty frightening. Last week I found a man hanging in the woods, Union or Secesh I couldn't tell, but he'd been there awhile. But to tell you the truth, I'd rather forage than do housework. In addition to the food situation, all those things we kept stores of are pretty much gone, too, like scouring-sand and soap: we have plenty of ashes, but no fat, and if we had any, we'd eat it rather than make soap with it. It also means even if I had books I couldn't read them. I've cut pine-knots to burn at night, but the light they give isn't good, and I'm always terrified someone's going to knock one over, and burn down the house. The men sleep on the porch, and burn pine-knot torches to play cards in the evening. (Drunk, of course: Pappy Weevil's still seems to be the only going business left in the county. I think the boys provide him with grain taken from the Federals, as part payment for the resulting liquor.) When the weather turns—if the fighting isn't over by then—I don't know what we'll do.

[sketches]

MONDAY, SEPTEMBER 7

It's funny: I still miss Payne terribly (I wear his clothes, when I go foraging), but barely think about my brother Regal at all. I never really knew him, even in good times. Then when he rode with the militia he changed even more. He hated our neighbors for becoming Pa's enemies, and hated the world, I think, for no longer being what it was. I try to think of any book that talks about this change in the heart: in *Sense and Sensibility,* the Dashwood Sisters are just too brave and good to turn sour that way, when they lose their home. Can you think of one?

Julia has cut one of Gaius's coats into a uniform jacket for Emory, and dyed it. (You can make a pretty good dye out of walnut-shells.) Sometimes I'll go into the nursery, and wonder, about Henriette and Tristan and Leonella. I try to think of some giant Mr. Thackeray in the sky, the Author who's chronicling their adventures, wherever they are, so they'll return unexpectedly in Chapter LVII, and we'll all cry, "Oh, my gosh, *that's* where they were!" and have Tristan fall in love with Mercy (they both being sixteen by then).

Until then, as Don Quixote says, "Patience, and shuffle the cards!"

Love always,
Susanna

[sketches]

Cora Poole, Deer Isle, Maine
To
Susanna Ashford

[not sent]

TUESDAY, OCTOBER 20, 1863

Dearest Susanna

President Lincoln has called for three hundred thousand more volunteers! Will is disgusted: "The man has frittered away the greatest gift—the greatest weapon—ever laid in the hand of a ruler: an army of volunteers who fight, not for booty, but for a cause they believe to be just. And what does he put to command it? Political hacks who can get his party votes, like Burnside and Sickles. And when they get their men butchered through sheer stupidity, and no one wants to play anymore, what right does he have, to continue the slaughter with men who have families to feed, and their lives to live?"

The fleet has returned. Uncle M and Papa will slaughter our bull-calf Saturday, so that we can begin with the cheese-making, while there is yet enough milk coming to do so.

Monday, October 26

Too tired, to write more than a line. But that line is, I miss you, my friend.

Tuesday, October 27

Last Friday the moon being full, I went with Will, as he sailed among the islands with provisions for the men in hiding. I have done this once before, ten days ago, with less of a moon, and later in the night. On both occasions I left Mercy with Mrs. Barter for the night, telling her that I feared to cross with my daughter by moonlight, which is true. Fig N–from Green's Landing, hiding on Spoon Island–is cutting wood there, which Will delivers and sells, the money to support Fig's wife and children.

Cheese-making all week, and heavy labor, cutting and mixing the curds. Mother no longer asks why we are in mourning, but I see her face puzzled sometimes. I dare not ask what it is that she has forgotten. In the evenings I read to her from the Bible, while Peggie churns butter, neglected in the press of all other work of the day. Always so tired, and it seems, never a moment to myself. The pasture is a glowing lake of goldenrod.

Friday, October 30

The Grand Recitation: the harvest of *my* summer's labors. Small girls hesitantly reciting "'The Kitten and the Tiger,'" boys parsing long sentences at the blackboard, or identifying State Capitals upon wavery maps that could be Arabia for all the resemblance they bear to the States of the Union. A dinner in my honor by the parents of my flock, which touched me very much. Yet, every cent of the money I made is already gone. Salt is forty cents a box at Lufkin's store, that was eight cents a box the year before last. The first week I came home, I remember flour was five dollars a barrel; it's now twenty-two, and thread is almost a dollar a spool. Mother and I both need shoes, and I've arranged to trade butter to Mr. Harrod in Southeast Harbor, to have ours re-soled. There are signs all over the island, asking us to donate a portion of our crops to the Army, as well.

It is cruelly cold tonight, but calm. Coming home across the bay, the stars seemed bright, like diamonds on a curtain, burning clear down to the horizon. Peggie, bless her, had the house spotless for Papa's homecoming, and together we read the Bible to Mother, who had a headache today, the worst in weeks. Will gave me, as he always does, a great quantity of newspapers, but even the news that Grant's army has arrived to break the Confederate seige of Chattanooga brought me no comfort. First, because it is so close to Greeneville, to Bayberry–*surely* you are not there, my rash girl?–to all those people I met and still think of, kindly and with terrible concern. And second . . . In September's battles there, when the Confederates trapped the Union forces in the town, twenty-five thousand men were killed or wounded. *Twenty-five thousand!* Nearly one man in three, of those who left their homes to fight!

I should read the newspapers, study the War . . . not turn my face from what is happening to this country, and to my home here on the island. Or as Papa says, I should read the Bible, to reconcile God's purposes with my doubting heart. I read *Vanity Fair* instead, and find in it the road-map to get me from day to day, and the laughter that lets me close my eyes at night.

And so we carry forward, my friend.

Love,
Your Cora

Susanna Ashford, Bayberry Run Plantation
Greene County, Tennessee
To
Cora Poole

[not sent]

THURSDAY, OCTOBER 22, 1863

Dearest Cora,

Still raining! In a way it's useful, because there's less chance there'll be anyone but me tromping around in the woods. I assume the Unionist bush-whackers are also sitting around under shelter somewhere, the same way the militia troop has all moved into the Big House. Some of them are perfectly nice fellows, and Emory–and the nice ones–serve to keep the others in line, but I am very tired of hearing their remarks as I pass them. I barricade the door of my room every night. That's where I am now, with three pine-knots burning, as much to keep me warm as for light to write by.

Julia and I spent the day washing. One of our few remaining neighbors, Mrs. Gitting, showed me how to make soap out of "chimney pinks" (I think they're also called bruisewort), but you can't preserve it in jars the way you can with regular soap. Still, there was plenty of lye. Every man in the troop came loitering around the kitchen, asking that we do his shirts or socks, as well. Of course Julia said we'd be delighted to, and lectured me about how these men were defending our homeland, and providing food for us, and being washerwomen for them was the *least* we can do. Mrs. Gitting lives five miles away, at the foot of Scanlon's Mountain; she told me she and her children sleep in the woods, their house has been raided by bush-whackers so often. I think it's her son who sometimes robs my traps.

[sketches]

SUNDAY, NOVEMBER 8

Happy birthday, my dearest friend! And, a little relief: the regular Confederate Army is moving north into this section to drive the Federals out of Knoxville if they can, and to draft whoever they can find. Most of the militia has high-tailed it into the woods, which means I can scrape the corn I saved for seed. When I hide portions of the provisions the men bring, Julia chides me, that the fighting will be over soon, and this miserliness of mine, besides being selfish, is foolish.

How I wish there was some other way of getting news, than what someone says someone said to them the last time they were in Greeneville two weeks ago!

It is arctic up here in my room, as darkness falls, and the house seems ominously silent. I tore my blue dress—the last one I have—digging a hidey-hole in the cellar of the old Gordon barn, and there is no thread to sew on a patch with (and only the rags of the kitchen towels, to use for patching). Emory tells me, the bush-whackers hanged Case Mitchell outside of Greeneville yesterday.

Tuesday, November 10

I caught a pig!!!

Yours in triumphant joy,
Susanna the Mighty Huntress

Cora Poole, Deer Isle, Maine
To
Susanna Ashford

[not sent]

Wednesday, November 4, 1863

Dearest,

The first storm of winter. Mother, Peggie, and I spent all the day in the summer kitchen, now icily cold, putting the last of the pigs into brine, while rendering lard and boiling the heads in the main kitchen. When the head-cheese was done, and all cleaned and mopped and scoured and scalded, Mother made corn-and-milk for dinner, as she used to when we were children. The wind howls, and when I crossed to the barn for the evening milking I could hear the sea running high beyond the woods on the other side of the road. Still, with my child sleeping at my side, I look forward with the greediness of a child myself to the adventures of Glaucus and Arbaces and the Witch of Vesuvius, and all those others destined to meet a thoroughly unedifying doom in the smoking ruins of Pompeii.

Monday, November 16

Evening again. Mother is asleep, at last, after a disquieting day. Much of the time she did not seem to know me at all. Soap-making all last week. My shoulders still ache from stirring the kettle. As Mother had an agonizing headache two days running, Peggie and I did not have her expertise to "prove" the soap, which I fear is too strong.

Peggie, too, is absent this evening, as she is many evenings now. She has begun sewing for money, pieces delivered from a woman in Belfast. This she takes to Elinor's as soon as the floors are scrubbed in the morning, and I do not see her again, sometimes not even for dinner. In many ways this is a relief to me, yet, her absence heightens the strange Robinson Crusoe quality of my days.

A week ago Saturday, Papa brought one of his Yale colleagues home with him, a Swiss gentleman who specializes in diseases of the brain. He examined Mother carefully, looked in her eyes with a powerful mirror, and tested her reflexes in all sorts of ways. Then he took us quietly aside into the parlor and said, There is nothing that can be done for her. He said had he seen her the very day she fell, it would have been the same. There is a slow effusion of blood into the brain. She will gradually get worse, and sleep more and more, until at last she will die in her sleep.

I feel sad, and very strange. I know not what has befallen you, my friend, in the year since I last heard from you. Nor do I know where Emory is, or if he still lives. All things seem suspended, waiting for this War to end; it's as if I am indeed stranded on an island of wraiths, unable to leave or to do anything to learn the fate of those I love. Like Lemuel Gulliver, stranded among the Lilliputians—or perhaps like Gulliver's wife, when her husband returned from his final voyage insane, unable to bear so much as the touch of her hand.

I can only think, that if that silly adventurer had a friend at his side, or access to books, he might not have so slipped his moorings and gone drifting away into the closed circle of madness. This is what they do for us, both books and friends: they remind us what it is to be human. As you wrote to me, they are the window into sunlight, even if we ourselves are shut in the dark.

Your friend,
Cora

Susanna Ashford, Bayberry Run Plantation
Greene County, Tennessee
To
Cora Poole

[not sent]

WEDNESDAY, NOVEMBER 18, 1863

Dear Cora,

I am ready to take a switch to Julia! She kept her mouth shut about the pig when the regular commissary men came through—and stole every atom of the food in our kitchen, not just the ten percent "tax" the Confederacy demands, *and* searched the grounds and found the hideout cache I'd dug under the burned ruins of the tobacco-barn—but when Emory and his men came back, she told *them.* She cried when I shouted at her, and hugged little Tommy to her and said, how I shouldn't be stingy because they were fighting for *him.* I only looked at her, and said wearily, "*I'm* fighting for him, Julia."

The regular Army caught three of Emory's militia and drafted them last week; it was two days before they could get away. Even Emory, when he has dealings with the regular troops about raids on the Federals, makes sure he leaves a reserve of troops behind him in the woods when he meets with them, and doesn't let the Confederate regulars get between himself and his line of retreat. "I wouldn't say so to Julia," he told me yesterday evening, "but I sure wouldn't put it past 'em, to give me a choice of goin' out to Virginia or gettin' my head blowed off." His boys spent the night in our house–it rained again–and he left us with a sack of peas and a half a flitch of United States bacon when they all rode off this morning. *And* they took all the firewood I'd chopped!

When they were gone we washed clothes–I will *not* be the camp washerwoman again and I don't care *whose* homeland they're fighting for!–and I waited til Julia was washing Tom, before I cut about a quarter off the bacon, and poured three or four cups of the peas into an old pot, and carried both off to one of my hidey-holes in the woods.

These past three or four weeks, if Tom's not too drunk, I've been "reading" to the family in the evenings–telling the stories out of the books I remember, in as much detail as I can, by the light of a pine-knot up in the room Tom shares with Tommy. When I do that I think of you, and the winter darkness closing in on Deer Isle again. I'm "reading" *Bleak House* now (you should have seen Tommy's eyes, when Mr. Krook caught fire!); as I wander down those fog-shrouded streets of Tom's All-Alone, I look for you, Cora, in the lighted windows. Tho' I know we can't ever speak again, it's good to see your face.

Love,
Susie

[sketches]

Cora Poole, Deer Isle, Maine
To
Susanna Ashford

[not sent]

THURSDAY, NOVEMBER 19, 1863

Dearest Susie,

Well, the house is "banked" once more; the shutters closed until spring. I had meant to wait til Papa came on Saturday, but the wind smells of snow, and today Will said that he would do it now. As I hear the howling of the northeast wind from the Bay, my heart tells me that Papa will not be here Saturday. Winter has truly come.

FRIDAY, DECEMBER 11

Heavy snow. I fear Papa will not be able to come tomorrow, either. Nor have any of Mother's friends visited in these busy days. In a strange way, being so much alone, with only Mother and Mercy, I almost dread any company but Will's. I fear I would not know what to say to a stranger, should I meet one.

I had meant to re-read *The Iliad,* yet I find the tale of war, and wrath, and men squabbling among themselves over glory and booty and female "prizes of honor," turns me cold: who was it who ever said that Achilles and his messmates were the heroes of anything? Mother has a truly fearful headache, and it is the first time that I have seen her frightened. Will brought newspapers as well as a bottle of laudanum, with accounts of bloodshed all over eastern Tennessee. Maybe this is the reason for my anger over Homer: fear that you may be caught up in what is happening there. Yet, when I read anything by Miss Austen, I find myself reflecting on how thin a line divides the Dashwood Sisters from Becky Sharp. Only luck:

good connections, benevolent friends. They are themselves powerless to alter their own circumstances without recourse to some man with a little money, to whose arm they can cling.

Thursday, December 24

Papa arrived, with little presents for Mercy and Nollie. Other than crying, "Papa, where have you been all day?" Mother was much as she used to be. We read the Christmas story in the Bible, and had a little feast of turkey and spoon-bread. Yesterday Will came to cut wood, and to make sure all was well here, and gave me the present he had bought for me in Portland: a copy of *Northanger Abbey.* I wept, Susie, thinking of how you enjoyed that book, and that Will would remember how I longed to read it. Will told me, that it being Christmas, the Provost Marshal has men out. They are watching for the deserters and evaders of the draft, who will be sure to be coming to see their families tomorrow. Yet, says Will, the children on Little Deer Isle have organized a warning-system and lookouts, and the Marshals have not caught a man yet!

The moon is nearly full, between the scudding clouds. I suspect—and fear—that Will is playing "Father Christmas" tonight, taking the *Lady Anne* between those tiny islets, with supplies and good wishes for those in hiding. I try not to picture Ollie on one of those little knobs of granite tufted with trees, living on lobster and sea-birds, until such time as he could come home alive. Did Mr. Dickens forget The Ghost of Christmas Never to Come? Or is its absence a part of his message: that such regrets serve us nothing? Only what actually *was,* what actually *is,* can teach us, rather than a sad legion of might-have-beens.

Thursday, December 31

Thank you, dear friend, for telling me to tell Will I longed for a copy of *Northanger* which he saw for sale in Portland: now I think of it as much your gift as his. It has propelled me, I blush to say, back into the sordid wallow of Udolpho, Otrano, Melmoth, and the Monk . . . an antidote for an anger too near the surface now even to tolerate Don Quixote's armed lunacy.

I pray 1864 will bring me word from you.

Your own,
Cora

Susanna Ashford, Bayberry Run Plantation
Greene County, Tennessee
To
Cora Poole

[not sent]

Friday, December 25, 1863

Dearest Friend,

I miss you.

Gray steady rain for days, with snow on the wind. There isn't so much as a berry in the woods, my traps have been empty for a week, and I've nutted out the trees for miles around. Emory rode in yesterday, with "the boys," and "for the day's sake," as Scrooge's nephew says, I "caught" the oldest of the hens I've been keeping up at Skull Cave, and contributed the poor old dear for Christmas dinner. We—the family—didn't get so much as a feather. Julia didn't care—she lives in a state of exaltation at her own self-sacrifice these days—but I did, and I know poor little Tommy is starving. Up in my room tonight I can hear Tom cursing, for of course Lyle Gilkerson brought him some of Pappy Weevil's finest for Christmas cheer. The men downstairs are quarrelling: they have their Christmas cheer, as well.

"Marley was dead, to begin with. Let there be no doubt about that." I don't remember the wording exactly, but I open up the book tonight in my imagination, and read it along with you, under your quilts in your little room behind the stairs, with little Miss Mercy at your side.

Thursday, December 31

Gen'l Longstreet's Confederates have retreated into the mountains, and there's a Federal troop in Greeneville. It doesn't seem to have changed anything. Monday Jimmy Deakins, who came back in the Federal wake and re-opened his shop, was beaten nearly to death by bush-whackers, half a mile from his own front door. At least now I'll be able to go into town—or maybe even into the Union camp—and see about a doctor for Julia.

[~~*I think about writing you*~~—heavily crossed out]

The men downstairs are celebrating—again—and I've pushed the bed up against the door, as I do every night. It's *far* too cold to open the shutters, to look out at the stars as I do in summer, or really even to go anywhere near the window; I can see the last twilight outlining the cracks. It hasn't snowed yet—and doesn't, really, not Deer Isle style snow—yet I feel, every night, as if I'm buried, with my invisible books, and the sketches that I hide behind the paneling in the walls, and the packet of your letters tucked under the floor-board. I hear Julia pass my door, and sometimes I hear Tommy, when he cries alone in the night and Tom is too deep asleep to waken and comfort him.

Please think about me.

Always your friend,
Susanna

[sketches]

1864

Susanna Ashford, Bayberry Run Plantation
Greene County, Tennessee
To
Cora Poole

[not sent]

SATURDAY, JANUARY 9, 1864

Dear Cora,

An argument with Julia as I was re-"reading" *P&P* to the family: "Now, you're making Mr. Bennet sound so nasty!" She said that about *Bleak House*'s Mr. Skimpole a few weeks ago—that Mr. Dickens never made him that evil in the Real Book: "Gosh, I'm like an innocent child in matters of the world, I have no idea how my wife and children live, but they manage to . . . Isn't that charming?" But at heart, aren't they both lazy? (And their daughters adore them both.) Is that what Hamlet means, when he says, "Let me make a note of this, that a man can smile, and smile, and be a villain"? Mr. Bennet is just nicer than Mr. Skimpole, that's all. It's been four months since Pa left, and there has been (such a surprise renders me faint!) no word from him. Some days I want to kill them all.

Julia, of course, is absolutely convinced that Pa's going to send us money any day. All I can say is, it better be in Union greenbacks. And then, she'd just spend it on new boots for the militia troop!

Then again, I'm the one who walks miles to comb the attics of empty houses for paper, and burns my fingers making ink, to write a letter I'm never going to send, to a friend who I know I can never see or speak to again. So who is the more *insane*?

THURSDAY, JANUARY 14

All day working on green dress. The blue dress (although it's so faded it hasn't been blue for a long time) having finally worn to tissue, Julia helped me pick apart the bodice, and sew it as a lining into the green, with layers of religious tracts ("A Voice from the Flames," "The Fleshpots of Sin," and "The Livery of Iniquity") in between, to cut the wind. It has been raining for nine days. Last night there was a tremendous fight downstairs, and shots fired—wasteful, considering how little ammunition they have. It's strange, not really knowing what's going on anywhere but here. Has someone invented a perpetual motion machine? Don't know. Has the earth opened up and swallowed Mexico City? Could have happened. I have great sympathy now for poor Dr. Manette in the Bastille (whose adventures I hope you've become acquainted with by now).

Maybe that's the reason I keep such careful track of the days, which I do with a stick of charcoal on the wall of my bedroom (see sketch). I feel that if I miss a day, I could suddenly lose a week, or a month.

My hens up in Skull Cave have quit laying, but I feed them what I can, and go check on them—and on Justin's books—every day, even in the rain. All the streams are high between here and the cave, rushing torrents. There isn't an acorn between here and the Georgia border, and I am sometimes in terror of meeting bush-whackers (or even some of our own militia boys). Still after the tumult in the house here, the silence and the smell of the trees, are almost as good as food. Yesterday evening I saw the fog moving down the mountain, like an army of silent ghosts. Breath-taking! I hope your winter days pass more quietly than mine.

Love from the Bastille,
Susie

Cora Poole, Deer Isle, Maine
To
Susanna Ashford, Bayberry Run Plantation,
Green County, Tennessee
Please forward

TUESDAY, JANUARY 12, 1864

[lost]

Susanna Ashford, Bayberry Run Plantation
Greene County, Tennessee
To
Cora Poole

[not sent]

TUESDAY, JANUARY 19, 1864

Dear Cora,

Night again, and drunken voices downstairs. Will I dream about this for the rest of my life? It's been cold enough to snow, but I foraged up to Indian Creek and Spaniard's Leap, just to see if by chance it had rained hams up there, but it hadn't. The trap-lines hadn't even been touched, except one that some bastard bush-whackers had stolen the string out of. It's so hard to get anything these days, hard to get anything to make anything out of, even. The farms and cabins on the mountains, where people gave up and left when their menfolks were drafted or fled to avoid it, have all been picked clean, even of things like rugs and curtains, let alone traps. Julia and I have been using hairs out of the horses' tails to sew with. Even the horses are stolen from the U.S. Army.

Yet the winter woods are so peaceful. Streams that were cataracts two weeks ago are down to trickles with ice, murmuring in the stillness. I keep careful watch on tracks, because there are men even worse than the militia boys up there (it's hard to imagine *anyone* nastier than Lyle Gilkerson). Only the presence of the militia here has kept Bayberry from attack. But the silence, and being alone to watch the clouds move across the mountains; being able to just sit for a time and sketch a pine-branch—it's like when I write to you.

Thursday, January 21

Found a dead man up near the Gilkerson place, someone I didn't know. I'm ashamed to say the first thing I did was search his pockets, but whoever had shot him had thought of that already. I built a blind, and sat there with the rifle Emory gave me, and waited. I shot two foxes before nightfall. Their meat tastes just awful, but the boys haven't managed to steal anything from the Army in Greeneville for weeks. I hid the carcasses and the skins in a tree in the laurel hell at the Holler. (I hide *everything.*)

Friday, January 22

Dreamed last night about Mr. Fox-Bait's wife, sister, and children. As soon as it got light, smuggled the shovel out of *its* hiding-place, and lost almost a day of foraging, to dig a shallow grave for him. The ground was nearly frozen, and my chilblains hurt like the Devil, but I did what I could. His shirt's a little big on me, (somebody else had already got his boots) but I don't care. While I was digging, I remembered Mrs. Willis at the Nashville Female Academy teaching us the proper form for a letter of acceptance to an informal evening party, and how to make facial restorative out of cucumbers, and I don't know if I should laugh or what.

In spite of all, your friend,
Susie the Grave-Digger

[sketches]

Cora Poole, Deer Isle, Maine
To
Susanna Ashford, Bayberry Run Plantation
Greene County, Tennessee
Please forward

WEDNESDAY, JANUARY 27, 1864

Dearest Susanna,

Forgive me, if my previous letter reached you, asking all the same questions that I will ask you again in this one, like a child tugging at her mother's skirt—as my beautiful daughter has begun to do. When I heard that Union forces had taken eastern Tennessee, my first thought was of you and your family. Eliza Johnson has written to me since, that the section is in turmoil, and I know that it is possible that my letter was lost. Such is my hope, rather than that, with the horrific conditions she describes, you have come to hate me as a Yankee.

So I write again: Are you well? Are you safe? If in fact hardship and bitterness have made it impossible for you to greet me as a friend—and if such be the case, please believe that I understand how it would be so—might you at least write me the briefest of notes, informing me that the correspondence is at an end. Thus at least I will be spared the wretchedness of doubt.

For myself, I am well. My mother is ill, and there are many days now on which she does not know me, nor where she is, though it was in this house that she drew her first breath. Such has been the storminess of the season, that Papa has not come since the New Year. My sister-in-law is estranged from me, and whenever the weather permits, carries her sewing and her child down to Elinor's, leaving me here alone. Were it not for Will Kydd, I do not know how I would manage.

I have had three letters from Justin, asking if I have had, by any chance or mischance, word of Emory, or of you. I hope there is at least someone at Bayberry, who might know where you can be reached. I do not know what you might have endured since last I had a letter in your hand. Yet I will say, that I hope.

Always,
Cora

Cora Poole, Deer Isle, Maine
To
Susanna Ashford

[not sent]

WEDNESDAY, FEBRUARY 10, 1864

Dearest,

I told myself, that having written two letters to you in the flesh—to a real young woman who might or might not be living in Greene County, Tennessee, who might or might not be too embittered to write back—it was childish to resume this correspondence with a phantom built from memories and the dreams of loneliness.

Yet without hope the heart dies, and even phantom comfort is better than the darkness in which I sit tonight. I pray that it is my letters, and not you, who are lost.

Mother has been very bad all week. Laudanum does not seem sufficient to quell the pain. Many hours I have spent at her side, and when sweeping, and cleaning the grates, keeping up the fires in the kitchen and in her bedroom—or making simple meals for myself and for her—I find myself always listening for sounds from her room. Saturday for the first time she did not recognize Papa when he came, though that might have been the laudanum. He was completely unmanned by the sight of her distress, and I spent as much time looking after him as her. What unspeakable relief, after Papa's departure Monday, when Will arrived, to chop the wood, and help me shovel out the stables, and dig out (yet again) the paths from the door of the summer kitchen to the houses of office, and the barn. What unspeakable relief, to talk to someone, [*~~to~~*—crossed out]

Thursday, February 11

How I abominate this soap! All winter it has burned holes in the clothes, if not carefully diluted, and my hands are always red and itching. Today Mother was very much herself. She helped me clean, and scolded me for keeping up fires in her bedroom, and for burning up all the kerosene, when it is so expensive. In fact, there is no kerosene because I haven't bought any: it is well over a *dollar* a gallon now! She had no recollection of her days of pain, nor apparently any awareness of its being February now rather than December—so similar are the winter days. She and I made a peach cobbler, none the worse for being made with maple syrup, and I am ashamed to say I congratulated myself, and thanked Ollie for understanding how I continued with life, in the very wake of his death. Yet perhaps the gods of the dead do have their revenge: each time I take an egg from the brine-barrel in the cellar, or open a jar of the summer's cucumbers, it is as if, with the scent of the vinegar, I hear my brother's footstep in the next room. Was it so for you, even six months after Payne's death? Does the hurt of loss ever ease?

Dear friend, wherever you are, take care of yourself, and know that you are always in my thoughts.

Love,
Cora

Susanna Ashford, Bayberry Run Plantation
Greene County, Tennessee
To
Cora Poole

[not sent]

MONDAY, FEBRUARY 15, 1864

Dear Cora,

Bad as it's been, having the militia permanently camped in the parlor, having them gone on forage is *worse*! Last night we were waked by hooves in the yard, and feet grinding stealthily in the slushy ice. Julia tried to keep me from getting out of bed (she's been sleeping with me, these last few nights) but I crept to the window and opened the shutters a crack. By starlight I could just see riders. Maybe they thought Emory had left men in the house. They didn't come in, whoever they were, but I heard them moving around for probably half an hour.

And of course, Julia won't hear of moving into town. When I spoke of it this morning she said, "Don't be silly, Babygirl, you know Emory takes care of us. And Pa's going to be back any day. We can't let him come home, and find the place deserted. If we weren't here, it might even be burned to the ground." I'm afraid I was scared enough that I got angry, and shouted at her, and she cried. After comforting her, it was almost noon before I was able to go out and check my trap-lines, not that there was anything in them. It was long past dark when I got home, and I heard a panther, hunting in the woods.

I'm scared, Cora–scared and so tired. Vexed as I get at her, Julia's braver than I. She's alone in the house, except for Tom and Tommy, and she goes forward with the housework, [~~*even in her condition*~~–crossed out] sweeping every floor, keeping the kitchen scrubbed clean, cooking the U.S. Army cornmeal and pea-meal that we've been living on all winter and that's almost gone. I don't want to and *will not* break into the seed-corn I have hidden–I *have* to be able to make *some* kind of crop! But I've been over this countryside, as far as I can walk and still get home by dark, and there is *nothing* to eat. I've dug up and brought home everything Justin ever told me the Indians ate, cattails and the roots of Solomon's seal and what-all else. If we get out of this without poisoning ourselves I'll be very surprised. There've been days I've been so hungry I've eaten some of the grubs I catch for the hens, and that's the truth. The hens are so thin, I don't even know if they'll be able to start laying come spring. [~~*And Julia will need*~~–crossed out]

Day is fading and I'll have to close the shutter soon. I can hear Julia talking to Tom in his room on the other side of the old nursery. Tom is so good about looking after Tommy, while I'm out foraging or cutting wood, and Julia's cooking and cleaning and even doing laundry, soap-root being the one plant I don't think I would eat. (But if the militia doesn't bring back *some*thing, ask me again next week.) Outside, the hush that lies over the gray woods is terrible. I brought my rifle up here, and I remind myself how frightened I've been, in times of genuine danger, and I'm still here.

TUESDAY, FEBRUARY 16

Well, we made it til morning. Silence all night. I feel like I could sleep for a week, but need to forage. My thoughts are of your mother's attic full of dried apples and pumpkins—and of you, my friend. The enclosed sketch is of me keeping watch by the window all last night.

MONDAY, FEBRUARY 22

Operatic drama! I didn't think anybody could misbehave themselves so badly they'd be asked to leave the Confederate militia, but Lyle Gilkerson did. Now that there's sometimes a little mail delivery again from the United States, families whose men went into the Union Army are getting letters from them—with money. A fellow in Greeneville told Lyle which families these were, and Lyle took about a dozen of Emory's men, rode into Greeneville one night, and visited these folks, horsewhipping one old man severely and confiscating several hundred dollars in greenbacks. The Unionist militia then rode into town, seized and hanged the informer, and went on to break into the houses of every Secessionist in town. When they couldn't find the stolen greenbacks, they stole other goods as "compensation."

I dearly wonder what Mr. Dickens would make of all this—or Mrs. Radcliffe, for that matter!

Your friend,
Susie

[sketches]

Cora Poole, Deer Isle, Maine
To
Susanna Ashford, Bayberry Run Plantation
Greene County, Tennessee
Please forward

MONDAY, FEBRUARY 22, 1864

[lost]

Susanna Ashford, Bayberry Run Plantation
Greene County, Tennessee
To
Cora Poole

[not sent]

THURSDAY, MARCH 3, 1864

Dearest Cora,

I got your letter.

I don't even know what to say. Except, forgive me, forgive me, that I can not write to you, not now, not ever. You sound so alone.

What happened to your mother??? How horrible–How can you bear it?–to live with someone you have known and loved–with your *mother*!–and have her not know you? I can't imagine that. As bad as things have been here–having to shove the bed against the door of my room every night, and pee into a bucket in the corner, and divide up grubs with my hens sometimes so they might have enough meat on them to start laying eggs . . . All these terrible things, and I realize, they are nothing, to what you must be going through, seeing someone you know turn into someone you don't.

Friday, March 4

I re-read your letter this evening, in this pearly hour when there's still enough light to see the writing. I can't tell you how my heart rejoices, to hear that the beautiful Miss Mercy is tugging on your skirt and asking you the same questions over and over again, as Tommy has recently begun to do to me. I'm so glad to hear that, though your Mother is ill, your Father is still well and teaching at Yale, and so sending you money. I suppose I should rejoice that Peggie is well, too, but I'd rather come up there and slap her for you . . . and then stay for dinner. (I'll bring some grubs.)

I wish it were possible for me to write. I wish I could find where to write to Justin, though I realize now I can't write to him, either, lest he in his turn write to you. My dear friend, I wish it were enough just to see your handwriting on paper again, to know that you are still there.

Love,
Susanna

[sketches]

Cora Poole, Deer Isle, Maine
To
Susanna Ashford, Bayberry Run Plantation
Greene County, Tennessee
Please forward

Tuesday, March 15, 1864

Dearest Susanna,

I send this in the hopes that with the Federal hold strengthening on Tennessee, a letter will at last get through to you, or to someone who can send it on to you. I ask only to know if you are well, and if your family is safe. I know not what you may have passed through since last I had a letter from you, over a year and a half ago, from Vicksburg; or whether you now have the smallest desire to continue correspondence with a Yankee. I know, too, that feeble protestations on my part of horror, indignation, or concern at the sufferings caused to you and yours by my country's invasion may ring bitterly hollow to your ear. I seek only to know that you are safe.

I am well. Snow still lies thick, and the house, in its shuttered mountains of spruce-boughs and snow, is dark, and stuffy, and smells always of smoke and cooking. Mother is no longer herself, save on short and infrequent occasions. Her manner frightens Peggie, and Peggie's fear communicates itself to Nollie, who is a fragile child, as nervous and imaginative as my brother was. Thankfully, Mother did recognize Brock for much of his furlough, and the weather was such that Papa, and Brock's wife and children, all were able to be with us: a bright oasis of brief joy.

Even with snow on the ground, the Army recruiters have returned, like midges, pestering every man not in uniform: mocking, cajoling, offering larger and larger bounties. Elinor and the Daughters of the Union are already organizing days of speeches. Too, the Provost Marshal's men are back, searching for the evaders of last year's draft. One man, hidden on Spoon Island, earns money for his wife and family by cutting wood, which Will Kydd brings across on the *Lady Anne* and sells. Several others fish for lobster, a profitless creature in the marketplace but at least serving to feed their families. Will is a great help to me, and a great comfort. For the rest, though Mother's condition is known on the island, we have had few visitors this winter. Her friends still greet her at church, to her childlike pleasure. Yet I feel their doubtful gazes on me, and have learned to wait for her in the sleigh.

My days are full of the most exhausting labor, my nights—once I have settled Mother—long. I am reading *David Copperfield* again, marveling at the cast of characters and yet sharply aware of who *isn't* in the story: of who isn't in *any* novel that I have read so far:

a woman who makes her own way in the world and yet remains a good woman. You asked me once, if I would have married Emory, were it possible for me to have the training a young *man* would get, for a profession? I admit that at times like this I feel imprisoned, and wonder if I will ever see my husband again.

Forgive me. The night is late, and I am woolgathering. I will seal this up now, and hand it to Will when he arrives. I pray it reaches you, my friend. I pray that I may still so call you.

Always,
C

Susanna Ashford, Bayberry Run Plantation
Greene County, Tennessee
To
Cora Poole

[not sent]

TUESDAY, MARCH 15, 1864

Dear Cora,

I forget which Roman poet it was, who said that spring's warmth stirred armies to life: the militia is out foraging again. Today I put on my brown dress (which is far too big for me and has only been turned twice) and walked into town, to find a doctor for Julia. It's eight miles and took me three hours. The midwife at the Yankee camp agreed to come out, if I'd do her sewing for her, which she takes in for the soldiers and also the camp whores and laundresses, black and white, of whom there are many! It was almost dark by the time I got back and I had to change clothes and chop wood; I'm going back tomorrow. Julia and I had a terrible fight about me working for the Federals, and she vowed she'd never let a Yankee midwife come near her and especially not one who takes care of the camp floozies, but as far as I know, Mrs. P is the only midwife in the county.

It's almost too dark to see the paper, and I'm too tired to sit up. I've never done sewing for that many hours, and my chilblains hurt so bad I want to cut my fingers off. Julia sleeps in here with me when the troop is away, but I hear her in Payne's old room—that is now Emory's—crying. It seems like no matter what I do, it isn't right.

Wednesday, March 23

Emory and the troop are back, which is fortunate, since we were out of everything but pea-meal and not much of that. As always, the minute no one was looking I took and cut as much as I dared off the bacon he brought, and scooped out handfuls of the cornmeal and peas. With the frost out of the ground, I've been preparing planting-grounds in about six places in the woods, to plant corn and squash, peas and potatoes all together, the way the Indians did.

I did sewing for four days for Mrs. P at the Union camp, and was very careful not to steal a single thing: not needles, not thread, not the food that they have so much of, though I did trade a little sewing on the side to repair stockings and shimmies, in exchange for beans, potatoes, and dessicated vegetables: desecrated vegetables, the men call them. Julia refused to touch any of it (they're exactly what Emory and his boys steal and bring here) and carried on as if I'd traded my favors for them, tho' these days I look even more like a boy than ever! In any case, it's three hours' walk into town, and three hours' back. And, they need me here.

But I got Mrs. P's promise, that when Julia's time comes, she will be on hand.

TUESDAY, APRIL 5

Your letter. I used to pray so hard, that one day someone would bring me out from town a letter with your handwriting on it, and now it fills me with such pain. Back when I did not hear from you, and there was no chance that I would, it was possible, to almost pretend that Emory wasn't your husband, that you didn't love him. Now the fact that I can't write to you because of him and Julia is like a chain around my neck. I feel its weight every time I move, and it strangles my words, when I want to say to you, "Be brave."

SATURDAY, APRIL 9

The last of Gen'l Longstreet's Confederate Army is moving out of Tennessee. The militia–of course!–made themselves scarce when a CSA forage detachment of them put in their appearance; they picked us clean of everything, even the wood in the wood-pile. Tom, who was as usual in his chair on the porch, cursed them (his jug of moonshine was the only thing they didn't touch), and their Sergeant said, "You ask your militia pals for food, when they get done skulkin' in the woods."

That was yesterday. Today Emory and his men rode in, for Emory to see baby Adam (surely no child has any business being *that* tiny at birth!), and to bid us good-by. When I walked him to his horse this afternoon, Emory told me that they would dog the Federal Army as it marches South: "We'll slow Sherman down, we'll bleed him, like picadors in a bull-fight, bleedin' a bull. And Joe Johnston and his army'll be waiting for him, the minute he crosses the Georgia line." I asked him, Did Julia know? and he put his hands on my shoulders and said, "You'll have to tell her. I've just said, that we're riding out for a couple of days. Will you do that for me?"

What could I say? *No?*

Cora, I wish there was someone who could advise me. But the

only ones who could are the ones who would be hurt—or who would be certain to tell you. I hate myself, and I simply don't know what to do. Please forgive me.

Your own,
Susie

[sketches]

Susanna Ashford, Bayberry Run Plantation
Greene County, Tennessee
To
Cora Poole

[not sent]

FRIDAY, APRIL 15, 1864

Dear Cora,

A man on forage for the Yankees brought a letter here this morning, from Eliza Johnson in Nashville. One of her friends in town had written her, that we were here at Bayberry. She asked, Did we want to come to Nashville? Tom used to work for Senator Johnson's newspaper in Greeneville, and now that the Senator is the Military Governor of the State, would see about employing him as a clerk. She said, that so many men are in uniform, that women are being used as clerks. I could do that, or work in her house as housekeeper. There was enough light left when I came back from the woods, for me to read it, and have the worst fight with Julia I've ever had in my life. After it was done I cried until I ached all over.

Julia will not hear of leaving. She says we are perfectly safe here, and called me selfish for even thinking of it, said that I didn't really mean it (she's always told me that I don't mean what I actually do mean), that I was just tired: How could I even think of exposing Tom, and poor Tommy and little Adam, to Yankee scorn and Yankee charity? When I pointed out that Tom had been a Unionist, she simply said, "How can you tell such a lie?" And then she cried, and clung to me, and made me promise I'd never leave her—and how *can* I leave her, Cora? Leave her alone here with a crippled husband, a two-year-old, and a newborn baby? She can't forage, she can't chop wood—and she never *will* leave, while there's the slightest hope of Emory coming back.

So I promised. But we can't stay here. *I* can't stay here. I remember what you wrote to me, back when Julia and Henriette were trying to make me stay on at Bayberry as housekeeper, and I wanted to go to the Nashville Academy. You told me that I had my own way to make, my own road to find. That if I were a boy and not a girl, no one would think twice about my right to make that decision. Tomorrow I must—I *have* to—write to Eliza. The only clean paper I know about, now, is the title pages and back signatures of Justin's books, up in Skull Cave. I haven't touched that paper, all this time. But it's there, and I think Justin would understand. I will go up the mountain, and write my letter, and find a way to sneak into town to send it.

It's cowardly, and wicked, but I have to at least write to her, and see what can be done. I can't go on like this.

MONDAY, APRIL 18

[~~*Saturday Lyle Gilkerson and his boys*~~—heavily crossed out]

Cora Poole, Deer Isle, Maine
To
Susanna Ashford, Bayberry Run Plantation,
Greene County, Tennessee
Please forward

TUESDAY, APRIL 26, 1864

Dearest Susanna,

From the newspapers I understand that the forces of the Confederacy have withdrawn from eastern Tennessee. Eliza Johnson writes me from Nashville, that the section is still in great turmoil: thus it is more than possible, that my previous letters to you have gone astray. I will write, then, and continue to write, in the hopes that either matters will become more settled, or that someone at or near Bayberry Run will eventually forward one into your hands. I do not ask for a resumption of our old friendship, though it was very dear to me. I understand that the horrors that have overtaken your homeland may have rendered it impossible for you to ever regard any Northerner as anything but a foe. Yet, if you would but send a brief note, that you and your family are alive and well, I would be most grateful.

I and my daughter both are well. I have been, through most of the past year, much occupied with my Mother, whose brain was injured in a fall. It is sometimes hard to keep cheerful, the more so because of the estrangement between my brother Ollie's widow and myself. I look forward to Papa's return, for the farm is much dilapidated, and the friend upon whom I much relied both for labor and for comradeship quite unexpectedly enlisted in the Army. As a result of this, it was not until last week that my Uncle Mordacai was able to help me remove the boughs that banked the house. It is a relief to undertake Spring Cleaning, even in the company with a sister-in-law who will not deign to speak to a "Copperhead." Owing to the scarcity of men on the island—for a third of our men have entered either the Army or the Navy, and of those that are left, nearly fifty are in hiding from the draft—it is not even possible now to hire help. Peggie and

I can not even do laundry, until my Uncle can next come and cut wood to heat the water. Without the discarded spruce-boughs, we would have been hard-put to heat the house on these sharp spring nights, or to cook.

Winter is hard in Maine, and its nights long. I feel that, like a camel, I have drunk deep of all those books that Justin sent me for safe-keeping, re-reading them twice and sometimes thrice, to carry me through a summer of days when I shall fall into bed too weary to do more than blow out my candle.

Please, if you get this, let me know at least where you are, and in what circumstances.

Until then, always your friend,
Cora

Cora Poole, Deer Isle, Maine
To
Susanna Ashford

[not sent]

WEDNESDAY, APRIL 27, 1864

Dearest,

Why do I feel that when I put this letter into that magic post-box among Justin's books in the attic, it will fly to you in some Gothic tower overlooking the roofs of Paris? I suppose it is an image I prefer to the one of you at Bayberry Run, cursing my letter as you put it into the stove. Or the one of your sister, or your brother Regal, doing so because you have been dead for a year. The other thing I have never encountered in any book—along with women who must entirely make their own way in the world, without assistance from even the tiniest annuities, who do not become either women of the town, or comic viragos—is a precise definition of where the line lies, between hope and insanity.

Are these letters to you insane? Either the one I wrote yesterday, to a house that may be a pile of rubble—or this today, to the friend who once sent me sketches that made me laugh, and words that let me know that I was neither alone nor mad: the friend who may not exist anymore.

Why did I never write—even in fancy—to Emory? Because I knew of no way to begin, that did not sound like reproach? Is that why you do not reply to me, dearest Susie?

Will I write to Will? What could I possibly say?

SUNDAY, MAY 1

Dear Susanna,

My apologies for the above. I think that looking after Mother has left me worn down, as if my nerves had been sandpapered. She is not the woman that I so deeply loved, yet daily, the hands that I hold are that woman's hands; the voice that asks who that little girl is, is the voice I remember. I am aware of feeling grief for her, like a well of darkness miles deep, but so constant is the need to care for her, and to support Papa's spirits, that I must train myself never to look into that well. Even in *David Copperfield,* I do not find this depth: this state of keeping the door firmly closed upon deep and genuine agony, because there is nothing else that can be done. All day I am busy and cheerful, and then without warning a single turn of phrase in a poem will eviscerate me with sorrow: I wept until I thought I should be ill, upon the words, "He said, 'She hath a lovely face.' "

For Papa it is worse. I would rather have remained here today, than accompany them to church, for I have been unwell. But in those moments of panic that Mother sometimes experiences, or with the sudden onset of one of her headaches, neither Papa nor Peggie can deal with her. And as she drifts farther from herself, Mother treasures more closely those things that she does remember: Papa, the church, and her friends. So we went, and so Elinor was able to come to me—the first words she has spoken to me in more than a year—and remark, that she had heard that Will Kydd had finally found the manhood in him to do his duty to his country.

Forgive me for writing all this, my friend. I am still so sick with anger that I shake when I think of it. I know she would not have known of his enlistment, unless she had had something to do with it; unless she had found the means, to force him to it. And so my one friend on the island is gone, and I fear that it was I, who handed her the weapon that she used to drive him.

Papa is calling from the summer kitchen, where the door stands open to the scent of the new-fledged woods and Peggie has set out the cold Sunday supper. We have always kept to the old New England habit, that it is as much a sin to cook on the Sabbath as it is to—for instance—write letters to one's friends, be they real, or imagined, or somewhere in between. I will dress again in my cheerfulness, and go.

Yours,
C

Mrs. Cora Poole, Deer Isle, Maine
To
Susanna Ashford

[not sent]

Tuesday, May 10, 1864

Dearest Susie,

I have prayed that you are not in the turmoil and horror of Tennessee. Now I take back those prayers. Better there, than in Virginia now.

Grant's army, a hundred and twenty thousand men, the papers say: eighteen thousand of them killed, wounded, or simply lost in the wilderness around Richmond, in two days of horrifying combat. Is your father there? Did you flee there seeking refuge, you and Julia, and Julia's child?

Or did you go to Atlanta, towards which another destroying army is now on the march?

Wherever you are, I know that you are in God's care.

Cora

Cora Poole, Deer Isle, Maine
To
Susanna Ashford, Bayberry Run Plantation
Greene County, Tennessee
Please forward

Wednesday, May 25, 1864

Dear Susanna,

I write in the steady hope that one of my letters will reach you, though I understand from Eliza Johnson, that the east of the State is still in great turmoil. Knowing—as well as one can from the newspapers only—the dreadful conditions now current in much of the South, I ask no more than word that you are safe.

Summer has come. Peggie takes her sewing—and her son—to Elinor's house, and often does not return until suppertime or later. Well I understand her resentment of me last summer. Mother has taken to wandering away, which is both frightening and, I am ashamed to say, vexing, as she will leave the butter half-formed in the churn, or the egg-basket lying on the ground. At least Peggie will remain to help on wash-days, though she left me today to do the ironing, which has left me—as you can tell from my handwriting—shaky and tired.

LATER

An interruption, to see to Mother. It is late now, and the house is profoundly still, as if cut loose from the earth and adrift in darkness. I have only just finished the butter, washed dasher and churn and paddles, and the mending all yet to do. It is my fault. I have been a little ill, and the medicine I took, though it promised that "no harm can follow its use, even when taken by the most delicate invalid," proved to be, I think, mostly quinine. I will be better by Saturday, when Papa returns.

They say the War must soon be over, one way or the other, but I find myself incapable of believing anything anyone "says," or indeed of thinking ahead at all. Tonight it seems that there is nothing but tomorrow only, and no world beyond what I can see from this table where I sit: to see that the animals are fed, that my daughter's hair is combed, and Mother is taken care of, as well as I can, for the time she has left. Time and events seem to have lost their meaning.

Please be assured that not a night has passed that I have not prayed for you and yours.

Always,
Cora

Susanna Ashford, Bayberry Run Plantation
Greene County, Tennessee
To
Cora Poole, Deer Isle, Maine

FRIDAY, JUNE 17, 1864

My dearest Cora,

What a blessing to hear from you, my friend! What joy, to know that you, are well! Both your letters came today! If there is anything I can do to help you, at this distance, and in our circumstances, just name it, and it is yours.

After being shelled forty-seven days by the Federals at Vicksburg, I can no longer claim to be the loyal subject of the Union that once I was. (*Are* women citizens rather than subjects? We don't vote.) But, here in Tennessee, there are still as many Lincolnites as there are Seceshes, and we have been robbed and stripped by both armies turn and turn about, with a perfect lack of distinction, so that as the English say, "You pays your money (only nobody has any) and takes your choice." I am still a Spy in Enemy Territory, for Julia is as loyal to the Confederacy as ever, and I will have to hide your precious letters under the floor-boards. What joy to have the opportunity to do so! Tho' the Federals officially hold this section, Secesh militia still occupies the ground floor of Bayberry, and supplies us, when in residence, with whatever they can steal from the Federals at Greeneville, a circumstance which has continued for so long that it is beginning not to seem odd anymore, like you living in darkness for six months out of the year.

I am more sorry than I can say, to hear that you have been ill, especially as you have lost the friend who gave you comfort. I believe that I have recently had your illness myself, owing to a mishap that befell me in April, from going alone on the mountain. I pray you are recovered, not only in body but in spirits. Please believe me when I say that you did what was best, for both your Mother and your daughter would have suffered, had your condition been allowed to continue.

I may not often be able to write, and my replies to you may be delayed. It is a long way into town, but please write me care of General Delivery in Greeneville, for I fear that Julia or Lyle Gilkerson—the head of the militia here—would destroy any letter to me from the North. It is good beyond words to hear from you again. I will reply when and as I can.

Always your friend,
Susanna

Susanna Ashford, Bayberry Run Plantation
Greene County, Tennessee
To
Cora Poole

[not sent]

FRIDAY, JUNE 17, 1864

Dearest friend,

I have re-read my letter to you twice, and pray it is cheerful enough to raise your spirits. You sound so weary, and I know perfectly well what kind of medicine consists almost entirely of quinine and claims that "no harm can follow its use . . . " etc. etc. It's exactly what Mrs. P in the Union camp gave me, to "bring on my periods" again after Lyle and his men caught me on the mountain. What other medicine would you be careful to take only after your Papa left for the week? Why half-kill yourself, to conceal its effects from Peggie, ironing and churning butter, when your hand shakes so badly that your writing can barely be made out? I am sorry, so sorry, my dearest girl, that you are in the position, to require such a terrible step.

"If there is anything I can do to help you, just name it . . . " Except tell the truth, my dearest friend.

Emory is back in the district. He shakes his head like a disappointed brother over my "affection," as he calls it, for Lyle, but he is careful not to ask about it. The last thing he and his militia need is a war with Lyle's bush-whackers. And from the first day that Lyle rode up to the house—with his men—after the rape, Julia has believed Lyle's story of "guarding those who're loyal to the South." Like Emory, Julia finds her life easier, with Lyle on good terms with us. Sometimes I still think about killing him, but I have only to look at that stinking cousin of his who'd inherit his command, to put that idea away.

I spoke of you to Julia, just after your April letter came, and she sneered, "What does she know about hardship?" and told me to tear it up. I said I wanted to keep it to draw on, though in fact I don't draw anymore. There seems no reason to do so.

I pray you'll write again soon.

Your lying friend,
Susanna

Cora Poole, Deer Isle, Maine
To
Susanna Ashford
c/o General Delivery, Greeneville,
Tennessee

TUESDAY, JULY 5, 1864

Dearest Friend,

You are alive! When I saw your handwriting on the envelope, I can not describe what I felt. So good to know that you are well—that, first of all. I do not know whether that joy was greater, or only just slightly less, than knowing that you will write again when you can. Thank you, and bless you.

Your comfort and cheer came at a good time. The season of preserving and pickling, boiling and brining, is at its height. Papa does what he can, chopping firewood and keeping the stove fed, and I live in hourly terror that he will sever his own hand in the process, or burn down the house. The anniversary of my poor brother's death has thrown Peggie into a deeper darkness of anger and resentment, and even her help detracts from rather than assists the process: I pray God to remove my anger and resentment towards her. Why were we not all created with mild and forgiving temperaments?

Her anxiety–and mine–exacerbated by the news of the War, bloody carnage both in Virginia and in Georgia, where last week thousands of men were slain at Kennesaw Mountain before Atlanta.

Wednesday, July 6

Cucumbers and peaches, although with sugar costing *fifty cents* a pound!–when Lufkin's store has it at all–most of the peaches, instead of being preserved as usual, I slice and dry for "leather." I slice my fingers, as well, and my wrist is so stiff that I can barely wield the pen. Silence has fallen on the house again, save for the crickets, and the whining of mosquitoes around the candle. I should go to bed, for we begin to harvest the corn tomorrow, yet, I greedily seek the pleasure of your almost-company.

I am horrified to learn that you were indeed at Vicksburg through the siege. Will you understand if I say, I am glad that at the time I was under the comforting delusion that your Aunt Sally had removed you elsewhere? The newspapers claim that the civilian casualties there were relatively slight–is this in fact the case? I am glad that you–and Julia–survived.

Thank you–bless you–my dearest, for your kind words about

my illness. Indeed, my foremost concern was for Mother, and Mercy. And oh, my friend, I am so sorry, if I read aright the circumstances of your own illness. There is literally nothing that I can think of to write, that would fully express my concern—or be of any help. Are you well now? I pray that your family was able to support you in this, at least. Thank you for your understanding—and for understanding that Mother and Mercy were not the only reasons, for my decision.

SATURDAY, JULY 9

All day at Uncle M's. The fleet goes out again tomorrow, sadly reduced, due to the sheer expense of cordage, and of salt to put down the catch, and mostly to the dearth of men. Many of the salt-sheds in Southeast Harbor are closed and empty. All about the island, one sees houses closed up, too, as women and children go to mainland families, only to survive. Mother was very bad with a headache this morning, so Peggie remained home with her and both babies, which made me deeply uneasy. I do not suspect her of wilfully harming a child, but often I have thought that, when left in charge of Mother, she doses her with laudanum simply so that she will sleep and not trouble her. There have been times when I was almost certain that she doses poor little Nollie, as well. He is fretful, and cries easily and for no reason, yet when I spoke of it to Peggie, she retorted, "So now you're accusing me of poisoning my own child?" I do not know what to do. Yet, when I have taken Mercy to the gatherings which I would fain avoid, she is often teased and tormented by the other children, while I am left, by their elders, strictly alone.

Forgive me for troubling you with these mundane conflicts, like the dreary *Iliad*s of snails. They are only the marks that I make on my prison-wall. It is good to know that you will know of them, and of me. A window, as you once wrote me, into the light. I have put a little oil on my chapped and aching hands, and will occupy myself with something frivolous and trivial, like *Les Trois Mousquetaires,* until Papa and Peggie return home.

Ever your friend,
Cora

P.S. I enclose Justin's three letters. The latest is dated from early March; I have had none since then.
P.P.S. Shocking news of a Confederate raid towards Washington; yet I find it harder and harder to bring myself to read the papers at all. I only feel helpless, and very angry.

Susanna Ashford, Bayberry Run Plantation
Greene County, Tennessee
To
Cora Poole, Deer Isle, Maine

THURSDAY, JULY 28, 1864

Dearest Cora,

How I wish I could say, "How I wish you were here!" But I care too much for you to even think it. On the walk into town early this morning I thought it, with the countryside so silent and literally drenched in dew, and all the birds singing, and later, as I worked my way from patch to patch of my little gardens in the woods. (Someone had gotten to two of them—every ripe ear gone. I hope they *choke.*) These woods are still so beautiful, each leaf and flower perfect, and as I walked back to Bayberry (after picking and hiding almost a bushel of corn, hurrah!) the fireflies were just beginning to come out. Do you have fireflies in Maine? I wish I could show you how beautiful the summers here are. The summers that don't include watching every second for bush-whackers, that is, and having the mountain picked so clean of game that you can't even trap chipmunks, and being down to the last needle at home and no thread and not knowing what you're going to find to trade for another one if it breaks. At least the rumble of evening thunder on the mountains is the same, and the scent of the rain.

It's so good to hear from you. I read your letter sitting outside the store in town, and again in the woods after I'd tended a couple of my little gardens. Thank you for your comfort and concern. I could not tell Julia of what had happened, and I'm glad that you know, and understand. You have to take care of your Mother–and your Papa, it sounds like–as I must take care of Julia and Tom: such are our lives now. Tom was crippled at Vicksburg, and is able to do little. And Pa, of course, went off to Richmond ten months ago. In February Julia got a letter from him, saying that (a) he was going to be back soon with lots of money; (b) President Davis was going to send him on a Mission to France unless (c) he decided to go to Mexico and work out some marvelous trading arrangement which would make us all very rich. Or maybe we could all come to Richmond and keep house for him. Heaven only knows whether he's there now, but my guess is, he's not. Pa is always very good at avoiding real trouble. Some people make it more difficult than others, don't they, for their children to obey the Fifth Commandment?

On the other hand, there's no Commandment about strangling your sister-in-law and I'm afraid I'd do it, if I even *suspected* she was dosing my child with laudanum to keep her quiet. I will say this for Julia, much as she exasperates me, she is a wonderful mother, patient and kindly, and Tom–though the only painkiller he has is moonshine and he sometimes takes too much of that–looks after Tommy like a gentle grandmother.

Thank you, by the way, for news, of which we have almost none. I guess tho' if the Confederate raiders had actually burned Washington, we would have heard.

SATURDAY, JULY 30

Evening again. The militia boys are all out "patrolling"—that is, riding around the countryside to steal whatever they can—so we did wash today: did I mention we use soapweed and chimney pink for lather? It works fairly well. I dry fruit, too, if I can get it—the peach orchard at the old Scanlon place produced handsomely, but it's a long walk. There isn't enough sugar to be had in Greene County to sweeten a cup of tea (if anybody had tea). (Or a cup.)

"The dreary little *Iliad*s of snails . . ." I like that. I wonder what the War in Troy looked like to the camp slaves? You know there had to be hundreds. Probably pretty much like Don Quixote's adventures looked to Sancho Panza. But I remember what you wrote to me a long time ago, about catastrophes not being like falling over a cliff. That they could be dealt with by climbing down, one hand-hold at a time. I can't tell you how many times I've thought of that, and how it's helped me.

I'm walking to town tomorrow, to see what I'll need to trade for a pair of shoes. There's a fellow who "buys" them from the Army. I'll mail this then. (It costs me an egg, to send it.) Julia of course hasn't been into town since the Federals arrived, and would rather go barefoot than wear "their" shoes.

You'll always be worth an egg to me!

Your own,
Susie

P.S. The Northern newspapers for once told some truth: there were very few civilian casualties during the shelling of Vicksburg. Some people didn't even move into caves, just lived in their houses, which took more nerve than *I* had. The seige didn't last really long enough for people to starve to death, though we ate some fairly strange things.

Susanna Ashford, Bayberry Run Plantation
Greene County, Tennessee
To
Cora Poole

[not sent]

SATURDAY, JULY 30, 1864
NIGHT

Dearest Cora,

Three letters from Justin. He was at Vicksburg, as I'd thought. Everyone on the mountain always said Justin has second sight: Did he know I was there, too? Or Emory?

The house is deathly silent tonight, worse than any Gothic castle in any book. There's no way of locking up the downstairs anymore—too many shutters have been broken, and the window-glass was all shot out over a year ago. So all we can do is shove the bed up against the bedroom door, and hope that if anybody prowls in, they'll leave by morning. Julia and baby Adam are asleep, as I sit here trying to make out the paper by the flickery light of a stick of kindling, burning like a torch in a hole I drilled in the wall. Usually Lyle's boys come in and camp when Emory and his troop are out "on patrol," but tonight—thank God!—there are neither.

Julia is used to me writing to you like this—to the Pretend-Cora—but since I've started actually getting letters from you again, I've noticed she watches me carefully. I know she's searched this room. She didn't find your letters—the loose board is under the leg of the old armoire—but I now keep them up at Skull Cave, in one of the boxes with Justin's books, except for your latest, which I carry with me, with my paper. More than once, she's taken away my paper, innocently claiming the need to use it for kindling, or cleaning the kitchen pot. I don't know what she's said of you, or me, to Emory, but I also notice that she takes care never to let me be alone with him.

I manage to snare woodchucks and squirrels now and then, and the hens are laying well. I've seen wild hog tracks, but even if I shot one, I couldn't butcher it out myself, and the men would take it, if I asked for help. I tell Julia I know of nests where stray hens sometimes lay out, but not that I'm keeping four of them up in Skull Cave. That way, I can trade the eggs if I need something (like postage to you), or, I'm sorry to say, eat them myself, when I go out to forage. I know if she knew of them, she'd only tell Emory, as she did with the pig, and they'd be gone. Trout are running well, too, and I never bring home all I spear. I dry one or two in the woods, and hide them. We'll make it through the winter somehow. I'm glad you get to keep all your corn.

Love,
Susie

P.S. They said in town today that Lucas Reynolds was shot as he rode back from Knoxville, because of his sons being in the Union Army.

Cora Poole, Deer Isle, Maine
To
Susanna Ashford, General Delivery
Greeneville, Tennessee

Tuesday, August 16, 1864

Dearest Susanna,

Thank you for your letter. Simple words, to embody the peace I feel, at knowing that there is someone, with whom I can share my heart. Papa tries so very hard to relieve me of some of the burden of looking after Mother, but he searches so desperately for crumbs of evidence that she is still as she was—or even that she is getting better—that every hour is to him a source of pain. If my words to you about climbing down that cliff in the darkness were of help—though at the time I wrote them I don't think either of us realized how deep that chasm is, or how appalling some of those tiny hand-holds—I come back, again and again, to the words you wrote me about your home: that you are reminded of that species of dream, where people around you insist that someone you know and love is indeed that person . . . only you know in your heart that they are not. I do not know which of my parents I pity more.

If there is any way to convey to Julia how deeply I feel for her situation, please do so. I only met Tom once, on the occasion of their wedding, but I liked him very much. How could I not, when I saw him and Emory together, shoving and joking like brothers? *The soul of Jonathan was knit with the soul of David . . .* Do you know, whether Emory was at Vicksburg or not? Or whether he knows of Tom's injury?

WEDNESDAY, AUGUST 17

An interruption, occasioned by the kettle boiling—one can make a fair substitute for tea or coffee by parching barley, and it has the advantage of not keeping one awake—which turned into an argument with Peggie about cleaning the bedroom china. I am teaching Miss Mercy to use these articles, and Peggie vehemently objects to their presence in the far corner of the summer kitchen. I suspect in my darker moments that this is because my nephew Nollie is slow, though only a few months younger than my Mercy, and has not the least concept of the matter. Or it may be that Peggie simply relieves her own unhappiness by picking holes in the conduct of others.

The summer kitchen is filled with tubs of laundry soaking, and the smell of lye. My hand smarts from a scald, but Mother, for once, is well enough to sit at the table, listening to Papa reading the Bible. The Book of Numbers—not, I would think, the most comforting portion of the Holy Writ, but it is the day for it, and Papa will not deviate from his schedule. Mrs. Greenlaw came to visit Mother—a rare instance, and I was careful to leave the house, until she was gone.

You ask, Are women citizens rather than subjects? I have noticed, in all the ferocious discussions under way now about giving the franchise to freed blacks, that Congressmen are neglecting half of that population—while half of the white population has for three years now managed farms and found food for their children, pretty much on their own, with nothing more than the satisfaction of having the Propaganda Societies praise them for duty well done. And some of us, not even that!

The Bible speaks often of the wailing of women and orphans in the wake of war, yet never does it recommend searching for ways to avoid war; even as it enjoins slaves to obey their masters, never decrying the evil of slavery itself. I trust that, being inspired by God, there is a good reason for this. Yet I find sharper food for thought in that portion of *Vanity Fair*, wherein it speaks of the Battle of Waterloo, and how each bold British hero left a trail of French widows, bereft for life in his wake.

I am so sorry, that to get this letter you will have to walk half the day, to town and back—*and* hide it under the floor-boards. I look forward to the day, when that will no longer be the case.

Love,
Cora

P.S. I will inquire of Aunt Hester about soapwort and chimney pink. They can't be any worse than the execrable soap Peggie and I managed to make last fall—which, thank Heavens, is running low. I will bespeak Aunt Hester's assistance this year!

Susanna Ashford, Bayberry Run Plantation
Greene County, Tennessee
To
Cora Poole, Deer Isle, Maine

TUESDAY, SEPTEMBER 6, 1864

Dear Cora,

Thank you for the wonderful, wonderful needles! And the fish-hooks! What better birthday present could I ask? Except your letter itself!

If you ask me, Peggie is very lucky not to have the bedroom articles in question broken over her head.

I did not say—and I meant to—how sorry I was, to read that Peggie is now a widow. I know how deeply you cared for Oliver. I remember in one of your letters, you speak of your brother Brock being home on furlough, and I trust that he is still well?

And please, tell me, if there is anything I can do—at this distance with Secesh militiamen all over the property—is there anything I can do, to make your life easier, with your parents? It was so hard for me to lose Payne and Gaius, Henriette and her children, but (does this sound insane?) my memories of them are unclouded. I remember them as they truly were. I don't pity you, but admire you, for your ability to keep cheerful—to make soap, and dry peaches, and comfort your Father, and teach Miss Mercy to use the bedroom china—under I think the most horrible conditions a human can endure. You have my deepest respect.

All the town was in a turmoil today, as Sunday night, the Confederate raider John H. Morgan was ambushed, shot, and killed. Despite the fact that there is a Federal camp close to Greeneville, Confederates are in and out of the town all the time. Gen'l Morgan was staying with the Williamses, who have one of the biggest houses in town (and have entertained plenty of Union officers, as well). He was shot, in dense fog, at the bottom of their garden, pretty much right in the center of town, and Julia is livid with rage, not remembering the number of Union men who have been ambushed, shot, killed, beaten to death, or hanged by Secesh partisans. The soldiers were saying, too, that Sherman has taken Atlanta.

THURSDAY, SEPTEMBER 8

No barley is grown in this part of the world (for reasons explained in the Geography lectures at the Nashville Female Academy, which I have forgotten). There's a plant here called Revolutionary tea that makes a pretty fair tea—Mammy Iris used to tell us that it's what people drank in the United States after the Boston Tea Party—and I've gathered that. I'm lucky in that Justin taught me about wild foods, because he was such a terrible miser he would sell almost the whole of his corn crop, and live on ramps and wild sweet potatoes! So even though Mrs. Gitting and the bush-whackers got most of what I've been raising in my woods gardens, I can still find food in this season, that they miss.

I will try to "read" *Vanity Fair* in my imagination again, (having now no access to the book) but so much happens, that I keep forgetting incidents. Others, like Becky tossing her preceptress's treasured Dictionary out the window of the carriage, are not to be forgotten under any circumstances!!!! I'm glad you have Justin's copy. I am consumed with guilt every time I raid his books for end-papers to write to you. This letter comes to you care of *The Meditations of Marcus Aurelius.*

Please give all my love to your poor Papa, and tell him that I remember him—and your Mother—in my prayers.

Love,
Susanna

Susanna Ashford, Bayberry Run Plantation
Greene County, Tennessee
To
Cora Poole

[not sent]

THURSDAY, SEPTEMBER 8, 1864
NIGHT

Dear Cora,

Thank you, thank you for the needles, and the fish-hooks—and I am sorry, that I mentioned our needs here: I won't do so again. I feel such shame, that I sounded like I was begging—and I *wasn't*!—that I want to send them back, but I can't. Julia talks as if everyone in the North is eating roast beef and ice-cream every day, and between courses asking themselves, "Shall we send food supplies to poor starving Southerners? No, let's feed them to our dogs." It doesn't sound as if you're teaching this summer—how could you, with your Mother to care for, completely aside from being a Damned Copperhead? And goodness knows what else Elinor is saying about you, and to whom.

I hate hunger. I hate war. And I hate Lyle Gilkerson.

And, I hate whoever it was, who went in and took all the corn from my gardens—all but one of them!—that I'd hoed and weeded and walked ten miles a day to care for, since March. When I came on that last one, after walking the whole circuit of them and finding each one cleaned out, I sat down on a log and cried, as I haven't cried in a long time. Whoever it is, they know the potatoes are there, and unless I stand guard over them, they'll come and get them, too, unless I dig them up before they're big.

Sometimes, when I'm prowling the woods with my bags and satchels, gathering berries and nuts, checking my trap-lines and fish-lines, passing the ruins of farms that I've picked clean even of the rag-rugs (that's what the satchels are made of) where people I used to know, used to live . . . sometimes it feels like I'm the last person on the face of the earth. That everyone else is dead, and I'm alone. *And I'm happy that it's that way.*

LATER. NEAR DAWN

Shooting. I don't know whether it was bandits come to steal the troop's horses and food, or Lincolnites. I had my rifle up here but the moon was down, and not enough ammunition to waste on shadows. From the window now, by starlight, I can just barely make out the militiaman walking patrol through the wasted ruin of Henriette's garden, waiting for daylight when they'll go after them. Julia is crying again—I hear Emory's voice, comforting her—and, closer, poor tiny Adam wailing in Tom's room.

Don't ask me what I'm feeling, Cora, because I can't even say.

Cora Poole, Deer Isle, Maine
To
Susanna Ashford, General Delivery
Greeneville, Tennessee

TUESDAY, SEPTEMBER 20, 1864

Dearest,

What on earth is a "ramp"? And, what you can "do" for me, to make my life easier, you are doing. Every letter I get from you raises my spirits, and scatters the shadows that sometimes threaten to swallow me. My ability to "keep cheerful" I learned from you, my friend, and from those dear unfailing friends to whom you introduced me: the Dashwood Sisters, and Miss Esther Summerson, and Eliza Bennet, and even the disreputable but indefatigable Becky Sharp, who never seems to let anything get her down.

I blush to remember, when first we came to know each other, that I had the *temerity* to regard novel-reading as a "childish flaw" in your character that you would one day outgrow! Now I see myself as having been one of those truculent illiterates who takes pride in "not knowin' nuthin' about book-learnin'," or perhaps more accurately, a bleak impenetrable soul like Claud Frollo or Miss Havisham, who boast to themselves that they are impervious to love.

Mr. Poole may have set before me the medicines that heal the heart, but it was you who convinced me to drink them. They remind me, too, that no condition lasts forever. That change comes.

Papa has returned to New Haven. Peggie and I work like squirrels, to store up what we can for the winter. She spends as many days as she can with Elinor, sewing and accompanying her to visit other Daughters of the Union, and various church groups and Ladies Aid Societies about the island. She leaves Nollie with Elinor's young sister Katie, along with Elinor's children, and I am certain that at every one of these meetings my character and conduct are subject for discussion.

Friday, September 23

I begin to feel quite wealthy, as provisions accumulate. All summer I have been making butter, trading some to Mr. Lufkin for necessaries like sugar and salt and wax to make candles, now that kerosene is so costly, and the rest, salting and caching in the coldest corner of the cellar. Today Jabel Dow delivered the barrels of cider and vinegar that Aunt Hester was so good as to have pressed with her own. For weeks now, after all the other tasks of the day are done, I have been peeling and slicing apples, and threading them to dry; a task done by others turn and turn about, with neighbors to help. While working, alone in the stillness of the summer kitchen by the light of the long twilights, I have adopted your method of "reading" while I work; seeing how closely I can recall every incident of *Emma,* or *Hard Times,* or Heaven help me! *The Monk,* starting with Chapter One, while Miss Mercy makes strange designs from the discarded peelings until she falls quite abruptly asleep on her cot. Mother, thank Heavens, has had a good week, but she sleeps a great deal these days. Mercy seems to accept that this is how Grandmother is—as I accepted, at her age, that all winters were spent by everyone buried in the dark, and as Emory once accepted that a father was someone who goes out and sleeps on the ground in the woods with his dogs.

How wonderful and how terrible are the things that children accept as the unavoidable nature of the world!

I have thought much about Emory lately; wondering if he is alive, even. Wondering where he is, and what things have befallen him, in the three years that we've been apart. Wondering if he has been wounded, or maimed, as your Tom is, and whether we will—or can—live in Boston again when he returns. Eliza Johnson has written me, very kindly promising that the Senator will find some employment for Emory, but I know now—as I did not before—how profoundly people can change, and *have* changed, from having been hammered in the forge of war. For this reason, Susie, perhaps more than for any other, I am grateful that our friendship has been resumed. It gives me the hope of other things.

A walk to Aunt Hester's tomorrow, who was so good as to take our butter into town to trade for camphor and turpentine, to do the mattresses before the onset of winter again. The air is sharp: frost soon.

Always your friend,
Cora

P.S. Convey my thanks to HIH Marcus Aurelius for the paper. I am grateful for his loan of it to you, beyond what words can express.

Susanna Ashford, Bayberry Run Plantation
Greene County, Tennessee
To
Cora Poole, Deer Isle, Maine

MONDAY, OCTOBER 24, 1864

Dear Cora,

A ramp is a sort of wild onion, that grows all over the mountains here in Tennessee. They can be cooked or eaten raw, though raw they're a bit vehement. If the Federal troops pull back to defend against the new Confederate attacks in the west (and take their cornmeal supplies with them!), they're what we may be eating all winter.

And, your fish-hooks work like champions!

We've had a sort of *Rob Roy* existence here lately. The militia lifted somebody's cattle over from Carter County (I didn't think anybody in the mountains *had* cattle anymore! *They* must have stolen them from someone in North Carolina), and last week about sixteen Carter Countians came to get them back. The house wasn't burned, so I'm pleased, but goodness knows what poor Tommy is going to accept as the unavoidable nature of the world. Julia, of course, is all ruffled up that those "damned Lincolnites" would *dare* refuse to contribute to the support of the lawful forces of the Confederacy.

I'd cheerfully sell one of the militiamen into slavery for a copy of *Emma*—or even *The Monk*. (Except it would probably take eight or ten, to make up the value of a book.)

The days shorten and grow cold. The last of Henriette's roses, in the overgrown wilderness of the old garden, has withered away. In addition to forage, I've made a little laboratory up at the Holler, to make enough ink to last me the winter. Boiling the stuff keeps my hands warm, and hereabouts I have to be careful, at who might see the smoke. Some evenings I don't get back til after dark. I wish there were a way to get the bugs out of the bedding here, but that's yet another thing on the list of, What to Do When the War is Done, like poor mad Miss Flite in *Bleak House,* anticipating Judgement Day. Last week I boiled my mattress-cover and blanket, and put smoke-smudges under my bed, nearly burning up the bed *and* the house in the process, but as long as we have big houseguests sleeping downstairs (and I will admit, they *do* keep other bandits away) we'll have *little* houseguests as well.

Your own, in spite of all,
Susie

Susanna Ashford, Bayberry Run Plantation
Greene County, Tennessee
To
Cora Poole

[not sent]

MONDAY, OCTOBER 24, 1864

Cora,

I don't know how much longer I can continue this. Every letter I get from you, I want to write back . . . What? I don't even know. How can I tell you that Emory, as far as I can gather, has not the slightest intention of leaving Julia, who clings to him like an imperiled Princess in a Gothic novel? Which is, I am sure, exactly how she sees herself and how he sees her. And if Emory left, what would we have? Lyle and his robbers? Emory, by the way, was *furious* when Lyle and his boys came in with the cattle–and of course, had eaten most of them before their rightful owners showed up. It was only due to Emory's diplomacy that our house *wasn't* burned.

And it's only the fact that I pretend that I actually *like* sleeping with Lyle, that keeps Lyle's band, which is almost as large as the militia troop, from murderous war with Emory's.

Julia keeps asking, When is Lyle going to *marry* me? It's very hard to keep my mouth shut. Lately at night—when he's lying there beside me drunk—it crosses my mind that the only way out of this that makes any sense is for me to die. I know you'll find out one day, when the War is over . . . Only, it sometimes seems that the War never *will* be over. Not here in Tennessee. The people who think a State has the right to leave the Union, still think it. And nothing the Federal government can do will make them say they don't think what they think. And the men who think Tennessee should be in the Union, are bound and determined to exterminate them, one man at a time.

And I don't want to live in that situation, any more than I want to live if you come to hate me for betraying you.

Cora Poole, Deer Isle, Maine
To
Susanna Ashford, General Delivery
Greeneville, Tennessee

WEDNESDAY, NOVEMBER 9, 1864

Dear Susie,

News reached the island today, that Abraham Lincoln has been elected for a second term as President.

So the War will continue. Not, I think, that anyone had any doubt of it, once Atlanta fell. But the conditions that you tell of, with such grim good-humor, appall me. And as you say, there is a vast list, of things ("Gammon and Spinach") that can not even be contemplated until the fighting is over. Not knowing what will be possible, I can not even plan or imagine. Last month notices went out here for a second draft. Almost two hundred men were called up: nearly half of those remaining on the island. Close to eighty of them simply vanished, joining the fifty or so already in hiding on the tiny islets of this granite coast. Fifty of those remaining hired substitutes. Mother's poor friend Jem Duffy, having mortgaged his house and farm to buy himself free from the first draft, was drafted in the second, and for the sake of his family–he has seven children, the oldest being eleven–he has sold both farm and house, and works now as a laborer . . . for those who have the money to hire him. I traded him two cheeses, to cut wood for the winter, and half of one of our pigs, for the labor of his wife, himself, and his oldest son, in butchering out the other two. All over the island, one now sees houses shut up, as those who can not make their livings either fishing or farming move to the mainland.

I am told, most curiously, that, so many men being in the Army now, in Boston and New York young women who can write a good hand are being taken as clerks, in both offices and shops. I would smile, if I did not know the cost of those victories in blood.

Thursday, November 10

Why should I not send fish-hooks to one who holds Open House for Secessionist militia, if poor General Grant is supporting the entire Confederate Army in East Tennessee, *and* their dependents, on his own rations? My local reputation as a Copperhead surely can not suffer more, even if the news were to become generally known.

I have not yet had the joy of reading *Rob Roy,* and dare not ask Papa to seek a copy of it for me in New Haven. As you can see, I, too, have been reduced to plundering my poor father-in-law's volumes of their title-pages and end-papers. Please send me your recipe for ink, as that commodity has risen to a *dollar* a bottle at Lufkin's.

FRIDAY, NOVEMBER 11

Dear friend, how I wish you were here! After Peggie left, and I had begun to render out the lard from the pig-killing, so that soap-making can commence Monday, Mother began one of her headaches, the worst yet, I think: staggering blindly from room to room, trying to beat her head against the walls. All the laudanum I dared give her seemed to have little effect, and even when she was half-stupefied, the pain remained. I did what I could for her, sitting beside her bed, holding her hand, then retreating into the kitchen to wrestle with wood, vats, stove until her cries brought me back. There was no one I could send for help, nor any way that I could leave her. The day was cold, wind blowing savagely, and though I did not want Mercy to see her Grandmother so, yet I kept remembering the story of how Emory, as a child, left his Father's cabin and wandered away onto the mountain in a storm. So I kept my daughter, silent and terrified, by my side.

Mother fell asleep, finally, hours before Peggie came home—and here I sit, with kettles full of cooling grease, in the dark summer kitchen as it grows cold with the howling of the wind outside, and I am so glad that you are there, my dear friend. Sometimes it seems to me that Mother will be in this much pain forever, and will never die. This afternoon, I did wonder, if—I can not write it, and I won't. But I did wonder.

I dread her waking up in pain again. By the sound of the storm, Papa will not be able to cross from the mainland tomorrow. And I must clean the summer kitchen yet tonight, and scald the pans from the evening's milking.

Tell me about *Rob Roy,* my friend, or *Quentin Durward,* or how to find wild sweet potatoes, before we sleep tonight, you and I.

Love always,
Cora

Susanna Ashford, Bayberry Run Plantation
Greene County, Tennessee
To
Cora Poole, Deer Isle, Maine

SATURDAY, NOVEMBER 26, 1864

[lost]

Susanna Ashford, Bayberry Run
Plantation
Greene County, Tennessee
To
Cora Poole

[not sent]

MONDAY, NOVEMBER 28, 1864

Dear Cora,

Adam is sick again, poor little fellow. He wasn't much bigger than a skinned squirrel when he was born, and at seven months it almost doesn't seem that he's grown at all. Usually he's such a silent baby, but now he cries with fever. Last night some of the men shouted to Shut that little bastard up! and others took umbrage at this (I heard all this through the floor of my room) resulting in a battle royal, that made poor Adam cry all the worse. Emory finally went downstairs and broke some heads. I think there was moonshine involved on all sides. I've been dosing Adam with willow-bark, which seems to bring the fever down, and wrapping him in wet cloths. Julia and Tom have taken turns, sitting up with him in the night. One of the men—a stringy old devil with a gray beard down to his waist—carefully gathered nearly a bushel of fresh horse-droppings from the corral and brought it to me, with the earnest advice that his Ma had always buried him up to his neck in it for fever. He assured me—unnecessarily—that they were absolutely fresh and still warm.

Last night, passing the nursery where Julia sat with her baby in her arms, I am ashamed to say I thought, If Adam dies, maybe Emory will go back to Cora . . . I wanted to weep, because I've become the kind of person who thinks like that, but I can't. And in any case, I don't think it's true. What Emory will do, when the War is over—if the War ever ends—I don't know. I don't even know what he thinks, or wants, or thinks is going to happen. There is a look the men have in their eyes, flat and a little glazed, as if none of them thinks beyond the War. As if none expects he will live to see peace, or anything but what he now knows. Sometimes it crosses my mind that they—including Emory and Julia—don't actually *want* the War to end, because they no longer know how to live in any other fashion. These days Emory is as careful to avoid being alone with me, as Julia is to keep us from any possibility of speaking unwatched.

This isn't difficult. Tho' winter is closing in and I did secure about a bushel of potatoes, I still go out to forage daily. I shot a woodchuck yesterday, and have seen hog tracks close to the house. Emory and his men hunt, as well as forage. Often, tho' he is living in the same house, we barely speak for days on end. Tho' I have heard there is a great thrust of men in the west, to take back Nashville, neither Emory nor Lyle is inclined to join the regular forces. At least Emory—unlike Lyle—makes his men cut wood for us.

Forgive me, for praying that Adam lives.

Yours,
Susie

Susanna Ashford, Bayberry Run Plantation
Greene County, Tennessee
To
Cora Poole

[not sent]

FRIDAY, DECEMBER 9, 1864

Dear Cora,

Bitter cold, rain, and a little snow. Nothing in the traps, and with the Federal troops pulled back to Nashville, the major source of supply for the militia is gone. I must be very careful, bringing the fish I've dried down to the house, lest Lyle ask, Where did they come from? Or Julia feel moved to confide to Emory that she thinks I have a hidden store that those poor militiamen really need more desperately than we do. We've argued half a dozen times over this, and she's wept, and called me selfish: "The only thing you've ever thought about is yourself," she says. "You just want to go away and draw or read, and you don't care about us at all." And it isn't true, Cora! Can't I care about Julia—can't I love Julia—*and* not want to be with her twenty-four hours out of every day?

It's been nearly two months since your last letter, but I know if I walked to town, there'd be nothing. The Confederates have surrounded Nashville, and no mail is getting through from the North. Even with the Federal camp gone, Julia doesn't like to see me walk into town: "Full of damn Lincolnites gossipping about what isn't their business," she sniffs. Every time one of Lyle's boys comes back from there, he's brimming with news about who "came for" whom.

Emory is away, "foraging." Lyle and his boys are camped in our parlors and the hall, and he's up here with me every night, and Julia's started asking again about when are we going to marry? Sunday I went up to the cave, and took a potion of pennyroyal and blue cohosh, which Mrs. P at the Federal camp had told me would bring on my menses if they stopped. It's so hard to tell, because even when I haven't been with Lyle, my periods will stop. The pennyroyal made me bleed a little, but it's awful, and I feel sick and queer. I wish there were someone I could talk to about this, someone I could ask. But, it would get back to Julia, or would get around town, and I *will not* have people saying that I sleep with Lyle only so he'll bring us food. Anyway there's no doctor in town.

I miss your letters. They're hidden up at the cave, but I know most of them, the same way I know books, and at night I "read" them in my head, the same way I "read" books.

Cora Poole, Deer Isle, Maine
To
Susanna Ashford, General Delivery
Greeneville, Tennessee

FRIDAY, DECEMBER 23, 1864

Dearest Susanna,

Although no newspapers have come to the island with details, Peggie announced with triumph—as if I had been praying for the contrary—that the Confederates have been driven from Nashville. I will take the chance that it is once more possible to write to you. One hears such terrible things now, about those who have been driven from their homes in Tennessee, camping in hundreds around the railway stations or on the fringes of Army depots. I pray that it is only the armies around Nashville that have kept your letters from me, and not that you are no longer on Bayberry to send them.

Snow lies thick here, and the night, though almost cloudless, is profoundly dark. I've made up the fire in Mother's room, and in the parlor, for Papa is expected sometime tonight, and there is a little chicken pie, and an apple tart—made with maple sugar—ready on the kitchen sideboard, waiting until he shall come in. As Papa's salary will no longer purchase the things we need—salt, which is *fifty* cents a box, over five times what it was at the start of the War!—I, too, have started sewing, stitching together caps and bodices for a woman on the mainland. I hate to sell the little time I have in the evenings by lamplight, that used to be my own to read. Yet, I would rather do that, than trade away the food I have accumulated. So, like you, I "read" in my mind and memories, for except on the most stormy nights, Peggie still prefers to seek Elinor's company. It is desperately lonely sometimes, listening in the silence for the small sounds from Mother's room.

I have made up the bed in Peggie's old room in the attic for Papa, where I would sit and read on winter days before my confinement. The last time he was here, though he feels it his duty to stay beside Mother during the nights, I could see he slept scarcely at all. I will offer it to him at least, "lest *he* disturb *her* . . ." though I am certain, she is not really aware, whether he lies beside her or not.

Saturday, December 24

We have had a pleasant Christmas Eve after all. Papa, Peggie, and I took turns reading the Christmas story to Mother, Nollie, and my darling Mercy—Mother even seemed to respond a little to the familiar sound of Papa's voice. Though Papa admonished us—with a twinkle in his eye—that it was "popish and pagan" to celebrate Christmas, I retorted that I had just happened by co-incidence to wake up feeling like making mincemeat pudding this morning, and it had *nothing* to do with it being the twenty-fourth of December. Though Peggie complained of the sacrilege, Papa and I went into the woods today and hauled in two sleigh-fulls of firewood—cut last autumn—so the summer kitchen is stocked again for the time being (the snow on it does not even melt, it's so icy in there). We saw a chickadee in the woods, hopping from branch to snow-covered branch, as if it were summer and human beings weren't at war. As I write this, Peggie is taking her bath and bathing Nollie in the kitchen, and Mother has roused herself so far as to tell Papa that a fire in the parlor is a great waste of wood and heat:

he looks as happy as if she were speaking words of deepest love to him, or telling him that he'd just been elected President of Yale.

I will bathe Mother next, and wash her hair, which has turned nearly all gray this past year. Thus I will close this, so that Papa can mail it, when he crosses to the mainland Monday. When everyone is in bed, I will sit up with my candle a little while, and read at least two staves of *A Christmas Carol*—or maybe three, for I so dearly love the Ghost of Christmas Present, with his images of happiness, and plenty, and laughter, and the love of good friends. One year soon may we spend it together: you and Miss Mercy, Emory, and I.

All my love,
Cora

Susanna Ashford, Bayberry Run Plantation
Greene County, Tennessee
To
Cora Poole, Deer Isle, Maine

SUNDAY, DECEMBER 25, 1864

Dearest Cora,

I am hoping that this letter will reach you safely. With the Union troops pulled out of Greeneville, rations were truly scanty here for a time, and we did eat ramps and wild sweet potatoes, and all of the fish I'd dried in the fall. When, at Christmas dinner this evening, the boys started toasting this person and that person in Pappy Weevil's moonshine, I had to bite my tongue not to propose a toast to Gen'l Grant, the "founder of our feast," since a good three-quarters of it was stolen U.S. Army cornmeal, bacon, and salt beef.

Enclosed please find imaginary Christmas presents for yourself and your family. The pink dress is for you—with new hoops and a satin petticoat—and the books, too: *Waverley*, *Rob Roy*, *Persuasion*, and *A Tale of Two Cities*. Also the quire of the finest notepaper, and pens, to write to me. (Julia says I'm selfish—this proves it.) The little pink dress (I hope the size is all right?) is for Miss Mercy, as is the limberjack—have you ever played with one? The book of sermons is for your Papa. It says, in gilt on the cover, "Guaranteed to be both Holy and Uplifting to the Soul, and Improving to the Mind." I have no idea whose sermons it contains. The other limberjack and the green-and-yellow toy horse is for Nollie, and the shawl and nightcap are for your Mother: I hope she likes green silk with yellow roses? That giant box is completely filled with propaganda tracts about how awful Confederates are and how they all deserve to be slaughtered in their beds. I know Peggie will just adore them. Being imaginary, all these things fit easily into this envelope—but, I would love to be able to see your face as they emerge, like a genie's smoke, when you open my letter.

Dinner is over, and I have prudently shoved the bed up against the door of my room, and will stay awake "reading" *A Christmas Carol* over in my memory, until things quiet down downstairs. When the Ghost of Christmas Present carries Scrooge on his tour of the world as it celebrates Christmas, I trust for the sake of Mr. D's more squeamish readers that they'll skip a militia-camp in Tennessee! When last I heard from you, snow had not yet begun to fall: I trust that the house is now safely tucked into spruce-boughs, that you got the pigs slaughtered and the cheeses made, and that the soap came out better this year than it did last?

I trust, also, that no storm kept your Papa from the island, and that your Mother is comfortable, and that the Christmas sermon at the church will not be too boring. And I trust—I hope—that you are all right? As Scrooge says, Christmas is a time for finding yourself one year older: it's hard not to take stock of what the year has brought. The only thing I choose to remember about this one is that it brought the renewal of our friendship. All the rest, I try to let go, like smoke in the wind.

Merry Christmas,
Susanna

1865

Cora Poole, Deer Isle, Maine
To
Susanna Ashford, General Delivery
Greeneville, Tennessee

FRIDAY, JANUARY 13, 1865

Dearest Friend,

Thank you so much for the lovely gifts! The pink silk dress fits perfectly, and is the precise shade to go best with my complexion, and, I can scarcely wait to read the precious books! Papa was both moved and Morally Uplifted by the sermons. The volume contained many of his favorites, and quite a number that he had read while a divinity student, but had never owned. He is most grateful. Mother, when we wrapped her in the lovely shawl, smiled and stroked the soft silk . . . and Peggie was so taken with the box of anti-Confederate tracts (which weighs quite eighty pounds) that she immediately carried it on her back all the way to Elinor's through the snow, for the pair of them to gloat over.

And the best gift of all is my laughter at the thought of these imaginary presents from you, at the end of a very cold and weary day. It has been storming all week, and today was the first day that I could snowshoe to Southeast Harbor for the mail, through a landscape like white iron. Little news of the fighting, which after the summer's horrors is now stilled. But word came in today that Will Toothaker, whose farm lies down the road from ours, died last week in one of the transports on the way to Richmond, of disease, without ever seeing an enemy. His young wife Lucy is left with four little daughters.

The harbor is frozen, the salt-sheds barely a line of marble hillocks against the black of the pines behind them: grimly beautiful, were it not for the thought of the wood remains running low again in the summer kitchen. By the time I reached home the wind had already begun to blow from the northeast, and I spent much of the day bringing in logs from the woods, where–thank Heavens!–Jem Duffy had left them piled in the fall. The wind howls outside now, and I know Papa will not be coming. I must finish my sewing, and put Mother to bed, and then perhaps will have some time to go back to the gaudy bustle of *Vanity Fair*.

"I know that the account of this kind of solitary imprisonment is insufferably tedious, unless there is some cheerful or humorous incident to enliven it–a tender gaoler . . . or a waggish commandant of the fortress, or a mouse to come out and play . . . or a subterranean passage under the castle, dug by [our hero] with his nails and a toothpick: the historian has no such enlivening incident to relate in the narrative of Amelia's captivity . . . " As there is none in mine. And then a few pages later I'm longing to shake that silly woman for not seeing how desperately her faithful Major Dobbin loves her, but instead clings to the memory of the handsome and quite worthless George . . .

As I cling to Emory? I tell myself, At least Amelia knows that her beloved George is dead. I tell myself many things. As you say, there are things that it is best to let go, like smoke in the wind: things that can not be helped, or at least can not be helped *now*. Things that are as they are. I am well; and, I have your letter, and your kind thoughts to see me through *my* captivity. I pray that your situation–which sounds horrific–is not in reality too intolerable, and that General Grant's supplies hold out.

Monday, January 16

A day of digging, of snowshoeing into the woods to drag out more wood. The wood I dragged home was the last of what Jem

Duffy cut this fall, and more will have to be chopped. Nollie is feverish—again—but Peggie insists on taking him to Elinor's with her. When I asked, Would she truly rather risk losing her child to pneumonia, than leave him here with me? she looked me up and down with incredulity, and said, "If you don't know why no decent woman would leave a child in your care, I can only pray for you." I was silent before her contempt, but when she was gone, I could not suppress the waves of anger in my heart. I would never hurt a living child—*never.* I know that as I know my own name. At the same time, tears poured down my face. Because of what I did last May? Or because it is clear to me now that all the island knows? Did I do what I did to save Mother and Mercy from the scorn and scandal, or because I feared to lose Emory?

I do not ask for answers, my friend; only for the relief that you understand my questions.

WEDNESDAY, JANUARY 18

The weather is clear, cold, and bright, though I will leave the rope stretched from house to barn, just in case. If it looks to remain clear tomorrow, we will soak laundry tonight. Clean sheets! Freshly-ironed chemises! Uncle M, God bless him, sent a man to chop more wood. With a cord in the summer kitchen and another out in the woods, I feel *invulnerable!*

Ever your friend,
Cora

Susanna Ashford, Bayberry Run Plantation
Greene County, Tennessee
To
Cora Poole, Deer Isle, Maine

MONDAY, JANUARY 16, 1865

Dearest Cora,

"Popish and pagan" indeed! I see that I should have sent your Father an imaginary hair-shirt and cat-o-nine-tails for Christmas instead of an imaginary book of sermons!!! Your Papa is lucky you served him a lovely mincemeat pudding for Christmas dinner instead of bread-and-water. *Dry* bread, weeks old.

As you see and will have seen, if you got my Christmas letter, we're still here, and will be, as long as Julia has breath in her body (she says). A few days after Christmas we had a frightful quarrel about moving into town. One of the churches in Greeneville got barrels of clothing and blankets from a "Ladies Aid Society" in New England, and, of course, God forbid Julia should touch Yankee charity! She clings to the belief that Pa will return any day. It's true, that if we were to leave, I'm certain that either the Unionist guerillas would burn the house over the militia's heads, or the militia would get drunk and burn it over their own.

FRIDAY, JANUARY 20

Brute cold again; nothing in the traps. No fishing, either, for the streams, even where they aren't frozen, run so low there are no trout, and I haven't seen so much as a bird for days. Thank God for the U.S. Army! Without them I suppose the Confederate militia would starve to death. This sort of existence makes much more sense of *The Iliad,* which I am "re-reading" lately. I used to wonder how those brave Grecian warriors found the time to fight over women (or each other's armor), and make long, tedious speeches, and stew over their honor, when they were locked in war with the Trojans. Now I realize that most of those ten years were probably spent the way the militia boys spend them downstairs: drinking, playing cards, and making long, tedious speeches about States' Rights and how the High Command should be conducting the War. (Did the Wily Odysseus have a moonshine still somewhere out behind the chariots? I'll bet he did.)

More than that, I'm trying to figure out why *any*one *ever* thought those men were heroes? I can't think of a single decent, kindly thing any of them did, except when Achilles finally gives Priam back his son's body—and then it's *only* because the gods "put it into his heart" to do so. Is that what New England preachers mean, when they talk about predestination?

WEDNESDAY, FEBRUARY 1

More rain. There's one officer we can trust to keep guard over the stairs, so Julia and I can haul hot water up to bathe—usually we just wait til the militia goes off "foraging," but the weather has been too bad for that. I'd pray for the earth to open up and swallow them, but with our luck, the house would fall into the resulting chasm.

MONDAY, FEBRUARY 6

Your letter, *hurrah*! I did not take mine to mail, having absolutely nothing to trade for postage, but have made an arrangement with Mrs. V, the postmaster's wife, to give her a day's help next month with Spring Cleaning and laundry, in trade for my next 5 letters. Isn't that clever of me?

I am glad you liked the gifts I would send you, could I do so—

and I especially liked Peggie staggering through the snow to display the pamphlets to Elinor, which I hadn't thought of. I trust she caught a severe cold *and* sprained her ankle?

Amelia Sedley has often been in my mind, as I've thought about your Mother–and, if you will forgive me for saying so, your poor Papa, too. But the heroine of *Vanity Fair* suffers from what all the heroines of any novel I've read have suffered: Amelia is not intelligent, nor spirited. She stays home and looks after her poor parents because there is nothing else that she *can* do and remain a "decent woman." Mr. Thackeray pities her, but never asks, "Why is the world like this?" Or more to the point, "*Does* the world *have* to be like this? Can we change it, and how?" What if Amelia did *not* bow her meek head and have everyone love her for her sweetness? What if Becky Sharp had dearly loved her son? Would Becky have been considered a heroine, if she were ambitious, and clever, and *kind*? Thackeray does not seem even to consider the possibility. "She could be a good woman, for five thousand a year . . . " Could not we all?

And Amelia Sedley had not *your* spirit, and *your* intelligence, and *your* education, my dear Cora. You will do your duty, and when it is done–whether Emory ever returns or not–you will find a way to honorably take care of your beautiful daughter and yourself.

FRIDAY, FEBRUARY 10

I am sorry to hear Nollie is sick–or was sick a month ago. (When I was writing letters to you that I had no hope of sending, I fell into the habit of thinking that you received my letters the very day after I wrote them, and forgot the weeks of travel intervening.) Little Tommy, who is now almost three years old!, also has been ill, on and off, most of the winter.

Oh, my friend, do not *ever* repine, that you made the choice that you did. Emory may return, and he may not, but your Mother has only those friends on the island, who would cut the connection with your family if it were proved that you let yourself be seduced: and this is something that *can not be proved.* Your daughter has many months—or, God forbid, years!—to live on the island, with your reputation as her only shield.

We all do wrong, my friend. Some of us do terrible wrongs. Yet, we are only doing what we can, with the information that we have, in the circumstances where we are. This is another of those things that I have yet to see truly elucidated in any novel (much less the Bible): that so many times, we *do not know* what the right course may be. I suppose this is why God is said to forgive *everything,* if asked with a truly humble heart.

Bless you, my brave girl. May the snows melt soon.

Your own,
Susie

Susanna Ashford, Bayberry Run Plantation
Greene County, Tennessee
To
Cora Poole

[not sent]

MONDAY, JANUARY 16, 1865

Dear Cora,

Thank you for your letter. Yes, we are indeed still here: sometimes Emory and his militia, sometimes militia and bush-whackers both, tho' on such occasions there is generally more fighting over accusations of cowardice (but not a one of them ventured down to Nashville to assist the Confederates during the seige). It is as if there are two wars going on: one between the armies of the Union and those of the Confederacy, and one between the local Union*ists,* who hate the local Seceshes, not only for their politics, but because of the terrible things they have done to the families of the Unionists over the past four years, and vice-versa. And I fear that whatever Gen'ls Lee, Grant, and Sherman agree amongst themselves, the fighting here will still go on, until the land is . . .

Is what? It is *already* a desolation, where men dare not work their fields for fear of being shot from the trees, and women and children sleep in the woods for fear of armed bands knocking on their doors in the night. It is only your letters, my dear Cora, that tell me the entire world is not what I see around me: hunger, treachery, callousness, and the eerie beauty of a world stripped of everything human.

Yet, Julia clings to this house, and clings to me. She begs me with tears not to leave her—or gets into arguments with me, that leave me too exhausted to think or feel anything. Sometimes I think I hate her, almost as much as I hate Lyle. And how *could* I leave her, with a crippled husband, a starving two-year-old, and a fading infant, among men who might scatter like startled rats at any moment, leaving her to fend not only for herself, but for them all? And, where would I go? Those who flee, sleep in goods-boxes and makeshift tents around the railway stations in Kentucky and Nashville, hoping for the charity of the Union troops as they march through.

Friday, January 20

A bad fall on my way up to the cave to feed the hens. Ice has made the rocks slippery, and it's hard to keep from leaving tracks that others could follow. Not just to steal the hens, but because the men know I forage alone. Lyle has said that he would kill me, if I went with another man.

Does he really think that the idea of *any* man—himself or another—is anything but nauseating to me?

Last night Unionist guerillas attacked the house—more, I think, because they thought we had some food here than out of political convictions. I spent an enlivening three-quarters of an hour loading rifles in the pitch dark, for the night was moonless. Julia, of course, had hysterics, but in the end we were the victors. Not only did they *not* succeed in burning Bayberry, but a lucky shot got one of their horses. *Meat* for two days!

Cora Poole, Deer Isle, Maine
To
Susanna Ashford, General Delivery
Greeneville, Tennessee

TUESDAY, FEBRUARY 28, 1865

Dearest Susanna,

You have forgotten one other thing that the Greeks did before Troy: they gossipped like schoolgirls! Homer, of course, calls it *exhorting* and *advising*. And you are quite right. I comb through *The Iliad* in vain for one Greek doing a simple kindness for another. You who are now living in an armed camp–is this the case with your militiamen? Did the Greeks before Troy spend much of their time drunk? Did they hold cockroach races?

Last week Eliza Johnson wrote to me, saying that her husband's recommendation would certainly procure me a post in the Patent Department or the War Office in Washington, as a clerk, at fifty dollars a month. I thanked her, and refused, for not only would the money not stretch to the hire of a woman to care for Mother, but know I can not leave Mother to Peggie's care. Not even to Papa would I say this. She is in pain most of the time now, and when the cleaning is done, the cows fed and their straw raked out, and the stove-ashes put by for next autumn's soap, I spend my days sewing or reading beside her bed while Mercy plays on the floor. The house is dark, the stillness such that on those few occasions when I do go into Southeast Harbor, or see anyone but Peggie and, occasionally,

Papa, I feel startled and confused, like a prisoner suddenly thrust into light. Sometimes I think I would forget how to speak, but for the lively conversation of the Bennet Sisters, and the Dashwood Girls, and d'Artagnan and his friends. You are quite right, you know, about *Uncle Tom's Cabin:* much as I still revere the book for what it has done for the slaves, I can not imagine anyone actually conversing in that fashion.

And thank you, more than I can say, for your kind words concerning the wrong I did. Each night I pray that you are right: that God does forgive, as we are taught.

FRIDAY, MARCH 3

It is base of me to repine that I lack simple things—like camphor, and tea, and washing-soda—when you lack meat and bread!!! Forgive me my referring to such. I am tired much of the time these days, and it renders me cross and thoughtless.

The island is still deep under snow, the harbors frozen. When he came in February, Papa crossed from the mainland on a sled. The newspapers are full of Sherman's "exploits" in marching through South Carolina: cities burned, farms wantonly laid waste. In this harsh weather I think about the men out on the islands, still hiding from the draft, and wonder, how they are kept supplied now. Recruiters still comb the island, to no avail. The men who are hiding in the cave on Little Deer Isle have a system of spies among the children, so that they can work their farms and spend time with their families. I am a loyal daughter of the Union: I should not smile.

Your friend,
Cora the Spy

P.S. Did you indeed write imaginary letters to me, when there was no way of sending them? I certainly did to you!

Susanna Ashford, Bayberry Run Plantation
Greene County, Tennessee
To
Cora Poole, Deer Isle, Maine

SUNDAY, MARCH 26, 1865

Dear Cora,

Such a luxury, knowing I can write this letter and Mrs. V will see that it's mailed! But, I now know that the only reason Hercules never helped with Spring Cleaning was because he chose to go to Hell and fight dreadful Cerberus instead—anything but a day like I spent yesterday! Mrs. V's boarding-house in town has been shuttered up (without spruce-boughs, but the effect is much the same) all winter, and she has apparently been too occupied cooking and darning socks for the Army sutlers and government officers to even keep the stoves clean, or to mop up tobacco spit in the parlors. The weather is fine at last, and everything was turned out of doors: furniture, carpets, dishes, clothing, curtains. We scrubbed the walls and floors, the chimney-breasts and hearths, white-washed the ceilings, black-leaded the stoves, beat the carpets and in between all that boiled pillow-slips, sheets, and towels in the laundry-tubs. I told Julia none of this. Not only is Mrs. V a Yankee-loving traitor, but it's for postage to send letters to you, not money to contribute to the militia! I felt excruciatingly guilty, coming home long after dark empty-handed, to her gentle sympathy. Mrs. V paid me a little, too, with which I bought powder and shot. Squirrels and woodchucks are awake again. I hid the ammunition in the old wash-house, with the gun.

I look around at all the things we need—and at poor Julia, doing what Spring Cleaning she can here—and I feel so selfish and terrible, for having earned money and squandered it for postage.

But, there was a letter from you!

Yes, some of the militiamen do show kindness toward one another, even tenderness. It's surprising, because the next minute the same man will be cursing fit to raise the hair on your head, or gouging and kicking someone who called him a name ("slighted his honor," I think is how Homer would put it). They'll guard each other's things, or share blankets if it's very cold, even with a man they don't like. I keep away from them. Some are only boys, younger than I am, fifteen or sixteen: children, when the War began, with the brute, cold eyes of killers. I wonder sometimes what will become of them?

Not a night goes by, that I do not think of you, sitting in that hushed room at your Mother's side.

Yours,
Susanna

P.S. They say in the South, that it takes two Confederate soldiers to keep one draftee in camp. I can't imagine it's much different in the North.

Lottie Barter, Town Landing, Isle au Haut
To
Cora Poole, Deer Isle

SATURDAY, APRIL 8, 1865

Dear Mrs. Poole, Maria Kydd send to tell me to tell you she heard to-day Will is dead in Virginia

Yrs Lottie Barter

Cora Poole, Deer Isle, Maine
To
Susanna Ashford, General Delivery
Greeneville, Tennessee

MONDAY, APRIL 10, 1865

Dear Susanna,

Sad news today, and my heart is heavy. Saturday I got the news that my friend Will Kydd is dead.

TUESDAY, APRIL 11

Your letter is a comfort. I have written to Will's mother, asking if I can be of help, though I know not what help I can be.

The work of the dairy has redoubled—Mrs. Brown and Mrs. Black have both calved, and we have now four goat-kids, as well, to the unending enchantment of Mercy and Nollie. Both children are of an age to find Paradise in the barn—and their own doom, unless watched constantly.

THURSDAY, APRIL 13

It begins to appear that spring has indeed come, though the nights are still cold and the roads little more than crevices of mire between the hills. Mother's friends from the church will still sometimes call, for which I am profoundly glad, though I can tell by the way they look at me that they have heard—something. And of course, each and every one has something to say on the subject of laudanum. When I went in to take Mother her supper, she was asleep, and I will not wake her; Mercy and I shared corn-and-milk, and with luck I will–

Later

Peggie came in with a newspaper that someone had brought across from the mainland this morning. General Lee has surrendered in Virginia to Grant.

Friday, April 14

Early morning–even before I usually go out to milk. I have slept little, thinking of what it means, that the War is done. Thinking–for the first time in years letting myself think–about Emory, and when he will be home. When he left–and I can still see him stepping out the door and walking away down Blossom Street–he did not even know that I was with child, and now Miss Mercy can sing about mocking-birds and di'mon' rings, and "help" me with the milking. For four years now, I have carefully plucked out every small shoot of hope, lest it grow bitter thorns or poison fruit. Yet now I hope, wildly and unreasonably, like a child. Oh Susie, I have missed him so!

Oliver's Colonel wrote to Peggie, after Gettysburg, a kind letter, if brief. Poor man, nine-tenths of his regiment lay dead on the field. If Emory was killed, sometime over the course of the past four years, who would write to me? Peggie said, "Now I suppose you'll welcome back your traitor husband, though he killed your brother." How can I even lament her hatred, when it is she who was widowed?

Saturday, April 15

I crossed to Isle au Haut, to see Will's family. The man who took me over was one of those whom Will helped hide out on Kimball's Island. When I came back the men at the Landing had a newspaper. It said, Abraham Lincoln was dead. One man was weeping. Another said, "Well, Old Abe had it coming, that's for sure." I have worked all afternoon—butter, scrubbing, baking for tomorrow (though like Christmas, Easter is regarded here with suspicion as "popish"), and sewing—and as I work the thought comes back to me, again and again, that he is dead. Why this terrible grief, for a man I never met? Yet as I write this, Susie, I weep as though my heart is broken.

Monday, April 17

Dawn again. Black darkness and silence but for the ticking of the kitchen clock. Even Mercy still sleeps. Mother was very bad yesterday, and so I did not go to church with Papa and Peggie. I understand the service was one of profoundest thanksgiving and deepest mourning. Last night after I had put Mother to bed, I saw light burning still in the attic, and climbed to see Papa sitting up in his little cot. He said, "Brock will be home," and our hands closed over one another's in thankfulness. Though Brock was wounded slightly when New Orleans was taken, back in '62, and later ill with malaria, so far as we know he is safe. He wrote us from Virginia, where he is now stationed, in March, and Betsy has heard from him only two weeks ago. And yet I am forced to reflect that everything is only, "so far as we know." There is in fact no safety in this world. War took Ollie, yet Mother is as surely lost to us, who never carried a musket in her life.

Papa leaves for New Haven after breakfast. I will have him carry this to town. I pray now that your life, too, will be able to return to conditions of safety; that you won't have to hide your food and your books; that your Pa will come back from wherever he has been, and sort things out at Bayberry. That you will at least know what is possible, and what can be done. Did the prisoners in the Bastille feel this way, when the walls were broken down?

Please write to me as soon as you can, and tell me, all that is happening there with you.

Much love,
Cora

Susanna Ashford, Bayberry Run Plantation
Greene County, Tennessee
To
Cora Poole

[not sent]

FRIDAY, APRIL 21, 1865

Dear Cora,

Rumors are flying that Gen'l Lee has surrendered to Grant. As soon as I get my "patches" cleared in the woods for crops, I will walk into town to ask after this. There has been almost no forage for weeks, and I move warily in the woods, and dry the fish I catch in two or three different caves. Now that it is spring, it's easier to catch grubs for the hens, and they begin to lay well. The rumor is also that several Lincolnites were killed over in Cocke County, for accepting the proposed plan of "Reconstruction." The Seceshes vow they will kill anyone else, who does likewise.

Sunday night, April 23

The rumor is *true.* Also that Richmond has fallen, and that Abraham Lincoln was killed. I remember writing to you from the Academy in Nashville, when everyone was saying that the Yankees had been driven back from Fort Donelson, and that this victory meant the end of the War. I remember how I felt then, strange and disappointed. But, Payne and Gaius were already dead. I think it's been a long time since I felt anything. It's as if I'm dead—and have been dead for months—and everyone has been too busy to notice.

Susanna Ashford, Bayberry Run Plantation
Greene County, Tennessee
To
Cora Poole, Deer Isle, Maine

Wednesday, May 10, 1865

Dear Cora,

So good to get your letter! It was worth the blisters and the burn on my hand, and scrubbing *lakes* of tobacco spit out of Mrs. V's carpets, to know I can write this without worrying about how I'll post it! We've had the news here—I had to walk into town one day to confirm it. Julia is still convinced that it is a lie, put about by traitors to "dishearten" loyal Confederates.

I am more sorry than I can say, to hear of the death of your friend Will. There were times—it sounds silly and horrible to say this—that I was a little jealous of him, because he was able to see you every day. But tho' I never lost my belief that the Union must be preserved (despite forty-seven days of Mr. Grant's attentions at Vicksburg) I had a sneaking admiration for Will, for helping the men who evaded the draft. Like Mr. Poole, piloting men over the mountains. Is there anything I can do, or say, to help you with this? Anything I can give you, but my deepest sorrow and sympathy?

As I said, I don't even think Pa was in Richmond when it fell. Like a tom-cat, Pa likes a comfortable chair, and I suspect he left before Grant's army closed in. Julia expects daily to hear from him. Each time I hint to her that we'd be safer in town–and with the Federals out hunting the militia, and the militia attacking the Lincolnites, it would be safer almost *anywhere*–Julia cries that Pa will soon be home, and I must be *patient.*

What is happening here, is, I'm sorry to say, exactly what was happening a year ago at this time, [~~only~~–crossed out]. Every morning I hunt. I have five little garden-patches in the woods, where I hoe the new-sprouted corn, weed around the pumpkins, pick up every grub and insect I find for the hens. I wish they could eat the bedbugs at Bayberry: they'd be fat as observation-balloons and lay eggs the size of oranges! I check my trap-lines (usually empty, this time of year) and fishing-lines. (I bless your name as I unhook every fish from every hook!) Julia keeps our rooms swept, and mends clothing, and looks after Tom and Tommy. The militia forage, or get drunk, or play cards, or fight (each other, not Lincolnites or the Union Army or anything). At night I bring home all but one fish or two, and a couple of eggs ("I found them . . . darn hens are laying out *some*where . . . ") and chop stovewood for the next day.

Well I remember how magic the barns were, to Payne and myself as children–much more ramshackle than yours in New England, I'm sure, with missing slats and holes in the walls you can see daylight through. I told Payne stories about the wars between the Woods-Fairies and the Barn-Fairies (I was secretly in love with the King of the Barn-Fairies), before I packed my heart up, bag and baggage, and moved to fifteenth-century Paris. You are right; it is a Paradise, and the thought that Miss Mercy might be pulling cows' tails, and sticking her little hands into snakes' holes and down the corners where the rats hide, and climbing up onto the ridgepole the way Payne and I did, raises the hair on my head. Put her in a room in the house and lock the door on her until she's eighteen and knows better!

Your own,
The Queen of the Woods-Fairies,
S

Susanna Ashford, Bayberry Run Plantation
Greene County, Tennessee
To
Cora Poole

[not sent]

WEDNESDAY, MAY 10, 1865
LATE NIGHT

Dearest Cora,

It's so clear to me Will loved you, and you him. You wrote once, late at night, "I'll give this to him when he arrives," and then it was, "A friend on whom I relied has enlisted," and you could not even write his name. I loved Art, and Justin, too, and worried so much about which of them I'd choose.

A horrible squabble with Julia, when I came back from town last night with your letter. Mrs. V told me about the Ladies Aid Society sending clothing and household goods, for we are dressed in rags and worse than rags (including the blood-stained dress that Julia mended for me when I "fell on the mountain," which I can barely endure to put on my body, only I must because there's nothing else). Julia will not move into town, nor accept "Yankee charity"—"They'll poke their long noses in our business," meaning, the Yankees won't want to give us clothing if it's going to go straight onto the backs of the Secesh militia, or be traded to put powder and ball in their guns. When I told her, look around at how we are living here, she wept so violently that she collapsed. I went outside while Emory tried to comfort her. In time he came out to me, and said, "You mustn't upset her, Susie. She's so frail, and she's terrified you'll leave. Promise her you won't. She needs you so."

It was the first time—literally—since he came to walk me home, in Vicksburg when I'd climbed to Sky Parlor Hill on the day Grant's men came up—that Emory and I had been alone together, and I looked him in the face. I wanted to say, *CORA needs you so. Cora is the one YOU promised not to leave, not to part from until Death.* I said nothing, but either he has some of his Pa's Sight, or I was madder than I'd thought, for he looked away from me and said, "Julie says you write to Cora. That true?"

He wouldn't meet my eyes and I know Julia still searches my room for your letters, so I shook my head and lied, "No. What would I say?" He mumbled, "I can't go back, Susie. You know that. And anyway, she's likely forgot me by now, and layin' in some other man's arms." I couldn't say what I had guessed from your letters, and only said, "If you think she's been untrue to her marriage-vow, Emory, why don't you write to her and ask?"

"Maybe I will," he replied.

I write this to you because I have to: you the Pretend-Cora, who lives in a Gothic house in Paris, or is the Queen of the Barn-Fairies, and who understands things I don't even understand about myself. Who understands that I'm crazy, and selfish, and bad, but that I'm trying to do my best.

How right you were when you warned, how easily a woman's freedom may be lost. Not even through her own folly, but just by being at the wrong place, at the wrong time, like me on the mountain.

I know he won't write you.

FRIDAY, MAY 12

The Unionists attacked Bayberry last night. I'm told they also hanged a man outside Sevierville in retaliation for Seceshes beating a Union man who was suing in the courts for lands that had been confiscated. Sometimes the view of you through that little sunlit window—of cows and goat-cheese and Miss Mercy singing "Daddy's gonna buy you a mocking-bird"—seems just as far away as the gardens of Pemberley.

Please forgive me.

Yours,
S

Cora Poole, Deer Isle, Maine
To
Susanna Ashford, General Delivery
Greeneville, Tennessee

TUESDAY, MAY 30, 1865

Dearest girl,

It was entirely unnecessary and unkind of you, to mention the things Nollie and Miss Mercy may be getting up to in the barn! It reminded me too vividly of what Oliver and I did, that gave Mother gray hair and earned me many a whipping—because, of course, like my daughter, I was the guiding spirit of those expeditions to discover barn-swallow nests up under the barn eaves (with a thirty-foot drop to the ground!), and perilous experiments with hoisting one another up on the hay-pulley.

How odd. I was laughing just now over the memory of being sent to get the paddle so that Mother could spank me, and it seemed that I saw that stern prophetess of my memory—who quoted Proverbs even as she shut me, smarting, into my room to impress upon me *never* to lead my tiny brother into danger again—saw them blend, without grief, without regret, into the withered old lady who sits silently shelling peas on the other side of the table from me. And I remembered—of all things—the Ghost of Christmas Present asking Scrooge, Had Scrooge never walked forth with the Ghost's brothers, all the Christmases—all the years, more than eighteen hundred—before that day, that night, that time? And it seemed to me suddenly that I can see Mother-Then and Mother-Now united.

To everything there is a season, and a time for every purpose under Heaven.

If there is anything that you can give me, dear friend, this is what I would have asked for: the keys of these images that unlock the door into memories, and lead me to the peace I feel now.

Is there anything that I can give you, send you . . . that will not call down Julia's accusations of "Yankee charity" onto your head?

Thursday, June 1

A time for every purpose under Heaven . . . A time for blackflies, which cause me to question Noah's wisdom in taking *all* insects into the Ark! A time to weed the garden, and tie up the pea-vines, and pluck bushels of snails and caterpillars off the leaves of cucumbers, tomatoes, squash. Yet, how perfect the spiral shell of each nasty little leaf-glutton! Surely these creatures must have also lied to Noah in order to obtain passage? For why would God seek to vex, test, or plague a Humankind destined to keep His Commandments with such scrupulous care?

A time to milk, and churn, and put butter away in the cold safety of the cellar against the time of snow that even in this day's heat I know must come. (And oh, the selfish little song of pride and delight, at seeing the profusion I will have gathered!) A time to mend, and to sew endlessly into the evenings, to be able to buy salt and saltpeter to brine next winter's pork? My green calico having been turned once too often, so that the bodice shredded away in my hands as I unpicked the threads, I am cutting up the skirt this evening to make a new dress for Mercy, whose golden head I can stroke now without bending down . . . upon all those frequent occasions whereon she loses her sunbonnet. There is fabric enough in the skirt for a dress for Nollie, as well. The dress is one I made in Boston, and as I cut it, I am back in Blossom Street again, in that tiny, sunny parlor, waiting for Emory to come home only from a day at Brock's law office.

Saturday, June 3

A blessing and a joy! When Papa came home last night, who should be with him but Brock! A sadly thin Brock, whose flesh hangs loose on his big frame and whose hands shake, for he is far from recovered from the malaria. My brother will, I fear, not be well for a long while. The week before last there was a great Review in Washington, all the armies of the Union marching past the White House for the new President–and I can scarcely believe that it is *our* Mr. Johnson!–to look upon, and thank, before they scatter again to their families and homes. Brock was not well enough to march. He tells me, though, that President Johnson has declared an amnesty, for all those who fought in the Armies of the South, with only a few exceptions.

There is no reason then, that Emory need fear to return. I feel as if I have seen the clouds break at last, upon blue sky.

Monday, June 5

Mother died, in great pain, late last night.

Yours,
Cora

Cora Poole, Deer Isle, Maine
To
Susanna Ashford, General Delivery
Greeneville, Tennessee

Friday, June 9, 1865
Late night

Dearest,

A brief note, to let you know that I am leaving Deer Isle. I have made arrangements with Abel Lufkin, to forward your letters to me at Willow House, Chapel Street, New Haven, Connecticut. This is the boarding-house where Papa has rooms, and where he has written to arrange a place for myself and Mercy. Peggie and Nollie will be moving into Uncle M's house. If by any chance you should hear anything from Emory, please tell him to seek me there.

Papa has been so sunk beneath his grief that he has been able to do little towards the arrangement of Mother's funeral, nor towards the closing up of the house. Brock, too, is quite ill, and I have surrendered my room to him and Betsy, and am sleeping–in a welter of children–in the summer kitchen. I tell them greatly embellished stories at night about knaves and thieves, and the wars between the Barn-Fairies and the Woods-Fairies.

I will write to you again, when we come to New Haven.

Your friend always,
C

Cora Poole, Deer Isle, Maine
To
Susanna Ashford, General Delivery
Greeneville, Tennessee

TUESDAY, JUNE 20, 1865

Dearest Susanna,

A strange and curious change of plan. Today a letter reached me from Eliza Johnson, to whom I wrote at the time of Mother's death. Mrs. J is now in Washington, rather uncomfortably situated in a boarding-house because of the continued prostration of poor Mrs. Lincoln at the White House. She has asked me, Would I wish to come to her, as governess and tutor to her grandchildren? (Both daughters and their families, will be living with them: a total of five children, the oldest of whom is ten.)

Susanna, I will go! Papa expresses regret that he is unable himself to set up housekeeping—he will be supporting Peggie and Nollie at Uncle M's, and helping Brock until he is well again—but it is clear to me that he looks forward to returning to his old boarding-house in New Haven. Nor do I wish to become my father's housekeeper.

And to tell the truth, I know that Emory, when he returns, will fare better in Washington than he would in any New England town.

Last night I sat down and tallied up all those who had marched away from Deer Isle, never to come home. In 1861 there were 625 men of "military age" on our island; most of them with wives, and families already begun, or with parents to support. Of those, 277—just under half of the young men I'd grown up with—went into the service of their homeland.

One in seven of those men died, Susie. There were families in which two brothers entered together, like the Hendersons, and both young men killed. Others, like the Eaton girls, were split up and sent to different relatives—or, sometimes, strangers—because their mothers could not afford to keep them, once their fathers were dead.

Another 140 men—half as many as those who served—went into

hiding rather than leave their families destitute for life, gambling that after the War, they could return. Over 50—maybe as many as 80—paid $300 rather than risk death, and I can not come to any tally of the wounded, who will be no longer able to support themselves or their families.

The town is over $60,000 in debt, from bounties paid to the soldiers and their families. The fishing-fleet is crippled, for the expense of cordage, curing-salt, and mostly men. Many, many families have moved to the mainland, leaving their stony farms to be swallowed by the woods.

The Union has been preserved, and slavery abolished.

This is Victory.

Wednesday, June 21

My darling Mercy is three.

Brock, Betsy, and their children left yesterday for Boston. Peggie and Nollie have gone to Uncle M's. The cows have gone there, too, and Uncle M will harvest the crop here when autumn comes, to pay in part for the expenses of Peggie and Nollie. On Friday, Papa and I will be gone. I grieve to lose this last sweet summer here in Maine, but Mrs. Johnson truly needs help, and I will linger in New Haven only long enough to make sure that Papa is comfortable.

Last week Mercy and I walked into the woods, where the wildflowers bloom in their sweet profusion: steeplebush and meadowsweet, fragile trilliums and gorgeous Devil's paintbrush, clouds of butterflies wafting around our heads. It will be long, I think, before I come to Maine again, so I picked some Devil's paintbrush to press between the pages of *Pride and Prejudice,* to remember these years, this place, the things I found here and the things I lost. Three of these I enclose.

Needless to say, all of Mr. Poole's books will ride with me, south to our new home, until he can come to claim them again.

Write to me, I beg you—how queer it sounds!—at The White House, Pennsylvania Avenue, Washington—an address to make your sister snatch the hair off your head! And if—and when—Emory should communicate with you, tell him, this is where I am.

Always your friend,
Cora

P.S. My best wishes to Julia for her birthday—if sending them will not bring trouble down on your head for writing to a Yankee!

Susanna Ashford, Bayberry Run Plantation
Greene County, Tennessee
To
Cora Poole, Deer Isle, Maine

[forwarded to Washington]

WEDNESDAY, JUNE 21, 1865

Dearest Miss Mercy Susanna Poole,

All my kindest salutations on this the occasion of your 3rd (!) birthday.

Your very loving,
Aunt Susie

THURSDAY, JUNE 22

My dear friend,

The only comfort I can draw from your letter is the knowledge that by this time your pain will have lessened a little: that you are not going through the first awful hurt *now.* I am so sorry. I wish I could have been there with you; I wish I could be there with you now, to help in what I guess is a difficult process of packing things up—surely your Father will not remain on the island? I am so glad that he was there with you (he must have been, for summer had begun?), as well as your brother and, I hope, your brother's excellent wife (who had the good sense to tell you, three years ago, what happens when babies are born)?

Please, please, let me know, what your plans will be now. Will you return to New Haven with your Papa? (All to the good for Miss Mercy, as one hopes that by the time she is eighteen—1880!—it will be possible for *her* to be admitted to Yale!)

Indeed, *our* Mr. Johnson is now President of the United States, and not a soul in the house has a good word to speak about him—not even Julia, who bore her baby under his roof. I'm sorry Brock wasn't well enough to march. It would have been a splendid parade! Not a man in the militia would stoop to avail himself of Mr. J's pardon: "'They can keep their damn Reconstruction!'" They have bush-whacked and hanged more than one official the government sent out to implement Reconstruction and more than one Union soldier who has returned home under the impression that the War is done. To be honest, the Unionist guerillas have hanged a number of returning Confederates, too, in retaliation for the hardships their families suffered at the hands of the Seceshes. Many people in this countryside are still sleeping in the woods. The local Army Commanders have declared that bush-whackers are to be shot on sight and given no quarter.

I would cheerfully shoot on sight the so-and-so's who raided the corn out of *three* of my patches this week! It wasn't quite ripe so I am certain Nature will accomplish my revenge for me. But the rest of the patch will certainly be raided as the pumpkins and beans come ripe, so I might as well abandon work on them, and concentrate on hunting. I have been stretching and drying the skins, at one of my hiding-places in the laurel hell up behind the Holler. I hope to sell them in town.

SATURDAY, JUNE 24

Alas, generous girl, anything that you might send me would simply be confiscated by the militia. We do not do badly here. The one comfort about living in a camp of thieves is that we are unlikely to starve as long as *anyone* in the county has corn!

Thank you, for that image of your Mother as she was, and as she became in those last days of her life, united and at one. Strange to say, it helps me when the memory of what Bayberry was—of my childhood here—becomes too painful to bear. I tell myself, it is only the change of the season. That isn't easy now, but I will summon it back, and try to accept.

Did you lead your tiny brother into danger, you horrid woman? Shame on you! It was Payne who was always daring *me* to do things like smoke Pa's cigars or ride Caligula, Mr. Scanlon's stud stallion, who was about twenty feet tall and mean as sin.

Dear friend, tell me as soon as you know, where you will go, and what you will do.

All my love,
Susie

Susanna Ashford, Bayberry Run Plantation
Greene County, Tennessee
To
Cora Poole

[not sent]

Saturday, June 24, 1865
Night

Dearest,

It seems that I am always asking, How can I help you? and you always reply, most generously, that my letters—little enough, and so much of it lies—suffice. I remember how awful it was, when I was five years old, and Ma died: that horrible feeling that no one would ever care for me again. For months I wondered what would happen if Pa died, too, and relatives would split up Payne and Julia and me. I didn't think I could survive, if I had to live alone with strangers. I even planned how I would kill myself, by going up to Skull Cave and eating snakeberries, so I would be dead before anyone found me.

Julia comforted me, brushed my hair, promised me she'd never let anyone split us up. (I don't know what she could have done about it, at age ten.) When Pa married Miss Delphine, and Miss D would whip us, or lock me in the attic with the rats, or burn my drawings, it was Julia who hugged me and brought me food. (And I now realize that Miss Delphine was scared, and humiliated to see Pa bulling the housemaids and buying them jewelry when he went to Nashville—and poor Delphine was only twenty when she died.) I was Julia's Babygirl.

The militia is away—both Emory's and Lyle's—and the black woods and empty fields are terrifying, in this eerie peace. The moon's barely a day old and already set, the stars like an ocean of fire but casting little light. Nights like this I wish we could go sleep in the woods, as so many do, but with Tommy and Adam, and Tom settled in his chair, there's no way we can. As bad as I'm afraid, I can't leave them. The last time both bands were away like this, someone came into the house—several people, it sounded like—and slept in the parlor, and were gone by morning. I didn't think anything in the world would make me want to have Lyle Gilkerson under the same roof, but that was it.

MONDAY, JUNE 26

Oh, Cora——Emory is dead. Lyle brought word today.

WEDNESDAY, JUNE 28

I should write this down. Julia's finally asleep. I feel worse than I ever thought it was possible to feel.

Lyle says Emory was shot in battle, but it's pretty clear they were just stealing horses from a band of Tories over in Sullivan County. They buried him in the woods. Julia begged to be taken there and tried to walk there when Lyle refused to escort her. For two days, every time I'd move to leave she'd grab my wrist and plead with me: "Promise you won't leave!" Well, I did sneak out the minute she slept and went up to the cave to feed the hens: so strange, walking back through the Holler, seeing what's left of Justin's home, just a tangle of wild grape and scuppernong. I could see the place where I used to sit reading, and where Emory and Payne would clean their guns. Then when I got back here Lyle wanted me.

[~~*I think I'd give anything, to be able to walk into the woods and—*~~ crossed out]

Friday, June 30

My dearest friend,

So you will indeed go to New Haven with your Papa. I'm glad for you, more than I can say or even feel, just now.

Cora Poole, The White House,
Washington
To
Susanna Ashford, General Delivery
Greeneville, Tennessee

Thursday, July 6, 1865

Dearest,

A note, to let you know that Miss Mercy and I have arrived safe, and are ensconced, of all places, in a small attic chamber of the White House, which surely has the *largest* rats I have ever encountered, anywhere. I doubt that lodgings elsewhere in the house would improve the situation, as the whole place is very dirty, ramshackle, and—in spite of Mrs. Lincoln's notorious "refurbishing" during the War—astonishingly ill-kept. However, lodgings elsewhere in the house are out of the question, as the entire Johnson clan is in residence, one family per bedroom, with the guest bedroom in which the Prince of Wales slept doing duty as family parlor, dominated by a splendid purple-and-gold-draped bed . . . On which I sit, with the children, to do lessons.

Washington itself is blisteringly hot and muggy—worse than Boston—with unpaved streets, choking dust, and vast, straggling camps of newly-freed slaves spread around its outskirts. The stench of the place alone is enough to make one ill.

And yet—Susanna—I am free! I am paid fifty dollars a month—I am indeed on the government books as a worker in the Treasury

Department—with my board and lodging found. I work hard, as governess and tutor. Yet, to live without constant reproach is a gift beyond belief. I am a stranger and sometimes feel like an exile, but I am not an outcast, and Mrs. Johnson has said, that her husband will surely find employment for Emory, when he returns. I live in peace, and in hope.

In haste,
Cora

Cora Poole, The White House,
Washington
To
Susanna Ashford, General Delivery
Greeneville, Tennessee

FRIDAY, JULY 21, 1865

Dearest,

Thank you for your letter, both for its comfort at Mother's death, and its kind wishes for the lovely Miss Mercy. Though my grief still comes and goes, I am better on the whole. Alas, I find that there are a thousand times more perils in Washington and in particular in this rat-ridden, lumber-choked house for my child to get herself into, especially with such enterprising souls as the two younger Andies (ages 5 and 6) to contend with.

At the moment my duties consist of introducing the Two Andies (Patterson and Stover) and their sisters Sarah and Mary Belle (Stover and Patterson) to the alphabet, which I do as I was taught, by means of blocks. I scatter them over the parlor floor for the children to find and assemble into the words which I print on paper for them. Lillie, at ten, is well grounded in French and a little Latin, and will be placed in school in Georgetown in the fall. Young Frank—whom you tutored in Greeneville—is of course in boarding-school now. Together we read history, and dissect the plants and insects we find in the woods by Rock Creek. The duties also include sewing—what else!—keeping the Two Andies from leading their sisters into the bowels of the White House basement and abandoning the poor things there, and, in the evening, reading to Mrs. J—not a duty at all, but a very great pleasure. The President has been ill, and keeps much to his room. And, how clever of *you,* my dear friend, to hide the present you sent me last Christmas *here,* in the library of the White House: *Waverley, Rob Roy, Persuasion,* and *A Tale of Two Cities*! It seems poor Mrs. Lincoln was a great reader of novels, and was shocked that the White House contained no permanent library for the mental relaxation of its occupants. Bless her, for understanding, and remedying that omission! Although, I have found some rather extraordinary volumes of Spiritualism tucked away in the corners. But after four years—a new book by Miss Austen! Bliss!

Miss Mercy, by the way, can already find the letters for CAT, HAT, RAT (alas), and DOG. I have high hopes indeed, that it may be possible, by 1880, for her to be admitted to her father's *alma mater,* and may bring him pride within its walls.

There has still been no word of him. He was not, at least, taken prisoner: that much Mr. Johnson's son (and secretary) Robbie has ascertained for me from the Federal lists. And though records from Richmond are scant, so far we have found no record yet of Emory's death. I live in hope, and trust in God.

Your words about the Secessionist militia still in residence do not surprise me. Mrs. J and I have talked much about the conditions in Tennessee, and Mrs. Johnson has asked: Would *you* consider removing to Washington? She has always liked you, and says, that she could get you work, either here in the White House helping Martha as housekeeper, or in one of the government departments, where, nowadays, there are many female clerks. You would, she says, be welcome beneath this roof—and I can not but reflect that even with its current rodent population, it surely cannot be worse than your descriptions of Bayberry!

Please consider it, my friend. It would be good beyond words, to have you here.

Much love,
Cora

P.S. You dreadful girl, did you really smoke one of your Pa's cigars?

Susanna Ashford, Bayberry Run Plantation
Greene County, Tennessee
To
Cora Poole, The White House,
Pennsylvania Avenue, Washington

TUESDAY, AUGUST 22

Dear Cora,

Of course there are the biggest rats in the country there! It's the nation's capital! Please thank Mrs. Johnson for her generous offer, and the kind thoughts behind it. I'm sure she and you both know the reasons that I can not accept, with matters as they stand here. Julia hopes from day to day—though "hope" is too mild a word for her unshakeable conviction—that Pa will return before summer's end: "How can we abandon him, to return to an empty ruin?" There are times when I fairly twitch to slap that girl. But, we do not do badly here. I trust that, as the Federal hold strengthens on the countryside, it will even be possible for me to bring in an actual corn-crop instead of losing three-fifths of it to bush-whackers and thieves, may dysentery destroy their innards! Not to mention being able to bring a book down to the house without fear of having it used for kindling—though I'd have to hide it from Julia for the same reason. I improve daily as a hunter, bringing in rabbits and woodchucks, and a good part of my day is spent at one or another of my hideouts in the woods, stretching and drying hides. Julia has been ill lately, and I have been returning from the woods earlier each evening, to do at least a little of the housework that she is unable to accomplish, and to cook the meals for Tommy and Tom.

Good for Mrs. Lincoln! That is the best thing I've heard of her so far, that she understood that Man Doth Not Live By Bread Alone Nor Politics Neither, and took care to make sure the Chief Executive of the nation has, as it were, a nice bowl of cold water to dunk his brain in at the end of the day. What Spiritualist books were these, that she left behind? Did you read them? You behold me agog!

I am so glad you have a chance at last to read *Tale of Two Cities*—though for some reason the number of staggering coincidences struck me as rather higher in this than even Mr. D's usual. The fact that Charles Darnay would be able to fit into Sydney Carton's boots quite brought me up short: now that, I decided, is just *too much* to swallow! (Though I accepted without question the whole business about Mme. Defarge.)

You have no idea how good it is, to think about Sydney Carton's boots, and how you'll like *Persuasion,* instead of arguing with Julia about how much of our food to give the poor starving militia. It reminds me again that there is a world outside of these silent, beautiful, deadly woods. I await with tingling anticipation the account of the Spiritualist texts. Please give my kindest regards to Mrs. J, and a million kisses to Miss Mercy. (Tom has begun to teach Tommy his letters, too.)

Your loving,
S

Susanna Ashford, Bayberry Run Plantation
Greene County, Tennessee
To
Cora Poole

[not sent]

TUESDAY, AUGUST 22, 1865
NIGHT

Dear Cora—in your imaginary garret above the Gothic spires of Paris . . .

And now it's a real garret above the Gothic spires of Washington! How glad I am, that you are free! How I wish I could be with you—

If what? If Julia were dead? If Tom were dead? And then it would have to be Tommy and Adam, as well, tiny Adam who runs about the house and yard and smiles at me with Emory's golden eyes? Even if (as I pray God daily will happen) the Federals caught Lyle's troop and hanged the lot of them like the beasts they are, it wouldn't free me. Julia still adamantly refuses to take "Yankee charity" in town, or to leave this place where she was born and raised. And I can not leave her. Nor will I risk losing the only relief or happiness I have, by telling you how I betrayed you, how I have lied all these months. Forgive me. Please forgive me.

A sickening fight with Julia over this, triggered by the news that she told Lyle about my gun, and he took it, because they are short of weapons in their war against the Tory bands (who, after all, get *their* guns from the Federal government).

FRIDAY, AUGUST 25

More killings in Knoxville. A man who'd fought for the Confederacy had his skull broke by Unionists; another, who'd been arrested for shooting a Tory, was lynched when a Unionist mob broke into the jail. Lyle and his men have ridden out to "even things up," leaving their food supplies (newly stolen) in the pit I dug under the wash-house, one of the hiding-places where I used to keep our food hid from the CSA Commissary boys.

I have snares and deadfalls set all over the woods, and these are bringing in something, and the fish-lines still provide enough to keep us all from starving. Yesterday I walked into town with a packet of furs–mostly rabbit and squirrel, and very heavy–and traded them for salt, thread, and some cheap calico, for the boys are mostly in rags. I got paper, too, for poor Justin's books are pretty much stripped of their end-papers and title-pages. I feel guilty, for getting paper instead of more cloth–enough for an extra dress for Tommy. What do I really need paper for? Why even write these to you, that I know I will not send? Because I can't not tell you the truth, even though I won't let you see it after it's written.

Monday, August 28

I told Lyle this would happen, if he hid his supplies here. Early this morning Unionist bush-whackers rode in, burned the kitchen, and took them. Lyle–

Wednesday, August 30

Dearest Cora,

I've seen Justin. He came Monday afternoon, about a half-day after the bush-whackers burned the wash-house; Lyle and his boys had rode out after them, Lyle saying, they'd be back before sunset, though the moon is close to full. What with Lyle being furious, and another dreadful fight with Julia after he left, I foraged close to home. So I was here in late afternoon when Justin rode in with his dogs, or what remains of Justin. He has lost his right leg almost to the knee, Cora, and most of his right hand, and I knew, as soon as I saw him, that he would be no match for Lyle and his boys. I got rid of him fast and I wasn't very kind, but at least I got him out of here before Julia or Tom could see him, for if Lyle knew he was in the county, he would go after him.

After he was gone, though it was growing dark, I walked up to Skull Cave. I burned his books, each and every one, to keep him from ever coming back.

Cora Poole, The White House, Washington
To
Susanna Ashford, General Delivery
Greeneville, Tennessee

MONDAY, SEPTEMBER 18, 1865

Dearest,

Indeed I understand your reasons for wishing to stay in Tennessee, and respect them, though it would be a delight and a blessing to have you here in Capital City. Though I am seldom alone in this place—as crowded as quarters are in this great drafty barn, I must make firm arrangements to set aside my time of meditation in the afternoons—I often feel sorely lonely: ridiculous, given the isolation from which I come. Washington is beyond hellish in midsummer. The dust from the unpaved streets deposits a gritty film no matter how tightly one closes the windows, and the condition of the house—which was virtually looted by the crowds that came for President Lincoln's lying-in-state—resembles a wretchedly-maintained boarding-house. Even in the summer, petitioners crowd the hallway and straggle in a line down the stair, smoking, swearing, and spitting tobacco, so that the children and I come and go by the servants' stairway. I had not realized how accustomed my heart had become, to the woods and quiet of Deer Isle, nor how my spirit had settled into the peaceful routines of milking, gardening, washing. True—I almost hear you saying it, Susie—what my heart longs for is Deer Isle in the *summer*—particularly the summer wherein a sorcerer visited and magically slew every blackfly on the island . . .

Even so, when I grieve for Mother, and wish she was alive again, I mean, Mother as I recall her in her prime—dark-haired, majestic, drily humorous in her Biblical way—not the pain-wracked shadow of those last six months.

I am sorry indeed to hear that your sister has been ill. I hope it goes better with Julia now? I pray also that you will soon have word from your father. Papa writes me often, very short notes, I think because he looks forward to even the briefest replies, which I am careful to send him, thrice and sometimes four times a week. I smile, computing the number of eggs such a correspondence would cost.

If I were more certain of the status of these Spiritualist tracts I would send you one—Do they belong to the Nation? *Would* the Nation truly suffer, if I were to tuck an issue of *The Spiritual Telegraph,* or "The Grand Harmonium," into an envelope for your edification? There is among other things the Spiritual re-write of the Declaration of Independence, quite gravely declaring us independent of our bodies: something I wish I could be, on these suffocating nights whereon the whining of the mosquitoes is almost drowned by the scuffling of the rats in the walls. At least, the rats do *eat* such cockroaches as venture up to the attics.

Thursday, September 21

A grand banquet this evening, for such members of the Diplomatic Corps as have returned early to the Capital (Congress does not open until the fourth of December). The bustle and flurry in the house brings to mind your account of your Aunt Sally's dinner for Jefferson Davis all those years ago, down to the minute paper crowns on the fish course. Unlike you, I was pressed into service writing menus and place-cards in my most lovely, Hartford-Female-Seminary hand. Martha acts as her father's hostess, Mrs. J being unable—and, I think, unwilling—to venture farther than the threshold of her parlor. I volunteered to keep her company there, and Dolly brought us, from the kitchen, miniature versions of each course, which entertained the children very much. After the festivities, the President came up to sit with Mrs. J for a time—he is still poorly—and I asked him again, Was there any other avenue that he could think of, whereby I might uncover some word of Emory? The fighting ranged as far as New Mexico and California, and I understand that it will take some time, for all of the men to return to their scattered homes. The days pass in noise, and drown awareness of their passing by occupation with such matters as Congressional gossip—which Mrs. J and her daughters follow with the dry, keen interest of connoisseurs—and paper crowns upon fishes: and then suddenly a letter comes from you dated in August, and I think, September is nearly gone!

The President clasped my hand, and said, We will find Emory, my child, if he is above the ground.

September is nearly gone. The War's end in April seems tiny, like an event viewed far off through the wrong end of a telescope. Yet I remember as if it were yesterday, weeping for President Lincoln as I scalded the milk-churn and rolled pastry for a chicken pie. In my mind I see the summer kitchen, closed up now and shuttered tight, and the bare bedstead in Mother's room, as it looked when I made the last walk through the place, to make sure nothing was forgotten, nothing left behind. Snow will cover it soon.

In the same way I see Elinor's face, and Oliver, and poor little Nollie whom I would have liked to know better—and the loft in the barn, bare now of its beds of hay, where Will and I would meet one another. Enough time has passed that I can say, "He was good to me, and I was a fool in need of comfort." All these things, like the Ghosts of Christmas Present fading into the echoes of Christmas past: a stage-set struck, living, as you said once, only in my memory. It is time to move on.

I remember what you wrote me once, that before every door that we ought not to pass through, there stands an angel with a flaming sword. Now that angel has stepped aside, and opened for me a door whose existence I never dreamed of. I stand on the threshold, looking at the road stretching ahead of me, and I only wait here for Emory to join me, so that we may undertake it, hand in hand.

I hope that your silent, beautiful woods are becoming a little safer, my friend; that the squirrels you catch are fat, and the berries plentiful, and your Pa comes home soon.

Wherever we may be,
Always your friend,
Cora

Susanna Ashford, Bayberry Run Plantation
Greene County, Tennessee
To
Cora Poole, The White House
Pennsylvania Avenue
Washington, DC

Wednesday, October 18, 1865

Dear Cora,

I'm sending you the enclosed, not in the hope of forgiveness, but in the hope that you will at least understand that I did the best I could.

Emory is dead. I know this—I talked to the man who saw him shot, and who buried him. Don't linger for him anymore, Cora. Don't say No to the road that stretches before you, to the promises of what your new life will bring.

I'm sorry I didn't tell you all this before. I'm sending you all the letters that I wrote to you during the War—or wrote to the Pretend-You, after we could no longer get letters through. I don't even remember all that's in them, but they will explain what happened, and why I didn't write to you even when I could have, and why I can't see you again.

You have always been the only person who truly respected me; I am ashamed at how little I deserve that respect. Your kindness and your faith should have better payment, than what I've given you. Ensnared as I am by people who are still fighting a war that can never be either won or lost, who will not give up or let go—reading your accounts of the new life on whose threshold you stand—I know how terrible a disservice I do you, every day that I tell you a lie that will hold you back, that will keep you waiting for someone who will never arrive. You deserve better than that—and that is something that I *can* give you.

I love you very much. I'm just not very good at loving anybody.

Good-by,
S

[packet of letters enclosed]

Cora Poole, The White House
Washington
To
Susanna Ashford, General Delivery
Greeneville, Tennessee

SATURDAY, DECEMBER 23, 1865

[returned unopened March 30, 1866]
[burned unread]

1866

Cora Poole, The White House
Washington
To
Susanna Ashford, General Delivery
Greeneville, Tennessee

FRIDAY, JANUARY 12, 1866

[returned unopened March 30, 1866]
[burned unread]

Cora Poole, The White House
Washington
To
Susanna Ashford, General Delivery
Greeneville, Tennessee

MONDAY, JANUARY 29, 1866

[returned unopened March 30, 1866]
[burned unread]

Cora Poole, The White House
Washington
To
Susanna Ashford, General Delivery
Greeneville, Tennessee

TUESDAY, FEBRUARY 13, 1866

[returned unopened March 30, 1866]
[burned unread]

Julia Balfour
Bayberry Run Plantation
Greene County, Tennessee
To
Cora Poole, The White House
Washington

MARCH 30, 1866

Mrs. Poole,

Enclosed are the letters you've been writing to my sister.

I'm sorry to say she took her own life last October.

May God damn you and every other Yankee to the Hell you deserve, for eternity.

–J.B.

Cora Poole, The White House
Washington
To
Susanna Ashford

[not sent]

Friday, April 13, 1866
Night

Dearest Susanna,

Back during the War—I don't really remember when—I remember asking you, what is this capacity of the human heart, to sustain the flame of hope for years, without visible fuel. You were there—I *knew* you were there—and that sustained me, during the worst days I have known. I do not know how I would have survived them, without your laughter. As I wrote to you then—to the Pretend-Susanna who would invariably get my letters the day after they were written—so I write to you now. I hope you'll get this one.

Not to say, *Forgive me,* for the anger that kept me silent for those months—for you must have done what you did very shortly after you sent me that last letter, and you did not know how many months it took, for my anger to run its course. But to say, *Thank you, for setting me free.* Like Elizabeth Bennet—pushing her way through her anger at Darcy to re-read his letter and see what he actually said—I have forced myself to read and re-read your letters. I have indeed been lingering on the threshold of life, waiting for Emory. Had you not known of his death, and had the courage to tell me, how long would I have waited?

Justin has been in Washington since February. This evening, after I had read Julia's letter, he called: I think it must be true what everyone always said of him, that those curious gray eyes do see beyond the present and the visible. He said he had dreamed of you, walking away from Bayberry early one morning at first light; had dreamed of Julia weeping, and known that it was because you never would return. He had hoped, he said, that it meant that you had—or would—take the courage to leave that place.

And so I shall think of you, my friend: that you did take up your courage, and you did leave that place, and walk away into the dawnlight. But, the place where you went to—the place where you will be happy—has no mail delivery. Would I grudge you your happiness there, just because you could never write to me again?

I write you this last time, to tell you that I will be happy here.

Probably not in Washington. The country has changed because of the War, and will change more drastically in the wake of the bloodshed and death that it took, to settle the questions: Do the local interests of the States or the higher commands of the government have the right to say what is permitted and not permitted? And, shall men and women be subject to slavery?

My dear friend Will once said to me, that he found it hard to fight for his homeland, knowing that the fight itself would transform that homeland into something it had not been before. Those questions were answered, but the answers left a vast and bitter stain on the hearts of those who lost their husbands and brothers, their homes and their children's hopes. Politicians and men hardened by violence and greed now pick at the looted ruin of the South, and that poison, too, will spread down the years. The land that we hoped to save has changed, and like all change, the result doesn't look as we expected it would.

I think it will be years, before I return to Maine. I may never again walk along those roads where the houses I knew are shuttered up and empty. Justin has spoken of beginning again in the West—he currently makes his living driving a cab here in Washington—but it takes money to make a new start. President Johnson has promised to help us, as and when he can.

And so we will go on, dear friend, into this new homeland, that is not the place where I grew up. I will carry you with me in my heart, and read your letters—all of them—for what they are: letters from a time and place that are dear to me, despite the grief and pain. And I will be happy.

But my dear friend, I will miss you so.

With all my love,
Your friend,
Cora

1869

Mrs. Robert Broadstairs
100 Boulevard Sebastopol
2ème Arrondissement
Paris
To
Miss Ashford
c/o Galerie LaFontaine
10, rue de la Rochefoucault
9ème Arrondissement
Paris

THURSDAY, APRIL 22, 1869

Dear Miss Ashford:

At the exhibition at the Académie des Beaux-Arts this afternoon, I was struck speechless by your painting, *Federal Gunboats Run the Vicksburg Battery–Night.* It was not merely the beauty of the work which arrested me, but the resemblance it bears to a sketch in my possession, made by a dear friend of mine during the late American war. The clerk in charge of the exhibition directed me to the Galerie LaFontaine, where M. Taschler was kind enough to show me some of your other paintings–I was particularly taken by the *Barbarian Chieftain Shown How to Write*–and to forward this note on to you.

My friend and I were estranged after the War, and I was told by members of her family that she had died. Not a day has passed since then that I have not cursed both my anger and my silence–for the fault was mine, and the circumstances leading to the break, far beyond her control. Yet, not until today did it ever occur to me to ask, Was the report of her death the truth?

If it was indeed the truth, and my friend is forever beyond my power to ask her forgiveness, please have no hesitation in dropping this letter into the fire. I have no wish to cause further pain, nor to avoid the harvest of what I have sown.

My daughter, my father-in-law, and I came to Paris in November of 1866, in the household of General Dix, the new American Minister: my father-in-law as the General's coachman, I as companion to the General's invalid wife and governess to their nieces. Here I met—and this spring, married—an English gentleman, Mr. Broadstairs, the kindest and most scholarly of men. I am most happy.

Please do not feel any obligation to respond to this, if it will bring discomfort to you or to members of your family. Though I sorely miss my dear friend, I take great joy in seeing the beauty of your work, knowing with what pain all good work is wrought. Forgive me if I presume, but I bought your painting of the little Devil's paintbrush flower. It sits before me as I write.

Sincerely,
C.B.

Susanna Ashford
60, rue Lepic
19ème Arrondissement
Paris
To
Cora Broadstairs
100 Boulevard Sebastopol
2ème Arrondissement
Paris

THURSDAY (NIGHT), APRIL 22, 1869

Dearest Cora—
Dearest Friend—

The first letter that you wrote to me, back in May of 1861, you pointed out that were I my father's son, rather than a daughter (and a homely one at that), no one would question my desire or my right to seek my right work, the calling of my heart. That meant so much to me, more than I can ever say. During those awful last years of the fighting, your letters saved my life, more than once. When you ceased writing, I felt it was I, not you as you say, who was reaping what I had sowed. I never knew you'd written: I think my sister Julia must have had a friend in town who intercepted whatever you tried to send me. But to tell the truth, after my betrayal of your trust, I did not expect you to write.

In March of '66 I realized, that if *Julia* were our father's son, rather than a woman, not a man nor woman of my acquaintance would consider it right, for him (Julia) to keep his (her) family starving and in rags, only out of refusal to take help that was offered by those whose politics he (she) didn't approve. Does that make sense? It was *Julia's* choice, to stay on Bayberry—to live in the world of the past. She was not helpless. There were other choices she could make. And if you could walk on, and take your right place in the new-born world, and leave the past behind, then so, too, could I.

I send her money—I work as a copyist for law firms, to pay for my paints. She sends it back, so I know she's still on Bayberry, and can at least afford a postage stamp. Never, *ever* did I think, that she would write to you after I left, and tell you I was dead. I should have, though. It sounds just like her. I am so sorry, for the grief this caused you, on top of your other many griefs.

It is so good—*so good!*—to see your handwriting before me, the ink fresh and not faded almost to nothingness, like all those yellowed letters in my box. I have the five letters Justin sent me, as well—does he know? If not, please don't tell him of me, til I've spoken to you. He hasn't *married* anybody, or anything, has he? (I haven't.)

Do you know the coffee-stand at the Porte Maillot, where the road goes into the Bois de Boulogne? Can you meet me there tomorrow (Friday) at four? I'll be wearing a straw hat and carrying a sketch-book—here's a picture of me.

And don't get run over by a carriage on the way, which is what would happen to one or the other of us if Mr. Dickens were writing this story.

I realize, I have no idea what you look like, anymore—I haven't seen you since April of 1861! Carry a copy of *Pride and Prejudice,* so I'll know it's you.

Love,
Susie

[sketch]

A Note on Sources

Over the course of the two-years-plus during which I worked on *Homeland,* I lost count of how many sources I used: letters, newspapers, books on everything from soap-making to the history of slang, journeys through Appalachia and Maine and to Vicksburg and Washington, DC.

A few of my most hard-used sources were: *Andrew Johnson, A Biography* by Hans Trefousse; *The Civil War Day by Day* by E. B. Long; Noel C. Fisher's *War at Every Door;* Vernal Hutchinson's *A Maine Town in the Civil War; My Cave Life in Vicksburg* by A. Lady (actually Mary Webster Loughborough); and *Fighting Words* by Andrew Coopersmith. There were too many others to name or count, and Web sites beyond computation, for my intention was not simply to write about the Civil War, but to put myself—if I could—into the hearts, corsets, and shoes of two women who were out of step with the accepted views of those around them.

And there were many such. Despite torrents of propaganda on both sides, the Civil War was fiercely unpopular in the North, and the South was far from united about the decision of the various State governments to separate from the Union—a split particularly virulent in the eastern part of Tennessee. Little is written about these dissenters, and less still is taught in most college survey courses, let alone at lower levels. Men deserted, and dodged the draft, in droves; partisan fighting continued in Tennessee for months after Appomatox; in the North, as one Maine man recalled, "You had to be awful careful what you said."

It was a time of courage and sacrifice, but it was also a time of great turmoil, when men and women, North and South, strove to grapple with questions that had no good answers: human rights and national security, loyalty, survival, and the freedom to choose.

"The Volunteer's Wife to Her Husband," an early Civil War poem, quoted on pg. 95. Quoted in Nina Silber, *Daughters of the Union: Northern Women Fight the Civil War*, Harvard University Press, 2005; pg. 18.

ABOUT THE AUTHOR

BARBARA HAMBLY attended the University of California and spent a year at the University of Bordeaux obtaining a master's degree in medieval history. She has worked as both a teacher and a technical editor, but her first love has always been history. Barbara Hambly is the author of *Patriot Hearts, The Emancipator's Wife, A Free Man of Color, Fever Season, Graveyard Dust, Wet Grave, Sold Down the River, Die Upon a Kiss, Days of the Dead,* and *Dead Water.*